The Crack of the Bat

John Szydlo

ISBN 9798837698095 (pbk

Chapter One

I felt her sweet soft lips on mine. Our tongues were interlocked, and as I held her very close, I could feel her nipples getting hard. Her arms were locked around my waist. My shorts began to stir. It started off slow, but now was heating up. The warmth of the spring sun glistened off our faces. It was a very warm spring day at three o'clock on Saturday afternoon at the high school baseball field. Sounds of chatter traveled from people in the stands. You could hear the sound of the ball cracking off the bat. However, I was in my own world with the girl I loved for truly all my life. I felt goosebumps up and down my arm as I opened my eyes and looked down at the angel of my life. She was the one and only fair Cassidy.

"I want you so bad," I whispered.

My body had wanted hers for a long time. She opened her eyes and looked up at me with a smile. My body melted like butter, my legs wobbling. Her eyes were the color of a cool breeze coming off the ocean on a sunny day. The chatter of the people was getting louder and closer.

"Oh John, I want you too, but the game." She put her head on my shoulder as I brought her close with a soft bear hug.

She was right. The game had almost slipped my mind, as I stood there under the bleachers in my high school uniform. The thoughts of the coach coming to find me raced through my mind. The nice moment, in the only quiet secluded space at the time since people kept pouring in, would be interrupted.

"Oh yeah I almost forgot about the game," I chuckled to myself aloud. "Let's just go to the Motel 6 on the outskirts of town, get a room, and forget about the game," still laughing.

We were leaning against one of the smaller buildings used to sell snacks at the game. We could hear some stuff rattling around inside the building which looked like a shed. It was right next to the bleachers. Right behind the home plate in the baseball stadium called Pikes Field. She knew I was kidding. We had been going out since freshmen year of High School, but as Seniors, still had not rounded all the bases with each other. She was holding back from going all the way, but he was good about not forcing the issue. It was hard with all their classmates seemingly having sex all the time. She wanted to wait until she was married, but still wanted to strip down right there and make love to him right under the bleachers, as she was as into him as he was her.

"Oh, stop it, that day will come, Mister. How about getting the school into the playoffs with a win today?"

Her arms reached up around his neck as she looked up at him with her auburn-colored hair and light highlights. It was tied in a ponytail that went down past her shoulders. He looked down and could see her beautiful cleavage, as he had many times before. He was hard, but he had to go.

He gave her a quick kiss saying, "Alright, baby cakes. Sounds like a plan I can be part of. We still on for a burger at Murphy's later?"

She kissed back and then let him go. "Yes, good luck, and remember to keep your head down. Wait on those curve balls."

Cassidy played softball. She loved baseball and knew a lot about the game. She loved coming to all his games as he came to all of hers. He started to jog away, stopped, and blew her a kiss from a few feet. She caught the imaginary kiss in her hands and blew one back. He jogged up the ramp with a smile on his face, as everything was going great in his final year in high school.

Chapter Two

The television in the dark room is playing what looks to be a porno movie. A man sits on the edge of the bed continuing to watch the footage over and over, of two people having sex on the screen. Once it is over, he rewinds it and watches it again and again. It is late in the afternoon and the sun is peaking through the cracks of the curtains. The only light of any kind in the room is coming from the tube television on the dresser. That, and the glow of a cigarette every time the man takes a drag from his Marlboro Red. The sound is off, and he watches closely as if he knows one of the two getting it on in front of his eyes. Then suddenly, he hears a roar of bike outside the door. The man is not fazed as he continues to be drawn to the man and woman on the screen.

Outside, the engine comes to halt. Not even a minute later a loud knock on the steel door is followed by a man's voice.

"Yo, Blade Runner! Are you there?" A pause is followed by, "Open up the door, guy."

The man inside is trance-like as he smoked his cigarette with one hand and controlled the remote with the other. He rewound the video for the umpteenth time. Then another thump on the door as the doorknob twisted. Still no reaction from the man sitting on the bed, as the door opened allowing a stream of light into the seemingly ransacked bedroom. Clouds of smoke left the premises in puffs.

"Oh My God, Blade Runner. What the Fuck happened here?" The man in the doorway asked in a very concerned tone.

Still nothing from the man sitting on the bed. The man took a step inside leaving the light from outside to see where he was walking, as he stepped over some clothes. The room was trashed. Clothes all over the place. Books scattered all over the floor. VHS tapes looked to have been thrown. Empty bottles of whisky laying on the coffee table, on their sides causing the leaking on the carpet. Looked to be a bag of cocaine opened on the couch. The logo of the club, to which both of these men belonged, on a poster held up by one thumb tack. Other pictures were off the walls. Holes in the plaster throughout the room in the shape of fists. The man took another step into the room as he was trying to come up with something to say, but words would not come out. Blade Runner *still* paid no attention to him, as he focused on the tv. The cigarette ash fell to the floor.

"You ok Buddy?"

It was a voice that you are talked to in when you have some kind of breakdown in an asylum of some type. The man took another step and saw a foot sticking out from under the covers, as Blade Runner sat there in silence. He then looked at the television to see what he was staring at, and his eyes almost jumped out of his sockets. He took another step towards the TV as he carefully looked at the other person on the screen.

"Is that Holly? Holy shit, that is totally fucked up."

It was a guy they both knew. He then put it together in his mind and looked at the foot on the bed, still in the same position. He then saw the video rewind in front of his eyes, as the guy he knew was doggie styling Blade Runner's old lady. Then he felt his body going numb. The pit of his stomach started to turn. The thought of Holly under the blanket in that bed, meant he knew it could not be good. He proceeded with caution as he stepped over stuff on the floor, finally getting close enough to Blade Runner, who was still in another land just eyeballing the same video. It was like did not know he had company. His friend now was standing right in front of him and what he saw made him take a step back. His hands began to shake like he had never experienced before. He knelt down in front of him, looking at him still looking at the screen. He put his hand on his shoulder. Blade Runner was not wearing a shirt. His chest was covered with all kinds of tattoos, just like all the guys in the club. That included himself. He could see he was bleeding with multiple lacerations on his chest. Obviously, scratch marks from the woman in bed with her head blown off. He took the remote from him as Blade Runner gave it up with ease.

"It's ok buddy, we are going to get through this."

He placed that on the nightstand with the sawed off shot gun that was leaning up against it. "Shit," he whispered to himself.

He took the cigarette from his fingers, extinguishing it in a Joe Camel pool table-style ashtray. Then he walked back towards the door, like he was walking through a mine field, and closed the door. The TV light stayed on as Blade Runner was in a trance still watching. All while a woman his friend believed was Holly, his old lady, lay in the bed. He was pacing the room trying to think of what to do. He fished out a Pall Mall cigarette out of his pack from his leather vest. He flipped his Zippo and quickly lit a cigarette to calm his nerves. To figure out what their next move will be. Did he have to call somebody?

Chapter Three

Spruce Wood High School was winning the big game that afternoon against Taft. After five innings of play, Spruce Wood was winning 5-4. Cassidy has been cheering on Spruce Wood, and her love, John Malone, with his family who made many of the games. John has been on fire the last few games, and he's been having a great year. But the last five or so games, no pitchers have been able to get him out. In this contest he was 2-2, with both a double and a mammoth home run. This to go along with 3 RBI'S and he scored two runs. The playoffs could mean some better scholarships than what he had been offered from colleges at this time. Lots of schools wanted John to play ball for them. However, the family and Cassidy believed if they made the playoffs and had the chance to play against the best teams in the state of Illinois, perhaps some school would give John a full ride.

"Alright son, nice catch."

His father leapt out of his seat, clapping like a wild man. He was followed by the crowd as John stretched out for one to rob Taft of extra bases. John plays first base, and he has been improving his defense. He was the type of player that did the extra practice to improve his craft. Extra hitting in the cages. Plus, having the coach and some of his buddies hit ground balls to him after practice or during his free time. Cassidy even remembers going out to the local park by their houses to hit balls to her man until dusk. Cassidy and the whole Malone family were behind John. Helped him in many ways. They all believed he was something special. Especially at the game of baseball. John's dream was to play professionally.

The day was perfect in Spruce Wood, Illinois that Saturday. Not a cloud in the sky. Spruce Wood was a small town south of Chicago. It was out in the country just far enough away from the big city. It seemed like the whole town was on hand to watch this game. The town of Spruce Wood loved their local high school sports. Friday night lights on the gridiron was the town's bloodline. However, they also got jacked up for baseball and basketball. The town had not made it to the State playoffs since the early seventies. Which was about two decades ago. Plus, being in a small town meant everyone knew each other. Everyone had high hopes John would make his dream happen and make it to the pros. The town was like one big family.

"John is up fifth this inning. If they get a few guys on, I have a great feeling about this." Cassidy was talking to one of John's younger sisters. Stephanie was sitting right next to Cassidy on the end.

In the stands, John, the oldest of three, had his mom and dad on hand with his two younger sisters. Stephanie was just finishing her freshmen year at Spruce Wood. The youngest out of the three siblings was little Katie who was turning 5. She had an adorably crooked smile with teeth missing, and she was as cute as a button. She sat in-between her two parents who were in their late 50's.

"Come on Jake!" screamed Stephanie.

Jake was John's best friend as they had grown up on the same block, playing ball since the days of the sandbox. He was playing left field in this game. He was a guy in the field that was a jack-of-all-trades and played just about anywhere except catcher. Stephanie has had a crush on him since about always. Her cheeks were red, as her mom just smiled, - watching her watch Jake and rooting him on. Everyone knew except maybe Jake himself. Jake, a left-handed hitter, took a swing at a low one and out of the strike zone. He golfed it into the gap of center and right, as it hit off the wall. The Malone family, led by Cassidy and the rest of crowd, were on their feet rooting for Jake to get extra bases. Indeed, the chunky senior was able to get onto second standing up. "He's not very fast," their mom commented.

Their father was in very good spirits as he said, "Those golf lessons have paid off for the Jake-Meister." He smiled revealing those coffee-stained chompers he had.

In his day, John's father was a pretty good baseball player himself. He was drafted by the Oakland Athletics, but never made it to the big show. He was able to get on a triple AAA farm team called the Timber Jacks out in California. However, he was a pitcher who blew his arm out and never recovered. In his mind, he always wanted John to be a position player and kept him away from the pitching rubber. Then two quick outs by Taft, both strikeouts, got the whole family in a twist as they could not believe it. Then the next batter was able to hit a sharp single to right, to move Jake into third. Everyone stood up as John walked up to the plate, smiling as he watched them. To let them know he saw them. Just in case they missed his wave or hat tip, after the other two At-Bats. John's whole family, and his girl, stood up as if it was the best song from the band that night. They were screaming his name, which started getting lots of others to stand, clap, and root John and the team on. Everyone at the park was looking for their team to add more runs on, to increase their lead as they had been hanging on to the one-run lead for too long.

John was wearing the team colors of green and gray. The helmet was a wild forest green with the letters SW (standing for the town of Spruce Wood) in dark grey. The pitcher looked at the catcher's signals and took a quick look at first. Jake was no threat to run at third, so he ignored his two steps away from the bag. The infield was playing at normal depth since it was two outs. John batted from the right side of the plate. As he gripped his bat, he moved his bat in his hands with shoulders up while eyeballing the pitcher. The first pitch caught the outside for a quick strike by the man in blue behind the catcher.

"Boo," shouted the crowd.

John's dad stood up and yelled, "Come on Blue, what kind of call is that?"

The umpire ignored that as the Pitcher got the ball back from the catcher. John stepped back in the box, and he dug his spikes into the ground. Stallions was written on the mesh jersey across the chest of the uniforms. They wore gray tops and pants with green lettering. They had the Stallion logo on the shoulder. The second pitch John took outside for ball one. John stepped out of the box. He adjusted his batting gloves. John was a lanky tall guy, just over 6 feet tall. He had short brown hair spiked in the front. It was covered up with the helmet, but you could see his dark facial features. He had a medium-sized nose and bright hazel eyes, with which he looked at the whole field.

With the third pitch, he got the head of the bat out on it as it made a ping sound coming off the aluminum bat. The ball shot off it like a laser beam down the right field line. Jake came in from third with ease as the crowd itself shot up out of their seats watching the ball roll into the right field corner for extra bases. People were yelling for him to "Go, Go, Go!" John's family were high fiving, and some were hugging each other as John headed for second while the man on first was rounding third. The right fielder was playing towards center, so he had to run a long way to get the ball and finally threw it in after two runs crossed the plate. John was

8

on third with a stand-up triple. His whole team were whooping and hollering from the dugout, as the whole crowd gave him a standing thunderous ovation. Now it was 7-4 Spruce Wood.

Chapter Four

The man that came by to see Blade Runner went by the name of Saw Dust. Everyone in this club had a nick name. They called it their personal code name, like GI JOE. Some actually knew each other's real names. Only the President and the Vice President of the club knew *everyone's* real names. Saw Dust got his from filling up another club's motorcycle gas tanks with saw dust. It was a move that ruined a lot of expensive Harley Davidsons that day. Saw Dust was able to get Blade Runner out of his room and into the club's bar, inside the main club house. Many of the members had a charity ride that day so it was a ghost town. They called the few acres of land where their club house and most of their housing was, The Ranch.

They sat at the bar with an open bottle of Paddy, an Irish Whisky. Plus, a bottle of Jameson. Both bottles were opened as Blade Runner grabbed the Paddy and swigged it in big gulps. Saw Dust had a shot glass and poured himself a small amount. It had taken a while, but Saw Dust was able to get Blade Runner out of his room. He turned off the television.

"Come on, I'm buying so let's get a drink and wash away the sins for now," he had said.

Sawdust's words always had something to do with drinks. Any kind of pickle, celebration or just an average day… drinks was his answer to just about everything. This time it had worked as both of them left the crime scene and headed to the club house. Sawdust found out that it was in fact his old lady on the bed with her head completely blown off. Blade Runner had almost half the Paddy down, as he sat at the bar looking at himself in the mirror behind the bar.

"After all I've done for her," he said in a raspy voice as he shook his head.

In his reflection, he looked like he had aged about ten years. He was 45 years old. Today, he looked to be in his 50's. He had heavy bags under his blood shot eyes. He was noticing new wrinkles that seemed to have appeared overnight. Saw Dust sipped at his next shot while listening to his club brother.

"The tape I was watching was sent to me through the mail."

Saw Dust quickly asked an obvious question, "Who sent it?"

Saw Dust was much younger looking than Blade Runner. His mirror reflection was a man with high cheek bones. He had a beard trimmed to perfection like the guy from the beer commercials, The World's Most Interesting Man. It helped being only 29, as he had no gray in his slicked-back mop of hair and beard.

"No name on it, no return address," as his voice seemed to clear up from the Paddy.

Saw Dust said nothing as the President of the club continued. "I had it for a few days. I even told that bitch in there about it." He pointed towards the back of him, in the direction of his housing.

"First, we did a few bumps, which got us both in the mood. I went to town on her and fucked her brains out."

He lit up another cigarette and took a quick long drag as smoke blew out of his nose and mouth in a straight stream.

Saw Dust continued to sip his Jameson while he continued to listen to this play-by-play of the night.

"She goes into the shower, so I throw in the tape, and I can't believe the guy I see she is fucking." He stopped and took another drag.

Saw Dust is now paying attention as if they were repeating the winning lotto numbers on the television.

"I had time to rewind and watch it a few more times."

He paused again and took another drink from the bottle. The whisky ran out of his mouth to drown the 5 o'clock stubble.

"She comes out with nothing on, asks me what I'm watching, and she wanted to go another round with me." Taking another drag from his cigarette, "That's when I stood up and shot the bitch in the head."

Chapter Five

The best burger in Spruce Wood was from a pub called Murphy's. It was also the best watering hole in town to quench your thirst. This was a town where everyone knew everyone; a concept this pub was all about, as well. It was located right in the middle of the downtown area. It was a red brick building and on the front of the building was a green canopy that said "Murphy's." They had a beer garden right between the main bar and party room. Paver blocks on the ground in the beer garden gave it that old cobblestone road look. They had a tree right in the middle of the garden. Bird houses with live birds living in them. Lots of seating with TV'S hanging for people to watch the games outside.

Inside it had a horseshoe bar right when you walked in. High top tables along the windows. Booths on the other side of the walls with multiple tables scattered throughout the middle of the establishment. Then on the farthest wall from the entrance, they had dart boards set up. Plus, they had those old arcade games of Missile Command and Frogger. In the corner of that wall was an old-fashioned juke box. On the walls hung pictures of Spruce Wood from the olden days, mixed with neon beer signs.

The place was hopping, and John was holding hands with Cassidy, followed by his family, as they headed to an open booth. When they were a few steps into the main bar, everyone in the establishment cheered. The town was doing that for all the players that came there after the game. As they continued towards the empty booth, John acknowledged everyone with a wave. Cassidy spoke in John's ear as they walked.

"That's all about you, Mr. Baseball."

John smiled as his face turned red. He loved the attention, but still played coy and shy with people. He loved when Cass called him Mr. Baseball. She got that from the movie they watched together, Mr. Baseball with Tom Selleck. It was about a washed-up American baseball player going to Japan to play baseball. John noticed many of his teammates were already there, sitting down at tables. He high fived a few of them and noticed a few already had some beverages in front of them. He even noticed the mayor of the town and the sheriff sitting at two different tables with their wives. The atmosphere was lively as people were all happy that finally Spruce Wood Varsity Baseball was back in the playoffs for the first time since 1977.

Everyone crammed their way into the booth. Immediately a waitress in her 40's came by the table smiling and said, "Hello, Malone family."

Her name was Natalie and she lived on the same block as they did. She had two little ones herself. She waitressed for extra money to raise money for her own craft-making business. Stephanie had babysat her kids for the last couple years. Plus, everyone saw and talked to her at Murphy's. It seemed she was their regular waitress every time they came here, which was a lot. Everyone said hello, as she grabbed her pencil and pad. She had curly short hair with a freckled face as she was 100 percent Irish. She was of medium height wearing the Murphy's tee shirt with short shorts that showed off her long legs with low cut white gym shoes. You could see the rock on her finger as the neon beer light made the diamond glisten green. Mr. Malone ordered for everyone - a pitcher of Old Style for himself and his wife, and water for everyone along with a few pictures of soda, regular and diet cola.

On the televisions, they had most of the screens playing the White Sox. They had a few other sets with the Cardinals playing. John loved baseball and noticed the Cubs on one television. Then he wondered to himself, "Why would any human being want to watch that crappy team?"

The plan was to eat dinner with the family. Then maybe hang out with some of the guys from the team after they ate. Then he knew Cassidy wanted to watch some movies. That always led to some hot images in his head. She was smoking hot this day, dressed in very short shorts showing off her long tan legs. She had on an old, faded Orange Crush tee shirt. She had cut the shirt in half to show off her midsection with the emerald green piercing in the belly button. Her breasts were a perfect handful. She was also wearing one of his hats with her ponytail coming out of the back; a style that just made him wild. John's dad had the conversation steered around the first school they played in the playoffs, probably about two hours from Spruce Wood. John felt Cassidy's hand on his leg, as his dad's voice suddenly sounded like one of Charlie Brown's teachers. As he felt something move, he slowly looked at his gal smiling at him. They were jammed together in the booth which was fine with him.

Chapter Six

The Ranch, for the Venomous Vipers motorcycle club, was out in the country. The Venomous Vipers may have called their group a club. However, this group was a bunch of outlaws. They had charters all over the United States. They were not the biggest in the States, but they were growing with charters popping up all over like McDonald's restaurants. Their main business was pure blow. They mastered getting this product all over the States. They even started making their own supply in some of the states. They avoided other biker gangs as they stayed out of the big cities. However, they were still able to get their cocaine in the major cities because they contracted that stuff out to people who had connections in those cities. Sure, blood was spilled from time to time, but they were a gang that did not want the credit for anything that would tie back to them. Their members have been arrested on many charges. They even have members in prison. The authorities never were able to get the big fish of the gang. The lack of evidence was always the hardest part when trying to get a conviction. The Venomous Vipers were all ex-military. They were trained to leave nobody behind. They were trained to leave no evidence behind that would cause problems for members at a later date. If the authorities had evidence, they would find the right people to steal it. Witnesses were always dispatched as well. This group of outlaws were smart and well-trained. They had a lot of money backing them. They had people in position in high places as well.

Blade Runner and Saw Dust disposed of two bottles of whiskey. It was around dusk as the sun was retreating behind the trees of the ranch, and they figured it was the perfect time to get rid of the body. Both of them wrapped the body up in blankets and loaded her into the back of an SUV. They gathered her clothes, purse, and whatever else she came with. It all went in the back of the truck. They both hopped in the dark colored SUV and drove down the path to the woods, on the furthest point of the ranch.

"Nothing like a Viking-style funeral in the middle of the weekend," Blade Runner said in the front seat.

Saw Dust drove slowly over the rocky dirt path the club created throughout the ranch.

The SUV bounced up and down as the path went downwards, then went up a slope, and curved to the left. They could feel the body shifting in the back as the SUV was rocking.

"Bitch does not deserve a funeral," as Saw Dust guided the SUV to the site on the ranch, which they used to get rid of their problems.

"Let's call it a BBQ then," as Blade Runner laughed for the first time. The pit of his rage was still inside ready to jump out as Saw Dust was figuring out.

Saw Dust chuckled out loud and turned on the radio to keep his friend calm and cool.

"After we are done, let's go eat like Kings and drink until all the pain is gone, when all our brain cells are dead, and then some pink pussy for dessert."

"HELL YEAH," as a Metallica song came on and Blade Runner turned up the volume. Both jammed as the body shifted again and rolled to the other side of the SUV.

It did not take that long for them to come to the end of the road. Saw Dust eased the SUV on a section of high grass as the head lights shone on a machine that dug holes. It had a blue tarp over it. He coasted the SUV slowly and pulled up to a pile of dirt.

He put the vehicle in park as he said, "This is the end of the road as I would like to thank everyone for flying with Saw Dust airlines."

"Keep the lights on," Blade Runner said as he opened his door.

Blade Runner looked around as they already had a hole dug next to a pile of dirt. Inside the hole, they had their own makeshift grill. This was not their first rodeo or their last at getting rid of bodies. It looked like the metal grill on top of a Weber being held up by some piping. It was a regular fire pit. Lay the body on top of the grill. Set your logs under the metal grilling. Light it from the bottom and poof the body goes up in flames just like a Viking funeral. Saw Dust got out and had the head lights perfectly shining on the burner and dirt pile. He quickly lit a cigarette and headed to the back of the SUV where Blade Runner had the back hatch opened. They both looked at his former old lady, Holly, wrapped tightly in a bag.

"Had high hopes for you darling," as he smiled in the way the Joker did in Batman.

"I'll get the logs from the shed while you say your goodbyes." Saw Dust made his way over to a secluded shed, behind the digger and covered up by a weeping willow.

"This bitch does not deserve any goodbyes," as he spat on the blanket and looked around.

The sun was almost completely gone, and it started to cool things off. The trees were rustling from a distance and a breeze could be felt on the back of his sweaty neck. He was still worked up from all of this going down today. His intentions had been he was going to marry Holly. He wanted a big biker-style wedding. He never got a chance to ask the two-timing bitch for her hand. As he sat back down inside the back of the SUV, he had taken out a smoke and lit it up with his zippo. The breeze made the flame move, but it did not go out. He was remembering some good ole times when they first started seeing each other. How hot she was wearing that all leather outfit when they had met at one of those biker parties where all the charters got together. He even started to pet her head. Actually, he stroked the inside of the blanket touching her, matted with blood, hair. He looked out in the distance as the orange ball was now off the clock sending one ray of sunshine through the trees. Blade Runner snapped out of it as he heard Saw Dust yell to him.

"We are a go."

He was climbing out of the hole. He went to the shed, brought a canister of gasoline back, and he had just finished pouring it around the bottom the group called the rotisserie. Flames started under the metal grating.

"Let's get this done."

Blade Runner grabbed the body by the head and started dragging it out of the back of the SUV like a roll of carpet. Saw Dust came just in time to grab the leg part of the rolled-up body known as Holly Denniger. They then threw the body onto the grating like throwing a log in back of a truck. Saw Dust kicked the body straight on the grating as flames began to singe the blanket. Then Saw Dust gathered up some twigs and straw, like hay, and placed it on top of the body. Blade Runner stood there and looked at the blanket catching fire. He could see some of her hair sticking out of the blanket starting to singe, and he thought he could smell the wildflower shampoo she used.

Saw Dust interrupted his train of thought asking, "Any last words before we pour some more of this on her?" He had the canister of gasoline in his hands.

"Fuck no."

He grumbled as he took the gasoline and poured it all over the twigs and hay that Saw Dust just covered up. The gasoline hit the flames and poof the flames came alive and just ate the

15

dead body up. Within a few minutes, you could see the skull as all the skin just melted off Holly. Blade Runner had another cigarette lit as both just stood there watching. Saw Dust was admiring his handy work. While inside, Blade Runner's rage was building. Flames continued to burn as Blade Runner flicked his cigarette butt into the bonfire. He suggested they get out of there, as they walked back to the SUV. They knew the fire would eventually go out on its own as Saw Dust pulled away. He gave a look once more at his handy work, and then drove back the same way they came.

"Do we have to take care of any loose ends?"

What Saw Dust meant was would any of her family and friends come looking.

"No," said Blade Runner looking off into the woods just collecting his thoughts.

As they drove on, all of sudden a beeping noise came from inside the SUV. Blade Runner opened the glove compartment and took out his beeper. He saw someone was calling him and he did recognize the number. The beeping freaked out Saw Dust for a second, but then he saw the beeper come out of the glove compartment. He was back to cool as he drove on back to the club house.

"Who's calling you?"

"Not sure, but I'll find out when we get back to the house." The SUV started rocking as they were driving over the bumpy part of the trail.

Chapter Seven

Late that afternoon before Blade Runner and Saw Dust put Holly Denniger in her eternal place of rest. Before everyone went to Murphy's to celebrate the big victory. The phone company had one of their vans on a country road working on one of the telephone poles. The road was a two-lane highway, Route 33, the main intersection of a small rural town called Drumleen. Drumleen was approximately 20 minutes outside of Spruce Wood, the nearest town. Spruce Wood was not a huge metropolitan city. It was more like a small suburb. But it had way more people than Drumleen, which was basically made up of farmers living in that town. Besides farmers, they had one small general store called Mary Jane's tucked away off the main highway. Most people would not know the little grocer existed as they passed it by doing the speed limit or faster.

Drumleen was also home to the Venomous Vipers biker gang, the Southern Illinois charter. Acres of land were owed by the biker gang. The telephone company van had a yellow bell on the side of the truck. In bold black print above the logo were the words, Illinois Bell. Its flashers were blinking quickly and surrounded by orange cones. The van looked normal from the average person passing by. They had a guy high up in the air on a ladder leaning against a pole, looking at the transformer. He climbed up the ladder and then went up the pole from those metal rungs that were inserted into the wooden pole. He looked normal in his neon vest, hard hat, and tool belt. Maybe a very small percentage of people would notice that the van is not the regular van used in the Illinois Bell fleet. It's an older Ford Econoline utility van. Illinois Bell had just acquired a whole new fleet of vans. People would think maybe they are still using some of the older ones. This van had another guy inside the van. He was hitting buttons on a computer that was in the middle console of the van.

In the back of the van, a greenish glowing light was shining. In the back of the van, they did not have phone wiring stacked up in those round wooden wheels. Or compartments that contained parts. However, it did have some fancy computers and monitors going on. They even had a guy in the back of the van with headphones on looking at the monitors. Afterall, it was a surveillance van.

"How far are you from the target," a man in his early 30's inquired into the microphone of the head set.

He was clean shaven with a round nose, fat cheeks, and short thinning brown hair combed to the side with perfection. Then he heard back from the guy in the field.

"Should be at the target in five minutes, over."

The FBI has been trying to infiltrate the Venomous Vipers for a very long time. This charter and many more across the states have been under surveillance. But they had no hard evidence, just hearsay. Blood has been spilled. Bodies have been piling up. More drugs are on the street.

17

All their charters were secluded. It was hard to get eyes on them and what they were doing. They were unable to break any of the drug dealers they busted in the streets. They were scared for their own lives and those of their families. However, the authorities knew that the Venomous Vipers were distributing the drugs to the dealers.

They got lucky with undercover agents in some of the charters. They were able to get a man on the inside of the Southern Illinois charter. He was the biker gang's prospect. He did all the meaningless tasks. He did the dirty work none of the members wanted to do. Over the last few months, he was able to provide some great intel to the FBI. He was able to tell them a way they could get into the ranch undetected. They were praying this mission would still work because they lost contact with this agent. Before they lost contact, the agent told them this particular day would be perfect for our guys to get a listening device and camera installed. Most of the club were headed out of the ranch this weekend. The FBI was gambling that the undercover agent did not give up any information to the Vipers about today's mission. They had faith in this guy that he would rather die and give them nothing if he was found out.

"Suspects are leaving in SUV, over," a man from the FBI dressed in all black with night vision goggles whispered into his radio.

The sun has been going down and thus the night vision googles on. He made his way through rough terrain and a thick patch of trees which blocked out most of the rays. Now he was crouched down in between two dumpsters next to one of the trailers.

Then the guy inside the back of the van said, "We need you to get in that club house which should be the biggest building on the lot right in the middle of everything, over."

"Roger that," as he quickly scanned the area for people on this ghost town of an evening.

After going up the hill for almost a mile through the woods, finally he could see all these trailers. It looked like a trailer park. However, in the middle they had a huge building which was two stories high and had to be the club house. Surrounding that they had a horseshoe of buildings that were also two stories tall and looked like apartments. The place was huge with barns out on the outskirts with big fields in between. They had a wooden fence surrounding the whole compound.

"Ok, easy like a bunny hopping down the Easter trail," the FBI agent thought.

He quickly lurched from the dumpsters and ran along one of the trailers avoiding the lights they had along the rows of the trailers. He crouched down as he tiptoed at a quick pace, feeling like the Grinch as he peeked out along the edge of the trailer at the road that probably would take him to the main club house. His name was Terry Long, and he loved his job. He always wanted to be some kind of spy. He loved James Bond movies. He loved to be behind enemy lines with everything on the line. He has done it overseas in the Middle East. Those were some scary times as an Army Ranger. The things he had to do. The things he saw. Bikers, or any domestic threat, did not scare him. He quickly ran in the shadows as he dove on the ground and rolled to avoid a light that was on a top tree branch, giving the place great light in that section of the ranch. The undercover agent had told them that he believed no cameras were placed around the housing area. They basically had security cameras around the perimeter of the property and the main club house, but he did not want to slow down and find out. Terry was 32 years old. He looked like he was younger. He was just under six feet tall and built like a rock all muscle no fat on his frame. He moved like a panther from trailer row to trailer row. It did not take him long as now he crouched down in shadows looking at club house and seeing the cameras. Plus, the skies were now dark, and the area all around the club house was lit up like Vegas in a way.

"I have made it to the Viper nest, over." He spoke quietly into his radio set.

The man in the van responded, "Stand by two minutes, over."

Terry leaned up against one of the trailers and crouched down. He had a backpack on his back, leaning against the tin metal of the trailer. He checked his clip on his gun. He felt the cool

18

breezy air blow on his face. He felt the wetness of perspiration on his back. He adjusted his night vision googles. He peeked out from the side of the trailer and suddenly darkness prevailed over the ranch. All the lights went out as Terry hightailed it over to the door of the main club house. He saw everything while running a full sprint about 50 yards. He crouched down by the door figuring he was going to have to pick the lock. Instead, he tried the knob, and he was in luck as the door was unlocked, and he peeked his head in the dark room. To him he could see everything with a greenish glow.

"Show time," he said to himself as he entered.

Chapter Eight

All of them had ordered burgers as Murphy's had the best in town. The patty was bigger than your head, combined with a scrumptious buttery sesame seed bun. Natalie put down multicolored baskets of steak fries down first. The hot steam rose from each basket. Mouth buds watered around the whole booth. Then she brought them all cheeseburgers. John and Cassie added bacon to them. All of the burgers came with the standard tomato, lettuce, and they made their own pickles at Murphy's that were fresh and very tasty. Natalie asked if the needed anything else, but they shook their heads with satisfied grins. They were only halfway into their beverages according to the glass pictures on the table.

The games on TV were pretty good. As all of them were one run affairs with the teams they were rooting for having the lead. John's sisters have been eyeballing the video games as they would dash over there as soon as they were done. Probably with only half the burgers finished since they were gigantic. Mr. Malone, John's father, was a big baseball fan. He read all the papers about the regular MLB. But he knew about high school baseball other than his own son's team. He was up to par with many of the teams that qualified for the Playoffs.

"You have to watch Donohue's slider, son. It's his wipe out pitch so you might have to get to him early in the count," referring to the next opponent John was going to face in the very first round.

"Dad! Get a life. How do you know all this?" His son said this with a smile as both of them had their own creative banter as father and son.

The father then laughed and shook his head. He took another swig of Old Style from his mug and attacked his burger.

"Son, I know all, and I know you will do well."

For the next ten minutes all of them listened silently to a Green Day song playing on the jukebox. The Malone family mauled down their burgers like they hadn't eaten in days. Nobody complained as everyone was very satisfied with their feast. Only a few fries remained in the baskets when they finished. Everyone pretty much finished their burger. The daughters left the lettuce and a slice of tomato on the plate with some remaining ketchup where they dipped the fries.

"We were a little hungry," they joked as Natalie was taking empty plates and baskets.

John's mother got up to let her daughters get out of the booth. They immediately raced to the video games as they had been waiting patiently with their quarters ready. Mr. Malone ordered some more drinks for the table. Everyone was at the end with maybe a sip left with melting cubes in the soda glasses.

"Honey, I'm going to say hello to Fred," Mr. Malone said to his wife, feeling his knees crackle, getting out of the booth.

Fred was the Sheriff of Spruce Wood. He had left his wife sitting alone and was talking to the Mayor of the town whose wife had just strolled to the bathroom. It was a small town, so Fred and Mr. Arthur Malone were friends since the sand box days.

"Hey Arty."

Everyone called him that, except the kids referred to him as Mr. Malone. They had been each other's best men at their weddings. They had remained best friends for all these years in their beloved town.

Cassie was talking about how she had to call her parents before they left. John was looking at a poster on the wall about a band called Ardara coming next week to play live music. He was semi-listening, watching the games, and then saw it look like the cook put some money in the pay phone. When he was done zoning out, he asked "Were we watching movies at your house or mine?"

He looked at her angelic face of an angel, as they reached for each other's hands. What a perfect night he thought. He could still hear the cook on the pay phone talking loudly over the music, as a Tom Petty song was on the juke box.

Chapter Nine

Back inside the clubhouse, Saw Dust went to the washroom while Blade Runner dialed the number that was on the pager. He stood behind the bar, and it rang three times on the other end, before finally a female voice answered.

"Murphy's."

"Someone just paged me," Blade Runner cleared his throat and spoke in a raspy voice.

There was a pause, so Blade Runner quickly interrupted the girl, knowing who had paged him.

"Probably, Brad?"

"Can you hold, please? I'll check."

The background noise on her end disappeared as he thought about why the lights were not on outside when they pulled up. The thought was quickly knocked out of his head when a guy's voice spoke up on the other end.

"Dude, let me call you back. Are you at the club?"

"Ok."

Blade Runner hung up the phone and fished another cigarette out of his pack as he looked at himself in the bar mirror. He looked like a beaten man in dire need of sleep. He took a huge drag out of his cigarette and stared at his dark jet-black hair, greasy like a guy working at the local lube joint. It was pretty long past his shoulders, slicked back with all kinds of split ends. The stubble on the face was salt and pepper. He was wearing a plain black shirt with a light blue faded sleeveless jean jacket. On the back was the Venomous Viper logo of a snake wrapped around a Harley. In the front he had his code name, Blade Runner, on a patch sewed to the jacket. He wore dark blue jeans with big black steel-toe construction boots. His arms were filled with all kinds of dragon tats spitting out fire. He actually had a dragon that went throughout his whole body. With lots of other dragons and deadly snakes with barbed wire that made the President a scary individual with wrestler-like huge arms. The phone then rang again. By this time, he was crushing the cigarette butt through other old butts in the ashtray that looked like a skull. He did not say anything as he knew it was the cook again.

"He's here."

"Ok," as Blade Runner's big beefy mitt wrapped around an empty bottle of paddy as blood was dripping from the palm of his hand and as he crushed the middle of the bottle with one hand.

His face was now fire engine red in the mirror and seemed to glow in the dim lighting of the club house.

"He just finished dinner so I do not know how long he will be here for."

A dark raspy voice grunted the words, "Keep him there. I'm on my way."

The man at the pay phone heard him hang up. An Eagles song was playing, and the atmosphere continued to be electric as every was having a good time. He could see the guy Blade Runner had an interest in. He was in the kitchen most of the night, but he had finally got out for a break. He had a bad feeling in the pit of his stomach. He hoped he'd get here soon. He hated being in bed with the Venomous Vipers, but he was deep in it. Favors like being a look out helped reduce what he owed to this notorious biker gang. They could make you disappear faster than a sneeze.

Blade Runner came from behind the bar and immediately walked out the door. The lights were now on outside, but that did not even cross his mind. He went back to his room. Grabbed his gun and some extra clips. He checked the clip in the pistol, ensuring it was filled and ready to go. He then walked out of his living quarters that were a downstairs apartment centered around everything on the ranch. He left the door open and quickly jumped on his bike. Only a few bikes were there since many were on a ride that weekend. The motor came to life with a thunderous roar. The headlight gleamed off a tree and the bike was set in gear. The motor roared while the gravel crunched under the wheels. He headed through the curvy roads and out of the ranch.

Chapter Ten

The guys from the truck were able to turn off the power to all the club's security features to let their agent move around without setting off any red flags. Terry moved around inside the dark club house like a ninja. It did not take long for him to install the listening devices, as they were small and stuck on things with ease.

"Testing 1, testing 2, testing 3. Can you hear me? Over."

From the van he immediately got feedback, as now he crouched behind the bar.

"Loud and clear," he heard in his earpiece.

All's he left was a camera over the bar area. He was admiring the Hamm's beer sign. It had that cartoon bear in a boat sailing on the water.

"Hamm's, the beer from sky blue waters," he was singing to himself as he looked from the sign to the Venomous Viper banner hanging behind the bar which gave him an idea of where to put the camera.

It did not take him very long to get the camera installed which he planted behind the banner looking out from one of the Viper's eyes. It was mounted perfectly in the middle where it could see the whole clubhouse which was very big. It was a room that had bar tables scattered around. It had couches set up in a horseshoe pattern facing a large T.V. screen in one corner. Pool tables on the other side. The club house was the place where these guys talked about their endeavors. True confessions came out. The FBI wanted all this good stuff on tape. The agent that got in the Venomous Vipers said lots of important stuff was talked about freely among members right there in the bar area. They believed their security was unbreakable. Except the FBI finally got a man through this crack down security. It was not easy as it took months to figure out. Terry was ready to leave when he heard the SUV pull up.

"Mom and Dad. I'm going to be a tad late for dinner. Someone's here," as he heard the doors slam.

"Hide somewhere quickly. We will have to turn the power back on, so they do not suspect anything."

Terry quickly hid behind the bar and whispered, "Roger that," as he heard voices getting closer to the doors.

He heard the doors open. He then saw the lights go on inside the club house. One guy went right towards the bar and grabbed the phone while the other guy left the room. He probably went in the bathroom or the kitchen.

The man inside the back of the van was the quarterback monitoring everything about this mission. He talked into his head set to the guy on the actual pole.

"We have a phone call being made. Have you been able to tap into their lines yet?"

The guy on the pole was having all sorts of problems.

"That is a negative. I'm in the process of changing out a few things that have been badly decaying due to weather issues."

"Fuck. Don't let me bother you. Finish what you are doing. These calls might not mean anything."

The guy in the front seat of the van on the computer said over his shoulder, "Lights and power are back on inside. I was able to disable their security for the time being with the power being back on."

"Excellent."

About ten minutes later, the guy on the pole could hear the roar of the Harley Davidson coming towards the country road. He looked down and saw from how high up he was, the head light flashing through the trees. He noticed the sloped curvy road in the trees from the light of the motorcycle. He had one more wire to connect to have the lines officially tapped in. "We have some company coming our way from inside the ranch," he said into his head set.

The quarterback of the operation came back quickly and said, "He'll probably pass us by without even noticing anything."

Blade Runner did see the van. He did see the flashing lights. He even saw the cones. But he roared by them without one thought as he zoomed by the van, putting it into a higher gear and he was off heading towards Spruce Wood.

Inside the club house, Saw Dust comes out of the bathroom. He's walking through the hallway where both walls are covered in pictures of motorcycles through the years. Thinking Blade Runner was still there, he spoke out loud.

"I would not use the bathroom. I did not give it a courtesy flush. I just let it linger and it has taken over the bathroom. Damn tacos I had for lunch." He saw nobody in the clubhouse.

"WHERE DID YOU GO BLADE RUNNER? Leaving me here talking to my own self."

He puts his pack of cigarettes on the bar. Fished himself out one. In a fetal position, Terry has made himself as small as possible as he fit himself under a shelf. He's looking at Saw Dust's boots. Fresh dirt on them. At that moment, he carefully slid his knife out of its sheath. Saw Dust lights the zippo lighter, as you can smell the blue-orange flame.

"Well, I think it's time I set myself up with another drink," continuing to talk to himself as he takes a big drag of the cigarette.

He leaves it dangling in the corner of his mouth as he turns around and spots a nice bourbon he would like to indulge in. Grabs the bottle and a rock glass, then turns around to the bar and pours himself half a glass. He sniffs it first as he puts his smoke in an ashtray. He then takes a swig and keeps it in his mouth like he's some kind of bourbon whisky expert. He even sloshed it around.

Then he says out loud, " That is some good shit."

His foot moves as his boot is now touching Terry.

"What the fuck is that?"

Before he could look down, Terry grabbed the man's boot and with one hand sliced the tendon in the back of the left foot, with his blade. It brought Saw Dust down to the ground behind the bar like a ton of bricks. He landed hard on his back and could feel the back of his ankle sagging. Blood is soaking the back of his jeans. He sees Terry pop out from behind the bottom shelf.

"Who the fuck are you?"

"Probably now, your worst nightmare."

He leapt out from behind the shelf and had the knife in his right hand above his shoulder with a drizzle of his blood still dripping off the teeth of the dagger.

Saw Dust's eyes widened as he lifted one hand up to try to stop Terry in midair. His other hand was trying to reach for his own blade. But he had no time as Terry took his left hand and knocked down Saw Dust hand defending him. It landed right on the Saw Dust's chest as he brought the knife down right through his neck. He turned his head when contact was first made. Terry drove the knife in the perfect spot as Saw Dust immediately went limp. His right hand clutched at his own knife handle but unable to pull it out. Blood squirted up like a geyser when Terry pulled it out of his neck. Drops of crimson red speckled all over the agent's face.

Terry rolled off the top of him. His heart was racing. He managed to untangle his feet and stand up from behind the bar. He was sure that only two bikers went in the clubhouse in the first place. He knew Blade Runner walked out. He heard the bike roar and the noise disappeared in the distance.

"Fucking cock sucker," he looked down on the man he killed.

He took a bar rag from the counter of the bar and wiped his face. He was trying to think, but his mind was racing. He had to contact the guys in the van. He needed to get out of there just in case someone came waltzing in. He spoke into the radio, but nothing happened. Something was wrong. He took off the head set and found that it broke when he leapt from under the bar.

"FUCK ME!"

Inside the back of the van, they had tried 7 times to get in contact with the agent inside the ranch.

"Come on, Terry. Tell me what's going on, over." He quickly switched lines and talked to the guy on top of the pole. "Hey, what are you seeing out there? We lost contact with Terry. Ove?"

The guy on top had a view as he was up high. He could only see a small section of the ranch as it was surrounded with lots of trees. Lots of spruce trees with branches thick with needles blocking eyes from the outside. It was dark and that was the major problem, as he had nothing.

"Negative on anything no signs of movement."

The guy inside the van just shook his head as this mission had been looking promising, and now things were unraveling.

"Stay up there, keep your eyes peeled and your ears open. Hopefully he's ok and the radio is just fucked up."

"Roger that," he heard in his ears.

The guy in back of the van asked the guy up front, "What's our timetable up there?"

They had a time limit set up if the radio failed.

"He still has 15 minutes," the guy in the front seat said.

"15 minutes," the man in back of the van said to himself.

The 15 minutes would be a lifetime for the three of them. The waiting. Looking at the clock ticking away slowly. Hoping their friend can make it off the ranch and back to the van. Or they would be going in after him. The guy inside the van shut down the outside lights once again. Took out the power grid to the cameras of the club's security system. He kept the lights inside on so none of the club members inside would get suspicious. The thought that if Terry could get outside, he'd be home free and unable to be found by any of those meathead bikers.

Terry left Saw Dust dead behind the bar and headed for the door. He wanted to go the same way he had come. He started to follow that path and make his way through the trailer part of the Ranch. It was easy as the lights were shut down outside. His night vision goggles were on and he was noticing the trailers he stopped at. Crouching down, he looked to see if the coast was clear. He only stopped once and looked around to see if anybody was following him, or even just moving around the ranch. He took a deep breath and continued as he came to a fork in the road. Two paths. Both looked the same. He quickly made the decision as he sprinted towards the trees and down the hill.

He was going down the hill at a high speed. He could feel some branches brushing off his arms. He could see branches coming towards his face as he quickly ducked out the way. He was seeing a different path as he slowed down a tad, but he was still going down the slope of the hill at a quick pace. He now knew that he was not going down the same way he came up. He had to slow down more because based on the inside information he recalled, many of the surrounding areas were in fact booby trapped. Either he finds the path he came up in or manages to find the main road where they drive in and out. He tried to slow down, but his body was taking him down the hill faster. He tried to slow his pace down by grabbing a spruce tree branch, but felt his leg slip from the muddy terrain. He grabbed the tree branch and of all sudden it snapped. Now he lost both his feet as he slid down the hill on his back in a nasty free fall still at a high speed. He tried to reach his arms out, but he could not grip any of the roots from the tree as now the slide came up to a ledge on the hill. A spot where he hoped he could stop before he continued this bad journey down the hill.

Terry managed to grab on to a bigger root from a bigger tree as he wrapped his fingers around it, bringing his free fall to a sudden end. His feet felt the ledge of the hill as he then pulled himself up. His other hand grabbed on to the root sticking out of the hill. His night vision googles remained on, and he looked further down the hill. There could have been major problems as he may have been decapitated by many tree stumps coming out of the dirt like canker sores. He looked in both direction as everything was green from his vision. Everything was thick with branches of the many trees that surrounded the ranch. He took another deep breath and decided to walk the ledge in hopes of reaching the path of the hill he had taken up. He knew he was about 50 to 100 yards away now in his estimations, as he tip toed like a ballerina in between spruce branch. All the while, trying to avoid patches of slippery leaves caked on the rocks from the rain the other night.

He was back on track, as he moved along side of the ledge like a circus performer in the dark woods.

"Get the hell out of here and when I'm done with this day, I'm going to need the biggest drink they have at the bar."

He knew he had to make his way over a tree that was blocking the rock ledge to get over to the path he came up.

He looked the slope up and down. He then saw a small area that looked on to the main highway. He could see one of his guys up high above the telephone pole.

"Alright. about at the halfway part of this hill."

He took a step around the tree as he held on to the trunk while he maneuvered around it. When he was almost around the tree, he heard a snap. At first it sounded like a large branch cracking very closely. But then he felt pain shriek through his leg. Pain as something converged on his leg right above his ankle. He could see the shiny green teeth through his lenses wrapped around his leg like an alligator mouth that begins to devour your leg.

"Fucckking bear trap," he hisses.

He still held on to the trunk of the tree. He had one of his feet planted and could see the other as this trap ravaged right through his pants and penetrated right through the skin. Blood soaked up the pant leg in seconds. He felt more pain as he tried to move, but the trap was chained up to the tree and there was not much leeway in the chain. He then tried to open the trap with his left hand holding the tree with his other arm. Then he felt his foot give away as then his hand slipped off the trunk of the tree. His body slipped down the hill, as the bear trap held the other leg on the ledge. He dropped a few feet as his face planted in the ground. His free hand broke the fall but now he heard something click in the terrain. His hand felt like he pushed something in the ground. He thought, "no way," as he thought of something else the undercover agent had said. He moved his hand and then turned around to pull himself back up the hill. He hung upside down by the bear trap around the tree by his leg. Then an explosion occurred. The guy on the telephone could see a section of the forest go up like a fire ball lighting up the darkness. "What the Fuck" he said to himself as he tried to look at that spot with his binoculars.

"What happened, Terry? Show yourself buddy."

He could hear the guy in the back of the van in his ear, but he had nothing good to tell him.

Chapter Eleven

Blade Runner maintained a steady speed of 70 mph. He had the wind in his face and from time to time a bug would hit his clear visor glasses that wore wear at night. The whole machine vibrated at high speed, especially on the handles. His fingers tingled with a mild sensation as cars whipped by on the other end sounding like Imperial TI Fighters in Star Wars. The moon looked like a banana on country roads with some clouds, as the night grew cooler. An owl hooted in the distance as Blade Runner was coming towards the town limits of Spruce Wood. He figured he would have to wait for the guy that slept with his old lady. When he got the call, he knew tonight was perfect. He did not think about if it was going to be a good time or even a bad time. He did not really know what he was going to do. The machine roared and all his muscles were jumping out of his skin. The blood was boiling inside. His blood pressure had to be off the charts as he rode. To think of this guy having the balls to do that to him. To have even bigger balls to tape it. The guy probably did not send him the tape, as that is a death wish. His fingers wanted to strangle him as he watched his eyes pop out of his head. He was not into the theatrics of the situation. A bullet would do nicely as well. He felt the taste of revenge on his tongue, as he leaned into the turn that would bring him into Spruce Wood.

Valerie Malone was a middle-aged mother. She was a woman that did not look her age, maybe 5 years younger. She had a nice figure and a pretty face. In her kids' eyes, she was the best mum in the whole world. She did not think that her kids thought that. She was now talking to her son's girlfriend like they were pals. Her daughters enjoying the video games across the room. Her son was talking to a couple guys from the team while her husband finished up talking with the mayor and the Sheriff. She saw him go to the washroom, as he gave the look to Val letting her know it was time to go home. She was finishing a cup of coffee, because she needed a little pick me up after a few pints of Old Style. She was a well-balanced woman. She could fit in many circles. She can drink a beer or just enjoy some wine. She loved watching sports and knew a lot about the games. She was a tomboy when she was growing up with many older brothers playing sports. She even played sports in high school and college. Her love was always tennis. She actually teaches the sport at the local country club. That was not her main job as she was in the advertising world. She was truly well-balanced. Her daughters had other likes than just sports. She could roll with the punches in any direction. She was talking with Cassidy about movies. Romantic comedies was the subject. Say Anything was the topic for the last 15 minutes as they both laughed.

"Had to have seen that movie over a hundred times," she took a sip of her coffee as she remembers watching that with her best friend from high school. The movie was only from a few years ago.

"So you still hang out with her?"

"I hang out with her at least once a week. A lot of times, more than that as she's like a sister that I always had in a family filled with men." A sparkle in her eye showed their fun times together were still fun and very necessary.

Cassidy told her about her friends. How they hang out even though she spends much of her free time with John. Mr. Malone came out of the bathroom and immediately paid off Natalie without even asking for the bill. John caught Cassidy's eyes looking at him and they both smiled. They were talking about the White Sox, who held the lead late in the game. Natalie smiled and thanked Mr. Malone, as she knew the bill was taken care of and also had a great tip in the amount she got from him. Mr. Malone thanked her and told her to give the lovely couple two more sodas. He then headed back to the table to get his wife and the gals, which would be hard because they were kicking some alien butt in the Missile Command.

Arthur Malone stood in the bar, looked around, and smiled. His son talking shop with some of the other guys on the team and about the games on the television. He flashed back to the days where he played for Spruce Wood High. Arthur, who everyone called Art or Arty, was born and bred in the small town. He played baseball at one of the old churches with his friends. The summer days involved nothing but baseball, ice cream, and swimming that took all the hours during those long summer vacations from school. He was even thinking of when he had two pretty good seasons in the Minors. Nagging injuries stopped him from making to the big show. But, Arthur was also book smart and went off to college. Got his degree and met the love of his life in Valerie. Looking at her he felt she was out of his league at the time. That little hole-in-the-wall bar where with a few beers, he finally had the balls to go up to her and talk to her. She liked him and was waiting for him to finally break the ice. After that point it was pure magic. Sure, he would have loved to have been playing baseball. But a trophy wife, a best friend, and a great job were nothing to sneeze at. His degree was in business. He was a bigwig in the company called Wild Shamrock Enterprises, which dabbled in lots of business ventures. Arthur's arrival there tripled the company profits. He turned around the company without making cutbacks. The company actually expanded. He was well paid. He was a guy that gave back. He was a guy that would never showboat the fact that he had more money than others.

He too was middle aged. He was tall and had all of his hair even though it was salt and pepper on the roof. He stayed in shape. He and Val stayed active. Both loved long walks at night and to play tennis on the weekends together. Arthur loved playing with the kids. Especially John, who would still find time to go to the cages or throw the ball around in the backyard. Then looking at his two daughters, who kept him busy, playing video games. He was grateful to have all of his hair with the never-ending list of stuff to do. The list was large, but it was all stuff he enjoyed. He walked over and kissed Val on the forehead to interrupt the conversation she was having with his son's girlfriend.

"Look at this guy kissing me in public like that," Val giggled.

Cassidy could see the love these two had for themselves as a couple. She wanted the same thing for John and her. They had that right now, she believed. But she wanted this story book ending, as she could see both of them so happy. She knew this was no way some pretend job as well.

"I gathered up the women… the little gals," as Arthur did his one of many imitations from the movie The Blues Brothers.

"You go round them up and I'll meet you by the door."

Val stood up and said, "I need to hit the lady's room before we bounce," as she and Cassidy laughed.

"Sounds like a plan my lady," as he walked off towards the video games.

Arthur stopped and said goodbye to the mayor, who was ushering his wife out of Murphy's. Both gave each other quick a handshake. He kissed the mayor's wife on the cheek with a hug. Arthur rounded up his gals, practically prying them off the machines. Arthur played the ice cream on the way home card, and that seemed to always work. It was the one and only play that had a great percentage of working almost every time. All three of them met Valerie back at the table and said goodbye to Cassidy. John came over & said his goodbyes. He had his car in the lot, so he would drive him and Cassidy after they had one more soda. Natalie was at the table with two more pint glasses of cola with shaved ice inside the glasses that had Murphy's logo on them. Natalie said her goodbyes as everyone went their separate ways, leaving the two young love birds to watch the end of the Sox game.

Chapter Twelve

As the Malones drove out of Murphy's parking lot, they did not see a big guy get off a motorcycle. They did not see him check the clip in his gun as he stood by his big Harley Davidson. The one thing he loved, the only thing since the betrayal that took place. He looked at the back door of Murphy's from where he had the bike parked in-between two dumpsters. He had determination in his eyes to spill some blood. He felt a drag in his insides. He was breathing in fire that wanted to come out in flames. His eyeballs were popping out of his sockets. He had that look of a boxer. The look a ref has seen a million times. A look that could melt the opponent's skin. If the referee were a betting man, he would put his life savings just on this look. He started to walk towards the door, as he shoved the gun in the back of his waistband. His muscles throughout his body tensed up. Veins pulsated. It looked like his dragon tattoos would pounce on somebody. The parking lot was quiet. He could hear music coming from the doorway. His mind was blank. If you asked him that moment what band was playing, he would not know if it was Journey or Whitesnake. His skin was boiling. His fingers were twitchy as if he were stretching them as his knuckles were cracking. His nostrils flared as he heard many people talking and laughing having a good time.

Inside Murphy's, the game was close, but the Sox were trying to close it out in the ninth while hanging on by a thread.

Cassidy stood up and said, "I have to go to the bathroom." Both of them were almost finished with their colas.

John stood up and said, "Hurry back for the most important part of the game." They smiled at each other.

"When mother nature calls, mother nature calls," as she slid out of booth.

He helped her up and said, "Very true."

"We leave right after the game," as she looked up at her taller-than-her boyfriend.

He kissed her on the lips.

"Yes, because I can't wait to get you alone if you know what I mean." All of this in a funny voice as they both had their own 'sexy' voice.

Across the room, Jake, John's teammate, said "Get a room," as he faked a cough.

John smiled and sat back down. He went back to the game as the Sox were one out away from a victory.

The President of the Venomous Vipers walked through the back door of Murphy's. He had seen a door close, but not the person, as it was the women's bathroom. Cassidy did not see the big biker walk in as their paths just missed each other. This was not the first time the Blade Runner has been in Murphy's. It was not a joint he visited regularly. He had a few scrapes in this establishment in the past. One incident involved throwing a guy through the window. The local Police always tried to keep the Venomous Vipers from their small town of Spruce Wood. They even had a mutual agreement with the Police and the biker gang to leave each other alone. It has done well. The bikers have avoided Spruce Wood, while the Police does not look into what was going down in the ranch. It was out of their jurisdiction, but the local cops could make trouble on the outskirts. Plus, get the State Police involved. Or help the State Police.

John was watching the screen as he pumped his fist in the air. The Sox held on as he said to himself, "Yes, a great day in the baseball world."

31

He took another sip, his final sip, from the pint glass of cola. People in the bar were clapping seeing the win. He noticed a big guy walking through the arched doorway from the hall into the main part of the bar. His eyes went from the T.V. screen to the flames coming out of a dragon on his tattoo. He noticed the barbed wire and the scaly features on the dragon. In his head he wondered if all those tattoo drawings hurt like hell. He thought it was well done as the dragon looked fierce. For some odd reason he did not see the big biker reach for his gun from his waist band. He did not see him bring the gun out. He did not notice it until people were fleeing towards the doors. Some chairs came tumbling down. Some swear words were thrown out there. All this was going on as ZZ Top's "Legs" played loudly over the juke box. People started to scream about the gun, as more chairs tumbled. People were fleeing the scene like a hurricane was coming their way. However, John was frozen like a deer in headlights. He was watching all this go down. He seemed like he did notice teammates calling for him to get the hell out of there. He just watched as the gun was not pointed in his direction. He could see the Viper on the back of the faded jean jacket. It was the logo of the Venomous Vipers. It was a logo everyone knew in town. It was like seeing the arches for McDonald's. You see the Viper snake and you most likely want to get the hell out of dodge.

John could tell who the bullet was for, as he saw the man's eyes open wider. Saw him turn white as a sheet.

He tried to get up as he pushed his wife down in the booth and in slow motion he yelled, "GET DOWN!"

John was watching this in slow motion. As the man in the Viper jacket with the dragon tattoo saw him, walked his way, and squeezed the trigger. The wife ducked in the booth. John said to himself, "He's going after the Sheriff."

Then the bullet pierced the man in the left shoulder sending him back to a sitting position in the booth. More screams as people were jumping over fallen chairs and hightailing it out of the bar. John sat there in a daze to watch the man fire another shot. The man in the booth's hand went right to his left shoulder. He then looked up at the big motorcycle guy and he knew what this was all about

In barely a whisper he said, "Let's talk this out."

No words were heard from the big guy as another bullet came out of the gun. The man in the booth waved his hand to protect his body as the bullet went through the palm of the hand, and the bullet went through the wall just over his shoulder. Blood splattered in the air and landed all over the green booth. The Sheriff's wife was practically on the floor, with her man getting bullets deposited into his body. She folded into a fetal position crying and screaming. Words you could not understand even if you were right next to her. Sounded like a wounded animal. Then the man in the Venomous Viper jacket emptied the rest of his gun on the man without any words said.

He turned around and saw John shaking like a leaf in a dazed and confused state. Blade Runner was here for one man, the Sheriff, as he walked out of the bar with a brisk pace. Cassidy had locked the door in the bathroom and even turned off the lights, as Blade Runner lumbered past. John's knees wobbled as he sat, still in shock over what he just saw go down. Screams continued from the other side of the room. The Sheriff had multiple holes in him with blood spewing out through his shirt. Tables and chairs throughout the bar were tipped over. Broken pint glasses and food baskets caked the floors. After a few minutes of silence, the bartender peeked out from behind the bar and went for the phone to dial 9-1-1.

In the distance, from the back of the building, a motorcycle roared to life. Then it got louder as it drove away. People were huddled on the side of the building in between cars, looking to make sure the gunman was not coming after them. Some fled to the local restaurant next to Murphy's called Skippy's. It was a chain-type of restaurant like a Chili's or a Bennigan's. Some of the people locked themselves in the party room and dialed 9-1-1 from the phone inside. All while they hid behind the bar inside the party room with the lights off, trying not to make a sound so the gun man would not come in blazing. People at Skippy's immediately called 9-1-1 as they locked their doors as well. Through all this mayhem, one of the cooks leaned against the back door and watched Blade Runner leave the scene. He just quietly had a smoke as he knew he was only here for the Sheriff.

Chapter Thirteen

THE NEXT DAY

It was a restless night for Cassidy Sorensen as the remainder of the night replayed in her head over and over. The sound of the gunshot still echoed in her ears. The feeling that rippled through her body thinking the love of her life was shot. Then feeling relief when she opened up the bathroom door to see John standing, and then hugging each other so tightly not wanting to let go. Even with the screams in the background.

"SOMEONE CALL 9-1-1," was shouted over and over.

The shrieks of the woman whose husband laid in the booth, a bloody mess. Tears coming out like waterfalls from her eyes. Loud sirens in the background. Police cruisers racing to Murphy's. They screeched their tires to a complete stop. The door open with guns out. They ran into the bar like stormtroopers ready to shoot and kill if the suspect was still on the grounds. The paramedics and fire trucks followed. People stood outside the bar in complete shock, motionless. Many were wondering how this could happen in their town. Some whispered that it was the Sheriff that got killed. Some people just fled the scene because they knew which guy walked in that joint and fired on that Sheriff. They thought no way these people wanted to get involved in something like that. With people that can slaughter your whole family. They left their cars and walked home at a brisk pace. Police will get their tags from their license plates and send someone over to interview them the next day. They will deny seeing anybody and say they fled because they were scared for their lives.

Tears of relief during the hug spouted out. It seemed like a quick hug as the two of them were broken up by one of the officers and ushered out. Both Cassidy and John tried to hold hands, but another officer joined the one that had them heading for the exit. Outside they were asking everyone if anyone needed medical attention. The place was quickly cleared as the paramedics entered the building with a stretcher while running with their equipment in full sprint. Outside they started separating people in groups. Both Cassidy and John were separated for a quick interview to get their stories.

"I'll see you after we get through answering the questions," said John.

"I know."

They mouthed, "I love you," to each other as both of them were dragged to different spots of the back lot to get their stories by different officers of Spruce Wood.

She relived this moment over and over inside her head. That was the last time she talked to him. Minutes later John was put in a police cruiser, and it sped away into the night. She had another terrifying feeling, kind of the same one as when she heard the gun shots take place a short while ago. She tried to call his house later on that night. No answer except the answering machine.

"Hello, this is the Malone Family. No one is available to take your call at this time. Please leave a short message after the beep and we'll get back to you. Beep."

Cassidy may have slept for a few minutes, except she thought about that message on the answering machine over and over. John's mother saying that no one was available. The request to please leave a message after the beep, stuck in her head like some jingle on the radio or television.

Then in the wee hours of the morning she felt rage as she clawed her pillow. She eventually threw it across the room. She felt like she was left in an asylum somewhere. Even though her parents down the hall were sleeping like logs. Her mind was racing with numerous thoughts. Why did they take John away like that in that Police Cruiser? Why are they all not answering the phone? John, what the fuck? Call me now because I need to know if you are safe.

"Dear God," she said.

More tears flowed down her cheeks. Her eyes looked out the window on a dark summer night. It seemed like the longest night of her life. She continued as her back was against the bed rest, "*Please*, help John be safe."

Then the thoughts of that motorcycle group, the Venomous Vipers, and how dangerous they are. The worst thoughts in her mind came racing through. She imagined the whole family was butchered by those thugs. Even the poor little girls, those fuckers would kill their own family to keep them from talking. "Not fair," as she laid on her stomach and punched the mattress letting out quiet shrieks with more tears.

After the longest sleepless night she had ever experienced in her life, finally the sun came up. It was a new day. Cassidy was on a mission. She needed to see John. She needed to see him in one piece. She needed to see the whole family in one piece. She looked in the mirror as her eyes were full of red cobwebs. Under her eyes looked to be baggy even though she was too young to have them. You could tell she had a sleepless night. She brushed her teeth quickly. She skipped the mouthwash to follow. She threw some warm water on her face. She ran her fingers quickly through her hair. Then moved back to her room to change her clothes. Shorts, and a tee shirt. Threw some flip flops on her feet, and she was heading down the stairs. Her parents were still sleeping as it was relatively still early. Her sister was away at school. Staying on Northern Illinois' campus during the summer as she had a job. She stormed out the door and headed to the Malone house.

It was a beautiful day out with the birds chirping. The temperatures were perfect. Cassidy did not notice as she was walking in almost a full sprint. The Malone family only lived two blocks away. It was only a few minutes' walk, but today it seemed like it was forever. It was quiet as no cars were driving, and she did not notice an elderly gentleman sitting on his front stoop and drinking coffee while reading the paper.

She arrived at the Malone household which was a two story red brick house with black awnings right in the middle of the block. She tapped on the door lightly as if not wanting to wake anybody. However inside of her head she wanted to yell fire and get everyone up. She wanted to make sure everyone was ok. A minute went by, so she had to try the bell. She even used the knocker on the wooden door to send an echo throughout the house. She then noticed the curtains wide open, so somebody had to be up. She stretched her head, took a quick peek through the window, and saw no kind of movement. Now she was getting worried even more than when she was in bed just a short time ago.

She knew the Malone family kept a key in one of the flowerpots in the back yard. She wondered if they were all sleeping, after perhaps getting home extremely late from the police station. Perhaps they were still there. How long can it take she thought? She asked herself if the whole family would have to be present.

She went along the side of the house using a narrow walkway. Came to a metal gate, unlatched it, and headed to the back yard. She remembers the key being in a flowerpot right next to the patio table. She walked past the back stairs going into the house. She walked past the sheet metal bird feeder that had some sparrows in it. They flew away when they heard Cassidy. Then she saw the Marigolds in the brown flowerpot, but something caught her eyes. It was an envelope that had her name on it. She did not bother to go and grab the key. She felt like something, or someone, had taken her heart out of her while she was alive. She was scared and started to shake. Somehow she mustered up enough strength to go to the patio and grab

35

the envelope that was leaning up on the pole of the sun umbrella. She slid her finger through the opening as it came undone easily. She pulled out a piece of yellow paper from the white envelope that on both sides, had writing on it. It started with 'My Dear Cassidy.' It went on to say, 'I'm sorry I have to tell you this.' She collapsed in the patio chair as she read on. Her hands trembled as she read the long letter to herself. Minutes went by that seemed like an eternity. Her eyes, even though she was all cried out from her sleepless nights, left tears running down her cheeks.

"He's gone, they are gone," she said to herself. "Not coming back."

Chapter Fourteen

FOUR YEARS LATER
DANVILLE PENITENTIARY

The new President of the Venomous Vipers waited patiently in the visitor's room at Danville Penitentiary. He did not look like a normal biker. His blonde hair was cut short, and his face clean-shaven. Looked like more of an FBI agent, not the leader of a biker gang. The one thing you can probably link him to the Venomous Vipers by, was a tattoo on his neck. You could see the eyes of the viper peeking over his white polo shirt. He was wearing black dress slacks with dark socks and a pair of wing tipped shoes. He was lean and trim, but the short sleeve shirt had no drawings or exposed barb wire to raise any red flags.

He was sitting at a round metal table that had four seats welded to the circle, while he waited for the former President of the Southern Illinois chapter. It was a room with all these types of tables. They had two doors, both heavily guarded by County Sheriffs dressed in their dark brown slacks with light tan shirts exposing their shiny badges on their chests. The room held over 50 tables, ten of which were being used. Lots of wives bringing the kids to see that daddy was doing time in a nice up-to-date facility. One side of the room had windows looking out onto a nice sunny day. The bars on the windows distorted the view of the bright blue skies.

It has been about ten minutes of sitting there staring out the window. The new guy in charge of the Southern Illinois charter had never done any time. He had a clean sheet. He knew no one had anything on him as well. He was a guy moving up the ranks of the Venomous Vipers at a fast pace, as he was only 34 years old and sitting at the head seat. He was a guy that had launched many new ideas for the club in Southern Illinois and throughout the states. He was a guy that followed his father's footsteps. However, he was not going down the wrong path like his father did. His father was a guy that never rose in the rankings. He was a guy that was arrested and eventually killed in one of these institutions. No way, he would follow that path. He has followed the military path and did better than his old man there. He joined the Venomous Vipers, and it did not take long for him to pass up his father.

The doors opened and the man known as Blade Runner walked through being ushered by two guards. His hands were handcuffed in front of him, and he was all dressed in orange. Blade Runner was a big barrel-chested guy, but the guards looked like they played offensive line in the NFL, as they undid the cuffs to let him wander off for 20 minutes to see his visitor. Blade Runner rubbed his wrists where the shackles were placed and saw the man that took his spot as President of the Southern Illinois charter. He stood up as Blade Runner made his way towards him passing up some people saying their goodbyes after their visit with another inmate. Blade Runner's arms looked like two big bobcat diggers. However, his stomach was bloated. Both men hugged as guards looked on seeing if anything would get passed during the exchange of greetings. This even though the new President was searched, and pockets emptied, before he was allowed in this room. However, things do slip in, and these guards were not going to let something slip by their division as they went on with their conversation with the other guy who was already standing there.

Both men sat down at the circle table across from one each other. Blade Runner fired off the first question to the man that took his spot since being incarcerated.

"How's the club doing?"

The new President went by the code name "The Shining," because he loved the movie and he thought of the Sun and how he will rise in the east and set in the west. All his day-to-day operations running to perfection in his thoughts, as he was a guy that had a huge ego. He looked at Blade Runner and noticed his face resembled a catcher's mitt. A broken-in one with a face filled of wrinkles. Harry had caterpillars under the eyes.

"Everybody is doing well as we expanded the newer ranch and have just added a lot of new faces. May I say these guys are warriors, top of the line soldiers that can ride and mix it up with anybody."

The old Ranch four years ago was invaded and seized by the Feds. The Venomous had to move their operations. Some of them went to jail and have been out already. Saw Dust was blamed for the murder of the Fed. While Blade Runner went down for the murder of his woman and the Sheriff. Others just got simple drug charges that were small potatoes. The gang was able to get all the weapons out of there before the Feds charged in like gang busters. The Shining was the one that was able to come up with a plan when things went south when the gang arrived back from their charity ride. Blade Runner listened as The Shining went on about how they opened up shop in the middle of nowhere by a lake that led into a main river. He even told him how one of the members just got married down by the lake of the new ranch. Old Blade Runner knew about his old buddy Trapper, who looks like an old grizzly bear. He was the one that set up that trap, which was able to catch Terry escaping, who eventually blew up from the landmine which was his doing.

Both of them talked about the Club and certain members for the next ten minutes. Just basic stuff on who's doing what and how everybody is doing. Then they talked some business. Not big details just in case anybody was listening. The group overall was doing well as they're able to get the drugs to cities with no problems. They had an increase in sales. They had more dealers, and they had these dealers out-selling the competition and putting a lot of competitors out of business as their products were still better than the others and they were still making them on the cheap as well. All the charters were doing well. Then time was dwindling down, as the guards were going to give the warning that time was up very soon. Blade Runner informed him that the drugs from the charter were a big hit in prison. This The Shining knew about, as both of them have put in a solid plan to get that revenue channel operational. Not just at this prison, but many throughout the state.

"What about the plan for getting me out of here?" Blade Runner whispered as he ran his fingers through his greasy receding hair and leaned in to say this.

"We have something in the works."

Blade Runner was serving a life sentence for two murders, his old lady and the Sheriff. Illinois does not have the death penalty. In the last four years, Blade Runner has gotten the drugs in finally. He was able to build alliances with other gangs in the jail, since not many Venomous Vipers were in cells. Blade Runner shook his head in agreement as his eyes opened wider and asked him about the Malone kid.

"We still have not located him or his family."

Blade Runner's face turned bright red as his eyebrows went to the anger stage. Before he said a word, The Shining immediately continued.

"We found this guy, an ex-FBI agent, who I know is a hitman. Yes, quite a career change and for the right amount of money he is going to find out where the whole Malone family is at based on the Witness Protection list. He knows people in high top-secret places."

Blade Runner smiled, "Excellent, I want his head."

The Shining rolled his eyes inside his head as he nodded his head, YES.

"I'll make those arrangements. The guy will kill the whole family and then that business is done."

That moment the Guards yelled out, "ONE MINUTE WRAP IT UP."
Both Presidents hugged and that wrapped up their meeting.

Chapter Fifteen

SOMEWHERE IN UTAH

It was Summertime in Utah, and America's pastime was being played. It was an amateur Men's league playing fast pitch league ball in a small town outside Salt Lake City. These were players ages 18 through 40, playing the game they loved for free. It was a well-organized league and the play between the 8 teams was pretty competitive. The state did not have many regular ball leagues. In fact, this was the only one for miles. They had regular 12" softball which was popular as well around these parts. This league got many talented guys that wanted to continue playing the game they love. Maybe even get discovered by a junior college or even an Independent Minor League affiliate. Most of all it was filled with guys that came after their day job to get some exercise and enjoy the game they had been playing since they were kids. Each team had their own uniforms, which made some teams really look like a professional team. This game had the Knights versus the Cyclones. Both teams were 2-2 so far in the season. No score and the Cyclone's lanky tall first basemen just dug a ball out of the dirt and made a nice tag on the Knight leading off. The pitcher caught him leaning.

"Alright Jackie Boy!"

A player in the dugout was rooting his teammate on as the crowd appreciated the play. Clapping was heard from the crowd of ten to 20 people scattered all over the bleachers on both sides of the diamond.

Jack Young high fived a few teammates as he was up second in the inning. He took off the red cap with a tornado logo and put on a red scratched-up helmet. That same guy who yelled out cheers for Jack, had a lot of team spirit. He was dealing with an injury but made it to the game as he walked up and down the dugout yelling.

"TIME TO GET ON BOARD BOYS! LET'S DO IT," which got a few other guys joining in.

The pitcher was done with his warmups as balls were thrown in and it was time to play ball again. Up first from the inning was the left fielder, Ricky Dudley, a black guy born and raised in Salt Lake City. The field faced the mountains which gave this diamond a very nice scenic field of dreams. It was still sunny out, but the lights surrounding the field were starting to pop on as it takes them awhile to warm up. By the time it got dark, all the lamps around the field would be brighter than ever. First pitch, Ricky got a nice piece of it and fouled it back. The pitcher for the Knights was a farmer and he had a big Red Man chew in the sides of his cheeks as he spit a flying saucer loogie right off the pitching rubber and it landed in the grass. The Catcher gave the signal as the big six foot Hoss did his wind up and fired one outside which was a good eye by old Ricky as he had an even count. The Knights were dressed in gray with light blue hats. In Orange English lettering 'Knights' was spelled across the button down jerseys. This time the farmer wiped some sweat off his forehead, and then wiped his hand on his pants. He looked at the catcher, gave him the nod, and adjusted his fingers around the ball in his black baseball mitt. Then he did his wind up as he threw his hands in the air and did a pivot. He brought his leg towards the plate and fired a ball which Dudley guessed was perfect on the inside. He adjusted his hips and slapped the ball to right field for a single.

Then Jack Young stepped to the plate. Jack stood tall to the left side of home plate looking at the mountains ready to hit one over the fence way before the mountains. He chewed on his gum as he looked into the eyes of the farm boy. Meanwhile, Ricky had a short lead-off first. A few chants came from the Cyclone dugout.

"COME ON JACK YOU CAN DO IT! JACK ONE OUT OF HERE!"

The farm boy could see the eyes of determination in Jack's stare. The farm boy worked from the stretch and threw an off speed breaking ball low as the catcher nabbed it right before it hit the dirt. Jack stepped out of the box and eyeballed the third base coach who was touching himself. Giving the other team nonsense as he was giving the green light to swing the bat instead of bunting. He stepped back into the box and re-gripped his fingers around the bat. He waved it in back of him as he did the same thing and gave the farm boy a stare that said, "I dare you to throw me something," across the plate. Jack was up for the second time in this contest. His first time was shot when he was snared by the first baseman robbing him of extra bases. The farm boy seemed to like the catcher's call and took a quick peek over at first as Ricky was off the bag a bit further than the last pitch. The farm boy brought his hands to his chest, and then paused and delivered a fast ball. Jack's eyes lit up as he could see the ball heading to the outside corner. He made the adjustment and "CRACK" swung at it and it flew as it got the meaty part of the barrel. The ball flew and seemed like it hit a jet stream because it carried to the opposite field as the left fielder went back to the fence. After a ball, which seemed like it was still going. The farm boy threw his mitt on the ground and almost swallowed some tobacco juice he had forming in his mouth. The Catcher stood up and watched the ball like it was fireworks at the fourth of July.

Ricky pumped his fists around second yelling, "YEAH DOG, NICE SHOT BUDDY."

Jack did not watch as he set down the bat and ran to first before jogging around the bases. He first slapped hands with the first base coach as it was 2-0 Cyclones. Jack was greeted with a standing ovation from the fans. His teammates were lined up as they high fived him running back to the dugout. The one teammate who screamed nice play in the top of the frame was out of the dugout screaming his name again.

"WAY TO GO JACK WOW YOU NAILED IT BUDDY," practically hugging him as he tried to get back in the dugout.

The Cyclones were unable to muster up any more runs that inning. The farm boy struck out the side to make the score stand at 2-0 Cyclones. Jack was exiting the dugout with the regular cap back on his head and a ball in his hand.

He heard "HEY JOHN," which stopped him in his tracks as he looked up into the stands.

"COME BACK HERE JOHN, I GOT YOU A HOTDOG."

It was a middle-aged lady screaming at her kid. He was in a dazed state of mind as he was just looking at the little kid running towards his mother. One of his teammates asked him if he was OK, as he was right behind him. Jack did not answer. Then the teammate put his arm on his shoulder.

"Hey Jack, you here? Earth is calling, my friend."

Jack snapped out of it as he ran out to man his position at first base. He rolled the ball across the infield for the third baseman to field.

Jack looked back and saw the kid with mustard and ketchup on his face, as he bit into the hot dog. Those were people he did not know. But it was like he knew them before.

Chapter Sixteen

SPRUCE WOOD

She was dressed all in black. She was tall with long legs and had a body many girls would want to have. Guys wanted to have her. She was model-like. She could fit a rock band type. Maybe a motorcycle club. She wore her hair long as it flowed past her shoulders. She had it parted in the front. It was motor oil black with tints of red violet. Her once angelic face would make the lead singer of Kiss cream in his pants. Now she wore jet black lipstick on her pouty lips. Her green eyes were covered up with fake eyelashes and dark eyebrows. All these black features, and her skin looked like it never gets any sun, lily-white.

She strutted down the street with eyeballs coming from all the windows on Main Street. People walking in downtown Spruce Wood especially had problems taking their eyes off her. Almost running into parked cars or street poles. Some even almost getting hit by a car as a driver would blast the horn at some horny toad. A toad who would suck his tongue back in his mouth, turning red and embarrassed by nearly becoming roadkill. She stopped in front of Fast Eddie's Tap Room, reached into her little black leather purse, and fished out a cigarette. After that, a lighter as she lit up and stood there in a miniskirt with black leather pumps holding her up. After she put her cigarettes back in her purse, she retrieved her sunglasses and put them on. She looked like she had all the time in the world as she stood there, maybe even waiting for somebody. It was a beautiful summer day, and she wore her cut-off black Megadeth half-shirt that covered her perfect handful breasts but revealed her flat tummy, which had a shiny emerald piercing. She took a drag of her cigarette as you could see she had a tiny nose piercing that glittered from the sun. If you were not looking at her face and stuck in a daydream trance looking at the body, you might have missed the pierced tongue. As she used her left hand to inhale another drag out of her cigarette, you could see her arm was covered up with multi-colored tattoos all the way up. Her other arm had nothing. She looked like a bad girl who was about to be up to no good. One thing was out of place as you could see she had a tiny green shamrock necklace around her neck. Nobody would even notice it as she had a lot of things going on.

Across the street, a woman coughed and gave her a dirty look. She looked around and did not have a care in the world, especially for some old bat who is going to complain about smoking in the streets. Around the corner, a big hulky type of guy was walking up to her. He was a tall specimen at 6'5" with long tree trunk legs and tank shoulders. He had a belly overhanging his faded ripped blue jeans as he wore black steel toe boots. On this summer day, he wore a long-sleeved thin shirt that made his gut stick out even more. He had a boulder head with wavy brown hair. He was wearing shades and even had a bandanna around his head like a head band. He had the 5 o'clock shadow on the face as he whistled out loud yelling to her.

"There's my sexy bitch."

She finished her cigarette and extinguished it on the sidewalk with her shoe. She strutted towards the gigantic man who looked to be 5 years older than his real age. She then put her long arms around his neck as the big man picked her up and while he did that, he planted a kiss on her lips and spun her in the air. He put her down as he looked up at him, as he was taller by a foot. She greeted him in a nice sexy voice that would probably send any man's drawbridge up.

"How's my Hanky-Panky Bear doing?"

"I'm doing better knowing we are ready to have some fun."

He gave her a bear hug as she could not quite get his hands around him fully, but the hug lasted a few moments.

Her head rested on his shoulder as her sunglasses slid down the bridge of her nose. She looked across the street at Murphy's. Her eyes were like Superman's. As if she was using heat rays to melt the whole building kind of stare. They released each other from the hug. They held hands as one of his sleeves moved past his wrists. They headed into Fast Eddie's Tap. Above his wrist was the beginning of a snake tattoo, the tail part wrapped around the wrist. He pulled it down when he opened the door for his girlfriend.

Chapter Seventeen

VEGAS

It is six in the morning and one of the Vegas casinos is pretty much emptied like the slot machines have swallowed up all human life. The machines with all their noises and flashing bright colors can be seen and heard by a few. One Latino guy is vacuuming while a security guard walks around checking the time on his watch. It feels like he's been there for days. The graveyard shift is what this guy needs to pay the bills, especially doing school during the day. Time has stood still as he walks through a ghost town. Sure, tumbleweeds blow through. The tumbleweeds usually are degenerate gamblers, who are still present. The ones who have that cold blank stare as if their minds are completely gone as they press the button on the machine, zombie-like. They get free drinks, but they must be playing a machine or at a table. Not many tables are open as a man sits at a blackjack table.

"Hit me," the man at the table says.

"Busted," the dealer said with a smirk as if the money was going into his pocket.

The middle-aged man rubbed one of his eyes. Then pushed his thinning hair out of his face. He had the look of an old veteran quarterback. A round circle of skin on the top of his head surrounded by shaggy thinning hair. He has been gambling for about three days nonstop. His hair was greasy. His eyes were cobwebs painted red. Bags under his eyes & cheap Bourbon on his breath. He had a collared shirt with half of the buttons open. A striped necktie, very loose, looked more like a noose, than a tie. He slurred his words

"Hey good mannn, cann you do me a solid and run this ard to get me ack in the game?"

He dug out a credit card, placed it on the green felt table. and took a swig from his rock glass. There was only melted ice left inside it, sitting on a cocktail napkin.

The dealers knew who he was as he had been there the last three days. Maybe this guy only stepped out to eat a bit. Maybe taking a walk to another casino to play blackjack and come back, which many did to try restart their luck. Most dealers know these types of guys very well. They have heard the typical life story. The guy at the table told one or more dealers that he was fired just a few weeks ago. How he had just left his family at that time as well. On this shift, the dealer was another guy working that shift because he was moonlighting and owed money for a stash of misplaced drugs. Unforgiving people were huffing and puffing about to blow his house down. He had to take whatever he could to get some scratch and pay these assholes quickly. He had no time to listen to this man's shenanigans.

"Sorry, Mr. Young. You know the rules. We can't run your card. You have to hit one of the ATMS against the wall."

He pointed to them as he spoke. Mr. Young looked at the dealer. He then spoke with anger and without slurring.

"You love me when the money is flowing and then as soon as I'm broke, you kick me out of my seat like an old shoe."

The dealer was in his mid-20's. He was dressed like he was going to a wedding. White tuxedo shirt and black bow tie. Dark dress pants with the bad combination of white socks and black shoes. He had short orange-reddish hair cut like a bowl. He had a cheesy thin mustache below a crooked nose. He rubbed his pointy chin and glared at the man while towing the company line. Inside his head, he was screaming for the loser to fuck off.

"Sorry you believe that sir, but it's policy around here."

Mr. Young walked away. He was nursing the last few drinks he had in the wee hours of the night. He was feeling a tad more sober. He walked towards the ATMs. He walked past rows and rows of slot machines. All of them claiming to have the biggest payout on one spin. As he walked, he was thinking he had one credit card that had a few hundred left on it. His plan in his head was to use that money to win back all the money he had lost in the last three days. He walked past the Buccaneer lounge that was totally empty. He then looked at the television screen up top. They had on a sports channel showing some baseball highlights. Out of the corner of his eye he saw a lefty that hit a homerun for the San Francisco Giants. The kid looked like his own. It stopped him in his tracks as he continued to watch. It was the best time of his life back in his hometown when his son was knocking the ball out of the park in high school. Many memories came flooding back in his mind. He even had a few tears flow down the sides of his cheeks. Where did it go wrong? He then saw his reflection in one of the slot machines. It was a machine called Cowboy Up. The screen had a cowboy riding a horse with a lasso and below that it said, "Round up all the big money prizes playing this machine." He sat down because he needed a minute to think. He wanted his family.

Chapter Eighteen

UTAH STATE

Utah State was located in Logan, Utah. It was summer, so most of the campus had gone home. Some people stayed all year round. Either working a job or taking some classes. Most of the time it was both. In her second year at Utah State, Shawna Young was trying to find herself. She was hanging on by an eyelash before flunking out. Her parents paid for an apartment on campus which she made into her own Delta house. She was out the night before at The Pelican and she's been eyeing one of the bouncers who works the door there. They have planted seeds with some conversation. Greeting each other with a smile. Thrown compliments at each other. Finally, on a school night with The Pelican not as busy as it usually is during the school year, these two sat down together and talked the whole night. Since it was not that busy, he was able to have a few drinks on the job. When it was close to closing time, they added a few shots before they left the bar.

Shawna did not eat anything for dinner, so she was basically drinking on an empty stomach. She lived within walking distance, but the bouncer offered Shawna a ride home. His car was parked on the side of the building, kind of secluded as the parking lot was pretty much emptied and his car was blocked by The Pelican's dumpster. As they got in the car they were kissing and groping at each other. They took a break and he pulled out a joint, from which they both took turns taking a hit while passing it back and forth. They continued to laugh and listen to the music as a cloud of smoke flew out the open windows on the bouncer's old 1980's Cutlass Supreme. He rebuilt (and rebuilt) it again as if it was his baby and it *was* one hell of a muscle car.

The bouncer was born in upstate Utah. His name was Brad Doxby, and he was in his second year as an Aggie. He was just under 6 feet tall. He was of medium build, very slender and ripped though. His face had that hawk style nose with a lantern jaw. All gals loved his baby blue bright eyes that sparkled with his smile showing his also sparkling pearl white teeth. He had short curly blonde hair on top and he was a player. He probably scored with more women in his car than the football team last season on the field. He did not quite have a major yet. He averaged straight C's, which was passing and meant he still would get the degree.

"How about I give you a preview of what's going to happen at your place?"

She whispered this into Brad's ear as her hand rubbed against his leg. Then it made its way to his soldier in his pants. It was saluting, so she gave it a rub that sent shivers down Bradley's spine.

Shawna was a very pretty girl. She was very close to six feet tall. She had wide hips with long muscular legs. She had a nice big rack which people noticed first, as she always wore clothes that revealed her cleavage. It drove many Mormons crazy. Her face was round, but she had nice features which included voluptuous lips. A button nose and she was a brown eyed girl. She had a few well-placed freckles just above her dimples. She had long thick auburn hair that went down to the middle of her back. It was combed to perfection. As if she spent hours just running a comb through the hair. In front, her hair was parted right in the middle and drifted off the sides of her ears.

"Little Brad and I are all about a great preview indeed."

He went along with the sexy talk. Her eyes look all about mischief as she gave him a look that said, "I will show you." His pants started to unzip as she smiled, showing her tongue was pierced, which drove Brad nuts. Her head slowly went down as little Brad and her mouth met for the first time and liked each other immediately. Brad could feel his whole body conversing as his eyes grew big. His heart pounded out of his chest as he was experiencing something out of this world. He stretched his arms over his head thinking this is what life is all about. Her head went up and down working the love muscle to perfection, and he thought 'God Bless, America.'

After a few minutes he exploded and his whole body felt like fireworks as her head came back up. She sat back in the passenger seat and looked at the smile as if he was the Joker from Batman. She said "Well, shall we see the movie at your place," as if she knew the answer already. She buckled her seat belt, he turned the key in the ignition, and they were off leaving The Pelican parking lot in a dust storm from the tires kicking up gravel.

They went to Brad's studio apartment, which was a dump. They continued like animals on his blow-up mattress. She was on top of him, riding him as he was so deep inside her body she felt the Fourth of July tremor through her insides as she came multiple times. They continued like two animals ravaging each other in multiple positions until the mattress started to lose air. Screams and moans were heard throughout the apartment complex. With paper thin walls, one person told them to keep it down, as he banged on the wall. Sweat poured from both of their bodies as they started to stick to each other. The window was partially open as she had propped it up. The ceiling fan was stuck in the lowest spin. But they continued and laughed between themselves when they heard the banging. They unstuck from each other as he almost killed himself walking across the dark room with his clothes everywhere covering up old pizza boxes. But he got some water from the leaky faucet in the kitchen/bathroom. They rehydrated themselves while debating whether to go another round. Instead, they lay on the bed that slowly oozed air. He found another joint in the ashtray next to his floating bed, and they immediately sparked it. Smoking it, they talked about their lives, hopes, and dreams. Both of them were out of their minds; loopy, laughing, and carrying on like stoned drunk young people.

"Where did you originally come from?"

"You know... here and there," she said coyly.

He took another hit and passed her the roach with the clips, so she was able to take a hit without burning her lips. They lay there naked looking at each other, digging the way the blade of the ceiling fan circled like some helicopter upside down.

"For real. Where did you come from? You are not from these parts; I can tell you that."

He tickled her at the same time as she started giggling and coughing on the smoke. She was about to put the roach out, but he carefully took it away from her.

"Whoa baby, let me take one more little hit off that bugger."

He took another hit and put the finished roach in the ash tray that had many other finished roaches. They both started cuddling. They looked at each other, eye to eye smiling about the night she wished never would end. She felt so comfortable. She felt like this was a guy she could be with. She was high and loaded so she just upchucked her whole life story. Maybe it was good to get this off her chest as she had held it in for four years. She told them about how they were from a small town in Southern Illinois. How her brother witnessed a biker shooting the Sheriff of the town in the bar. He was curious and asked for more information. He was being a great guy, listening to her every word while holding her tight.

"We have some biker gangs that travel through this town time to time. They always have some terrifying names."

"Venomous Vipers," she whispered, thinking if she said it any louder, somebody might be listening.

"Never heard of them."

47

Maybe if she was not stoned, she'd be able to tell he might be lying. She continued to tell the story of how the whole family were sucked up that night and put into custody. Not arrested, but in protective custody. She went on to say her brother ended up going to court and basically put the madman away.

"Wow, you are like in a witness protection thing," he said, intrigued as the sun was coming up and he could see the room getting lighter.

"Then they made us move out here, and it eventually split my parents up."

She felt the heat radiating off his flesh as the room was stuffy and smelled of body odor and stale food.

"So, your real name is not Shawna?"

To him it sounded like the type of movies he watched.

She started to cry tears that came out of her eyes like small waterfalls. It's been four years of holding all of this in. There was a dam holding off the water until it just collapsed entirely. He held her tighter and rubbed her arm as she sobbed and whimpered, 'Stephanie.'

She told him every detail of the whole story as the sun rose fully that morning. As they both lay on the bed, the room looked worse in the light than in the dark. She told him about Spruce Wood, and all the people from the town. All the friends and some extended family they were not able to talk to for the rest of their lives. She told him how the family has been dealing with bad times in Utah ever since the government chose their new location. She finally pleaded with him and made him swear not to tell anybody as they cuddled the rest of the morning. She felt a burden was lifted off her by just spewing all of that out. Her head was foggy. She was very tired as she closed her eyes. She dozed off as he lay on his back with her face planted in his chest. He looked up at the ceiling fan with the smirk of a man with an idea, before dozing off himself.

"No worries baby, your secret is safe with me."

Chapter Nineteen

THE OLE NEW HOMESTEAD

The Young family, formerly the Malone's, were moved into a suburb of Utah. It was outside Salt Lake City, a very nice suburb called Cherry Heights. It was all newly developed housing. These houses were enormous three-story brick buildings. Each new house was on almost a half-acre of land. All the houses pretty much looked the same in each subdivision. However, the view from the backyard was breathtaking. A huge meadow of wildflowers was beyond your fence line, and then the glorious mountains could be seen in the background. It had a lot of Mormons in the neighborhood, who the family did not see eye-to-eye with. Their religion, their views… not their cup of tea, but Valerie, now going by Darlene, knew they had to blend in. They had. However, most people seem to give Darlene the look because all-of-a-sudden, she's a single parent. Raising her kids in a whole other world that is totally different. Before her husband left her for Vegas, it was OK. Now it seemed worse with the people surrounding her.

She sits out on the back deck as she loves the view. She has already popped her happy pills. Was also able to choke down her blood pressure pills, which was skyrocketing. She enjoys the summer morning after her night shift at the hospital. She became an X-Ray technician when they moved into Cherry Heights. She has her coffee as she sits at a table with a floral umbrella covering up most of the deck and the glass table. Over the last four years, she has aged ten. She looks like a skeleton head-to-toe as she hardly eats anything each day. Her face was invaded by wrinkles and bags under her eyes from not sleeping steadily each night. Just restless nights, and the sleep aids have not done what she wants. Except for night terrors that she cannot remember when she snaps out of it with a cold sweat. Cigarettes, which she smokes a pack of a day, with ease. On the deck are multiple empty coffee cans of Folgers with dead butts aging in the sun.

She wears a floppy white sun hat with sunglasses that look like she works for the Highway Patrol. She has on a simple red tee shirt with a pair of capris. She opens her book, sipping her coffee, and has the cigarette clinging between her yellow fingertips. Her feet are up in the chair as smoke lingers in the air. She's thinking about popping the cork on her wine bottle. It's the morning, and she does not have to be at the hospital tomorrow so maybe around the noon hour. Another reason she does not like the area is because it's a dry county and she has to drive far to the liquor store to get her stash of wine. She buys them by the cases. Only if her neighbors looked in the recycling bin, they would scoff at her. At times, she gets rid of empty bottles in the regular garbage just for that reasoning. Every time the garbage truck comes by and the bottles clatter with a loud bang, she knows people are whispering.

She tries to read, but all she thinks about is her big family she left home back in Spruce Wood. Every day since leaving, she thinks of someone or something from that town. She always compares food or prices and the overall towns to their new town of Cherry Heights. She misses all her friends and neighbors as it has been very difficult to fit in. She feels like a misfit toy from Rudolph the Red Nosed Reindeer. But most of all, her own family that went quickly to shambles since they arrived. It's been hard on everyone.

She had everything going for her in Spruce Wood. She knows her son did the right thing by testifying. It was her husband that wanted him to do that. In her head, way in the back of it, she knew it was the Christian thing to do. However, at the time and now going through the motions in life, she thinks it was a bad idea. This is what ripped the marriage apart in her thinking. The way her husband made their son testify. How much they preached to him about being a good person, is now dooming the whole family. All the late-night arguments she had with all of them, but mostly with her now former husband. The way she just wanted to kill him; it came to that kind of anger. She never had these thoughts. But the way he continued to stand up about how they did things the right way, has been something that has annoyed her. Something that made her crazy and she slapped the shit out of him. The man did not strike back. He just suddenly moved on and left a note. Technically they were still married, but with all the heartbreak they had been through over all the long months, it will never be the same. The love has walked out the door since they arrived in this awful state.

They did not even get to pick where they wanted to go. They did not even get to pick what they wanted to do as their new career. Now she's suddenly working in a hospital that took on a whole new world in her brain. She was the type that was scared to death walking into that kind of building. She had three children, but anytime else, she got the heebie-jeebies walking into that environment. Even if it was just visiting and leaving right away. She got through it. The pills helped with that.

She still tries to get into her mystery when the gate opens and makes a creaking sound on the side of the house. Then she hears the roar of a few machines fired up on the side of the house.

"Oh good, my cute lawn guy is here," she says to herself out loud.

This is what it has come down to now. The one small perk of the week she had. The one Mexican fellow who rides in on a standing mower. As she finishes the cigarette and drops it in coffee can next to the table, it's still lit with trails of smoke coming out of the can. The mower engine gets louder between the sides of the houses. She does not know what has drawn her to this man. It has been a very long time. The first time she saw Juan, she did get the guts to say hi to him and found out his name. Her body heated up. Pent up horniness trapped and needed to get out. She never had the toys. She felt like she'd break a thousand Mormon laws if she procured a few sex toys for herself. Instead, she did it the old fashioned, and popular, way in the bathtub. That 5-speed water pressure system really did the job. Probably better than the man she married. She thought 'ooh baby,' as Juan drove by along the fence line, and the clippings flew in the air as a blade circled at high speed.

Juan was only 5'8" tall, but on the stand-up mower, he looked like he towered over 6'4". He had dark olive-colored skin. He wore baggy jeans and had black boots. But it was the big arms with the sleeveless shirt that allowed the sun to glisten off his well-sculptured body. He wore dark sunglasses. His face was nicely chiseled out with distinguished features, and a perfectly "Rollie Finger" type mustache that was groomed to perfection. His hair was cut short as it looked like a chia pet just sprouting. Juan did the perimeter and then started making paths North and South through the back yard. She knew where she was going to be in the next few minutes. She gave him a little wave as he took one hand off the controls and waved back with a smile. She felt her breasts get hard. She kept the book in front of her like she was still reading the mystery, which she wasn't making any leeway in. Her body tingled, and a little drool came out of the corner of her lip.

"Fuck you, Mormon neighbors. I should just go invite Juan inside for a drink of water and have my way, as he's probably a beast in the sack," she muttered.

Minutes later, Juan was done with the back yard and out mowing the front. Darlene headed through the glass sliding patio door and headed up the stairs to her bedroom. She discarded her clothes, as she walked and fired up the bathtub. She thought this is going to take me a few hours of pleasure. Then after that, she can take a long nap and envision Juan doing her over-and-over until she explodes. Then on to some wine as it would be about 5 o'clock. Just in time for happy hour, or in her case, one happy evening of her and her friend, the bottle.

Chapter Twenty

HIGH SCHOOL

The only Malone kid that was doing well in Utah, was Katie. Nowadays, she went by the name Gretchen, which she had to get used to. She was the only one not missing Spruce Wood. She had the most going on of anyone in her family after four years away. She was only in grammar school when she left her hometown. Now she was a young woman in High School. She had fantastic grades. She made lots of friends. She even fell in love with a guy and had been dating him for over two years, together all the time. The whole Malone family always excelled in sports, and she was the best basketball player on the Varsity team.

She was upset her parents were having problems, but somehow it did not faze her in her regular daily life. She continued doing her thing and stayed away from trouble. She was pure as she wanted nothing to do with sex until she was married. Maybe it was the Mormon strict rules that got to her instead of the Catholic ways she had been brought up on. She was clean when it came to drugs, alcohol, or smoking cigarettes. Her only devilish thing was maybe liking desserts, as ice cream was her cup of tea. But she was a growing girl, and very active so the dessert did not ruin her fit and trim body. She was close to six feet tall, and the doctors said she was still growing. She had long muscular legs, but not tree trunk Amazon legs like some tall women get. She had long arms and her breasts had not fully developed. She was a tad on the flat-chested side of things. Her face was innocent with freckles, dimples, and forest green cat's eyes that glowed in the dark a little. She had strawberry blonde hair pulled back in a ponytail with a blue scrunchie tying it up in the back. Her nose was small with lighter features around the eyes, with a pretty smile. However bright, there were some crooked teeth that would need braces soon.

For Gretchen, the day started off with a basketball practice. Even though it was summer, the team still got in practices during the weekdays. After the practice ended, Gretchen got cleaned up and into a change of clothes. She met her best friend Molly in the parking lot, and they hopped in Molly's gray Toyota Corolla. As the car left the high school parking lot, Gretchen said as she fiddled with the radio. She had one word, as Christian rock jammed inside the newer used car belonging to her friend, and the car pulled on to a busy intersection.

"Tacos."

"We better be talking Salsa Amigos."

"You know it, girlfriend."

They headed to the mall to get burrito bowls at a chain place that had been popping up all over the West. Salsa Amigos was one step better than Del Taco and two steps better than Taco Bell.

It was a beautiful afternoon, and the music was loud. They both sang loudly with the wind whipping through their hair. They had the windows down as traffic was moving along at a good pace.

"We're going out tonight," Molly screamed over a singer yelling out some religion references while having a bad trip of some kind with some catchy lyrics.

It could have been a country song with those lyrics in a way, but it was an upbeat rock tune.

"My Mother will probably be passed out on the couch by the time we get back from the mall."

"ALRIGHT THAT IS YES," Molly screamed as her fingers tapped the steering wheel and she changed lanes.

It took them another ten minutes of driving to reach the mall as they both jammed to their favorite songs. They walked through the mall and headed to the eatery. Both were dressed in shorts and tee shirts with their hair pulled back. They figured they'd eat and then do some shopping. If they came across some guys, that would be a bonus. Both of them ordered the same thing and the food was up quickly from the middle-aged Mexican guy wearing a sombrero with tassels hanging down from the brim of the hat. Both of them sat down at a white round plastic table with their burrito bowls and fountain drinks

Molly quickly said, "OK, Therese just texted me and Bud is bringing two of his friends to her house tonight to watch movies and we are invited." When excited, she was very hyper.

"I hope it's not that guy he hangs out with that has those horn-rimmed glasses. He looks really creepy,"

Molly chuckled as her fingers hit the phone, sending a message back to their mutual friend. Then they continued to eat and drink their diet sodas as the sun came through the roof of the eatery. It had those greenhouse type panels as a roof which gave it that feeling you were sitting outside. The phone then chimed back, and she read the text out loud.

"It's Nickolas and Martin. Not the guy you're talking about, who is Tanner."

Gretchen felt embarrassed and turned red. "You did not have to tell her I said that."

"No Worries, I didn't," as she took a sip out of the straw.

"I call dibs on that Martin guy. I think he's cute when he wears those tight jeans with the black shirt. Those aviator glasses drive me crazy."

Gretchen had heard about him from Molly a few times. Molly's way was to wear the guy down to finally get a date with him. She was the type that would not take no for an answer. Gretchen felt like Molly was her sister, as they had an instant bond since she came to this state four years ago.

"Yes, well aware of that," and they both laughed.

"Do you have dinner plans?"

Molly said it very quickly like she was pulling out a gun at high noon.

"No."

Before Gretchen could say anything else, she had made plans for the both of them at Molly's house for dinner. then they would go out from there. It was Molly and her family that acted like family to Gretchen, more than her family at home. It was that type of feeling of family she had in Spruce Wood. She did not think of it like that. But she latched on like a pilot fish on a shark, to Molly and her wonderful family.

Chapter Twenty-One

AFTER THE GAME

That night, Jack's team was victorious, and he was a big part of that. He had a monster day at the plate. Defensively was not too shabby as well. Overall, it was a good night. Now he had to get to the car and race to his night job. He opened the back door of his Chevy Cavalier to throw his bat bag in the back seat when he heard someone speak.

"Hey, Jack."

It did not dawn on him for a few seconds that someone was calling his name. After over four years of being in the witness protection, that is one of the many things he found hard to get used to. Then for the second time, he heard an older man's voice.

"Hey, Jack Young... great game."

That somehow rang a bell as he closed the door of his older rust bucket car and looked at the guy. He suddenly snapped out of it as if he was just daydreaming, and politely looked at the gentleman.

"Yes, sir."

"The name is Rusty Mulligan, but people call me Big Red." The bigger middle-aged man extended out his hand and continued, "I'm a scout for the Tacoma Twisters and I have been liking what I see out there from you."

Jack extended his hand as he shook hands with Big Red, who had a soft big beefy hand with red hairy knuckles.

"Thank you, sir, I appreciate that," as Jack released his hand adding, "It was a great team effort."

Big Red's name fit him. He had a red beard, and hidden under a green Tacoma hat, was a mop of red hair. He wore a green and white tee shirt with bold green Twisters written across it. His arms were a prairie filled with red hair. His shirt was tight exposing his great big belly which hung over his golden belt buckle, that had a rifle on it.

"I like those well-spoken words son, but you might not understand. I want you to play for us."

He fished into his wallet, which looked like a black file cabinet, and came up with a business card. He handed it to Jack, who had just opened up the driver's side door and was leaning on it. He took the card and started reading it. Right then, behind Big Red, a few of Jack's teammates walked by.

"Great game, Jack."

The other asked, "You heading to the bar?"

"Thanks guys, but no, I have to get to work."

He waved his hand up at them as they said see you next week at the next row of cars in the parking lot. The parking lot was clearing out as a line of cars were trying to merge into the busy intersection. Jack had work on his mind, as he liked to be one of the first to get out of the parking lot. He did this to avoid this line, as he had a 15-minute drive to work, and he needed every minute to get there on time. This guy was holding things up. Jack looked confused as he did not know what to do with the card or what to say to this guy.

Big Red broke the awkward silence and said, "Listen, I don't want to hold you up. Take that card and call me. I would like you to come to Tacoma. We are an Independent minor league baseball team that will pay you some money for your services if you make the team. We offer free housing as well, so please take the card, call me, and we can talk."

This sounded very nice, but Jack was not soaking up all the stuff Big Red was saying. He just looked at him with a dazed look and nodded his head. Big Red spoke again.

"Go on now, don't be late to work," as he reached his hand out again to shake hands a final time.

"Now don't forget to call me soon, it was great meeting you. Great game again, son." as he released his hand from the shake and walked away into the partially lit parking lot.

"Thank you, sir, I will think about it and call you."

Jack folded himself up into the small Cavalier and put the card in the ashtray that had some ATM receipts and other stuff in it, before starting the car.

He did make it on time to the warehouse where he drives a forklift. He did think about the offer. He thought about a lot of things as he started to unload some semi-trailers. His family was torn apart. But he kept thinking of Cassidy and what she was doing. Then thought about that biker yelling at him in court telling him he would kill him. The completely red face, and the spittle coming out of his mouth. Which gave him nightmares still, four years later. But he kept thinking about the girl, his best friend at the time in the whole world. and how they were separated for life. He was not supposed to take any pictures with him. But he did have a picture of his girl. At his first break from work, he'd go out to the car and look at her on the visor. He would even do that before the games. The photo was of both of them at the local carnival and had soaked up many tears in the last four years.

Chapter Twenty-Two

VENOMOUS VIPER VEGAS CHAPTER

On the outskirts of Las Vegas, a man had just picked two girls from a catalog to join him in his motel room. It's a dump called the Roll of the Dice Motel. Many called it the "Roll in the hay" Motel. The man was short on funds, so he had to rent a cheap room in a dump that was far away from the strip. He was not going with expensive hot call girls. He was going with the budget buy of hookers, but he thought the pictures of the girls in the catalog looked hot. It never crossed his mind that the girls that would arrive would be someone else. Perhaps they will do. He was in the mood for a threesome, and he had picked a tall blonde who went by the name Asia. Then picked a Black woman who went by the name Saturn, like the car or planet. But she had some Jupiter planets as a rack in the picture. It was sort of a celebration that he had going down. He had organized a big-time deal that was going to get rid of some debt he owed. He was hoping for some extra scratch to win him some big money at the blackjack table.

It was a dry heat type of day, as the temperature was in the 90s and still rising. The Roll of the Dice Motel was one level and laid out in a horseshoe. It had rows of rooms except by the parking lot entrance which was the office. The parking lot was right in the middle of the complex. They had yellow parking lines going in a horseshoe pattern, so you could park your car in front of the door or window of your room. The guy at the time at the desk was on the crapper when a dark sedan entered the parking lot. He drove past the big Motel sign and immediately parked. The windows were tinted and rolled up as he had the air condition cranking on this hot day and parked with the engine running.

Inside, Brad was taking a shower. He was singing aloud to himself, "Come sail away with me." He did not know most of the song, so he just repeated the chorus part over and over.

He left the bathroom door open as water blasted off the sweat from the drive from Utah. His air conditioning on his truck has never worked. Plus, he still did not shower from sweating up the sheets with Shawna the other night. When he woke up, the bar needed him to go in and he'd had no time to shower. He just threw some gel in his hair and wiped his pits with his Old Spice that was down to the shavings practically.

He finished with his shower as the steam blew out in the air-conditioned room and he walked out of the bathroom. As he felt the nice cold air hit his body from the blasting AC, he heard a knock at the door. He looked at the digital clock and thought the two girls would not be there for another hour. He had a meeting set up late that evening for his deal. He walked by the television, grabbed the remote to click off the TV, and tightened the towel around his waist.

"Who is it?"

"It's about your meeting this evening, Mr. Doxby. I'm sorry, but we will have to do this right now as other business has come up."

A male voice was speaking outside the door, in an Eastern European accent.

"How the fuck did he know where I was staying?"

That he said quietly, but then more loudly added, "Give me a minute."

He quickly threw the towel on the queen size bed, where he noticed the bed frame had a grill of brass poles. They'd be great for having the girls cuff him to it so they can have his way with him. He threw on his jeans that were laying on the red shag carpet and opened the door as he slid off the chain and turned the knob. Sun immediately shone right in his eyes as the door suddenly smacked him in the head. Brad fell backwards, shocked and dizzy at the same time, as he fell to the ground on his back. The guy outside the door came waltzing in the room after he kicked the door, knocking Brad off balance. The stranger immediately closed the door as the sun quickly disappeared. Outside was a ghost town as not many people were even checked in, and the manager was reading the newspaper on the toilet still and could be in there awhile.

"What the Fuck, man?"

Brad covered his nose as blood was leaking out of it slowly. The pain made it feel like it could be broken, and it was hard to breathe as he looked up at a man dressed in all black. The man took of his sunglasses. He did not say a word as he took a quick peek in between the mini blinds to see if anybody witnessed him kicking the door open.

"SILENCE," the man dressed in black turned around and spoke. Suddenly he was holding a gun that looked like it had a silencer on the end.

Brad started to slide his bum backwards towards the bathroom with one hand on his nose. The other helped him scoot his butt across the shag carpet.

"Whoa, easy buddy. I don't want no trouble."

That seemed like it did not go well, as the Eastern European man fired a shot. It winged Brad in the right shoulder, and now his hand came off his nose and placed it right on the bullet hole. Warm blood oozed out between his fingers as some was still coming out of the nostrils. He went in a fetal position right in front of the bathroom and was grimacing in pain as tears started flowing out of his eye ducts.

The Eastern European was over 6 feet tall. He looked like a skinhead with a shaved head on top of a giraffe neck. He had albino colored skin, especially with the black clothes he was dressed in. He had a tight black tee shirt that clung to his well-oiled machine of a body. Like a Terminator. He had black Cavarricci pants with black steel toed boots. He had the Mike Dukakis eyebrows with beady crazy eyes. He had a tubular nose with a clean-shaven face. He grabbed Brad right underneath the arm that had a bullet hole in it and lifted him with ease with one arm before throwing him on the bed.

"GET UP!"

Brad shrieked with pain but did not say anything as he hoped to play dead and maybe this big bad hairless bear would go away. His nose continues to bleed into the sheets of the bed. All while he held on to his shoulder, trying to stop more blood from coming out as he held one of the pillows to the wound.

The Eastern European, still holding the gun, easily pulled up the small armchair in the corner of the room and sat down with the gun pointed at Brad in the bed. He leaned over as his face was looking at Brad like he was one of those close talkers bringing you into a long conversation. Brad could smell garlic on his breath as he spoke.

"Tell me everything you know."

"Who the hell are you," asked Brad, mustering up a sentence, as he continued to grimace in pain.

The Eastern European stood up and holstered his gun, as he slid it behind his back.

"Well Bradley, I'm kind of a contractor who was hired by a party that you seek riches from."

He put one foot at the bottom of the bed and rolled up his pants leg, so Brad could see him pull a knife out of the holster around his ankle. The steel blade seemed to twinkle from the bathroom lights behind him.

"They sent me here to deal with you, as I'm kind of like a business broker. However, as a contractor, I have a full list of duties."

He now held the knife in his hand and paced the room.

"I was told I would be meeting one of the local charter's top guys to tell him the information and work out a deal."

Brad could still feel the warm blood on his fingers as he was plugging the wound by pressing down hard on it.

"Yes, your friend the one who works as a drug dealer, yes."

"Yes, Kurtis"

"Let me tell you about Kurtis. I be right back so don't you leave that bed."

He took the blade of the knife and brought it down perfectly into Brad's wound. Brad's body just jerked, and his heart raced as he then brought the blade of the knife out of the wound, but he twisted it making the wound bigger as Brad howled in pain. Drips of crimson warm blood dripped off the set of teeth on the blade, as they trickled on the white comforter. The Eastern European wiped off the blade found on the jeans leg. Then the guy found one of his rolled-up socks, placed the knife right by his left pec on his chest, and stuck the sock in Brad's mouth like an apple in a pig at a pig roast. Tears flowed down Brad's cheeks as the Eastern European guy gave Brad his shirt. He threw it on the bed.

"Wrap that around your wound, yes."

Brad now wrapped his wound with his shirt, and the sweat gave his wound a quick sting. All's he wanted was a hole to open up under him and suck him into the earth to get away from this nut job.

"I be back in a jiffy, yes."

The door opened and the room was half lit by the sunlight once again.

Brad could feel the pain shooting through his body. It was a fiery pain. His stomach, all of a sudden, felt queasy. His head continued to pound like a jack hammer that he could not escape. As if it was just a woodpecker inside pecking constantly. He could hardly get a train of thought as he laid there just thinking he wanted to die. The Eastern European returned with a black duffel and closed the door. His bald head was perspiring, but now the cold air from the A/C blasted all over, and made him feel better from that brief time going in his trunk for this bag. Brad could hear the zipper glide open on the top of the bag.

"TA DA!"

He pulled out a head from the bag, with a very familiar face, and tried to smile.

"Do you like, yes?"

Brad's heart just stopped as now he knew that it was his friend who was working as a drug dealer for the Venomous Vipers. He was the one that got this meeting for Brad. Brad told him the story but did not give him the details. He had told him to give the charter his price, but now realized that it had not been a wise idea.

"What the hell is wrong with you?"

The head now was set down on the bed. The skin looked like it was turning blue. He had stuff coming out of his neck right where this psycho cut it. Brad just closed his eyes rather than looking at his old friend, Kurtis, who was looking back at him with eyes open. Tears flowed down his cheeks

"Why? OK. I'll tell you everything I know, and you do not have to pay me anything. Just leave me alone."

He left the head on the bed, which made Brad's stomach turn as he felt acid rising through his insides. So, he just closed his eyes. The Eastern European guy sat back down on the chair. He had the gun back in his hand that was resting on his lap. "You have the floor, so go ahead and tell me everything. Then I can get out of your hair, yes."

"I tell you and then we are good. We go our separate ways. I don't want to end up like him."

He grimaced in pain looking at his old friend.

"Of course, yes, we go different ways, yes."

He gave Brad a smile exposing his yellowish teeth. Tea and cigarette stains had left their evidence.

Brad started telling the guy all the details about the Malone family. He had lots of drinks that night and smoked many joints. Like in life, Brad had that selective hearing. When his ears were open, he could remember the dictionary. This he thought would be a big money maker. He told him about how he was sleeping with the girl. The father is here in Vegas. The mom works at a hospital when she's not loaded and passed out on the couch. The other girl is in high school. While the main character, her brother, works at a warehouse.

"Is that all? You are not leaving anything out?"

Brad was now sitting up in the bed, but still in pain. Still holding his shoulder. He nodded his head yes, as the Eastern European stood up from the chair and paced. The head still sat on the edge of the bed.

"What about addresses or phone numbers?"

Brad pointed to his bag on top of the desk in the corner. He walked over to it and rifled through some clothes until he found a manilla folder. He found all kinds of information he could use to track down the whole family.

"Very good work indeed."

He walked over to the bed, reading all the information Brad had found on his own.

"Glad you approve. So, we are good?"

"It's great work for a bouncer at a night club. However, you're fired."

Brad's eyes opened all the way. He did not have any time to react as his head went backwards. Blood and brain matter splattered all over the headboard.

"Sorry, I lied."

The Eastern European took his bag, as well as the manilla folder, and headed out the door. He left the head on the bed and Brad slumped over on the bed against the headboard. He put the do not disturb sign outside on the door. Then he put his shades on, got in his car, and drove off.

Chapter Twenty-Three

After drinking at Fast Eddie's Tap for hours, they had had plenty of beers, a few well-drinks, and many shots like it was a 21-year old's birthday. They managed to get a cab to get them out of town, and to the border of the next town over, where they found a nice hole-in-the-wall motel. The big fellow spoke in slurred words as they came through the fleabag motel's door.

"Let's get naked and fuck 'till the cows come home."

The place was a dump as inside it smelled like sweat and horrendous body odors. The man known as Anaconda rented the place only that afternoon and was not there very long as he went to town to meet his woman who he wanted right at this moment. They called him Anaconda because he had a tattoo of an anaconda with the tail along the arm. It wrapped around his chest and midsection ending in the picture of the scary head right above his belly. It had blood dripping from the reptile's mouth. Now he laid on his back exposing his bare-chested snake tattoo. His pants were rolled down his ankles as he had his dick out hard and ready.

"Come on baby light my fire," he sang as he started playing with himself as his girl was in the bathroom.

She was looking in the mirror at herself. A face she did not recognize. She had just as many drinks as he did, but she was unfazed. She heard singing, and she tried to sound sexy and add some feeling to it.

"Just a minute, my sexy man beast."

Then she heard "Yabba dabba doo," from Anaconda's favorite cartoon, the Flintstones. He did his best Fred Flintstone and went back to singing the Doors song, of which he only knew one line.

"Come on Cassidy give it a few more minutes," she whispered to herself.

A big smile came over her face when suddenly the Doors song came to an end. She walked out of the bathroom with her clothes still on and looked on the bed to see the big fellow passed out snoring logs as his dick went limp.

"My poor baby fell asleep, and I was going to ride you until I rocked your fuckin' world."

She found his jeans, pulled them off his legs, and took out his cellphone from the pocket.

She has done it again, as she crushed a few pills and put them in his last drink at the bar. They got to the motel and like clockwork, he was out before any festivities took place. She went through his phone. She took out her phone and took pictures of some contacts. Looked through some text conversations and took her time reading it all. Finding the stuff she wanted and shooting pictures of it with her phone. When she was satisfied, she put her phone away in her purse. She stashed his phone back in the jeans where she found them. Then she took out a piece of paper that was pre-written and put it on the nightstand. She messed up the covers as she was setting her stage. Making it look like something went down. Threw a few pillows on the floor. She reached in her bag and put a pair of panties in his hand that she wore the other day. Something he can sniff because he was a pig and liked that sort of shit.

"Now the part I hate," as she reached in her bag once more and pulled out a pair of wax lips.

She then fished out a tube of lipstick and ran it over the wax lips. She hated this part as she had to get close to his junk. Seeing him naked was revolting and made her insides swirly. She took the waxed lips and stamped Anaconda's penis a few times, leaving the imprint of a lip mark. She did it like stamping a box "fragile" or "sold." Then she did the same thing on top of his forehead and on his chest, yes right on the snake's mouth which she imagined turned him on. She has never actually slept with him. But in his mind, he has fucked her multiple times. She stood up, took her bag, and walk towards the door. She blew him a kiss and turned off the lights.

"Good night, sweetie!"

The next morning he'd wake up and read her note saying she had to leave and apologizing. She had some sweet nicknames in there as well. She called him 'sweetie thang' and 'cuddly bear.' Snake Mountain was his favorite. Then a P.S XOXOXO, Call me next week. He would wake up in a confused state of mind. But sniffing the panties would bring him visions that never actually happened. Then seeing the room and looking in the mirror to see the lipstick in a few spots, was a job well done. He always wished he could remember. But, then he would smile and let her fill him in the next time they met. As she would indeed tell tall tales.

Chapter Twenty-Four

"Obviously, I want to be your husband someday and play baseball, professional baseball."

"That's the order you should keep it in."

They both laughed as they sat in front of Cassidy's house on a swing. It sat on a wraparound porch at her parent's house.

The night was gorgeous as they swung on the swing cuddling each other. It was mild out with a little breeze. Crickets and the squeak of the swing along with these two on the swing in love with laughter. The full moon gave a nice light on most of the backyard they were facing. They each had a nice glass of lemonade on the small table next to the swing with a lit candle next to that. They loved to talk about everything. Especially future plans for their dreams, and how they wanted to make each other's dream come true. They looked in the sky as they held hands. Her head was on his chest, and she could hear his heartbeat. Both of them spotted a few stars twinkling in the night.

"Do you remember when we went camping?" she said.

"I remember you could not put up that tent."

"Shut up! That was your bone headed mistake not learning how to set it up before you borrowed it from your pal, buddy boy!"

The swing swung slowly back and forth as they both looked like they were starting to doze off.

"If we had more light to see the tent to set up, we would have been OK, but no… Someone was running late."

His point was too late as she had her eyes closed and was asleep.

"Figures when I'm winning," and just laughed to himself.

The swing was still swinging as he held her tight. She had a little bit of a snore if you listened closely. He had heard it a few times over the years. The night was calm as the whole neighborhood was asleep. It was one those moments in life you could not forget. He thought maybe this moment could be in that comic strip, "Love is." He closed his eyes as he nearly drifted off himself. He heard some footsteps on the wraparound wooden porch. They seemed like they were getting closer and closer. Then they stopped. He had not opened his eyes, as he could feel a presence looking down at them as the swing now was still. He opened his eyes, and he heard a click as the barrel of big silver cannon was pointed right at his head. He could feel the cold steel on his forehead jabbing him, as he looked up and saw Blade Runner. Cassidy was still asleep, and it seemed like she was having some good dreams as he could see a grin. He put his hands over her head as if to protect her or make sure she did not hear anything. Then a dark deep voice whispered in the night, grinning with a crooked smile.

"I told you mother fucking rat boy, I would come back and kill you."

Suddenly he woke up in a cold sweat. His body trembling and heart racing. It seemed so real. As he composed himself, he saw he was in his room at the house in Utah. He could see little streaks of the sun making way through the cracks of the drapes. He looked at the time as he had only been sleeping for four hours. He sat up and wiped the sleep out of his eyes. His heart was back to beating normally, as he thought about that dream which was so real. It was actually an old moment between them years ago which seemed like an eternity now. It was like something or someone downloaded the old memory of the two and just added that crazy biker.

Thinking of that guy made his heartbeat faster, as he took a deep breath. He wanted to go back to sleep, but a dream like that will linger in his mind. He now had the urge to dial her number. He has done it, but only to get her voice mail. He started to tear up as he exited the bed to head to the bathroom thinking about her. The closeness they had on that swing in a way made it seem like he could smell her hair. Some wildflowers scented shampoo. Instead, he came to the realization it would be better to just head to the batting cages. Take 100 swings and put the rest of the stuff out of his head at least temporarily. As he brushed his teeth, his mind was made up. Then one last thought came through his mind about that biker. It took two years to get the image of him out of his brain from just seeing him on the street, popping up like some ugly weed on the lawn. It was his mind playing tricks on him as most images were not even close, especially somebody riding a motorcycle. But the way the engine grew louder as they kicked it into gear, made him shiver like the last leaf on a tree.

Chapter Twenty-Five

"Yes, I found him," the man said into his phone.

He was sitting drinking a cup of coffee as he listened to the person on the other end.

"I'm actually looking at the man as we speak."

He took a sip out of the coffee mug as he continued to listen. He was looking at a man playing on a slot machine at one of the hole-in-the-wall casinos off the main strip. It was the kind of place that seemed appropriate for desperate people trying to win back their dignity. Or go home.

"Ok, I'll wait until you transfer half the money into my account before any business is complete. Do we have ourselves an understanding?"

Seconds later he said, "I'll be waiting for the deposit and then I will start."

He clicked the button to end the call without saying goodbye to the person on the other end.

He thought to himself this will go easy as this guy is down on his luck and will be easy to erase from this planet. A waitress came to his table, and her hand was shaking due to definitely being scared of this guy. He kept his eyes on the guy the entire time, never looking at her.

"More coffee, sir?"

"No, may I have the check please?"

Like a cowboy in an old Western movie, she pulled the check from her apron pocket like pulling a six shooter out of her holster.

"Here you go sir, have a nice day," fleeing the scene like her life was in danger.

To him, it felt like he was being watched. He pressed the button on the slot machine to see it roll and turn into nothing. No change except to his dwindling machine balance. He quickly pushed the thought out of his mind as today would be the day he turned his luck around. He was thinking of calling his son to have him wire some money to him. He knew he needed an excuse as this was not the first time he borrowed money off his son. Even when he took that autographed ball of all the White Sox signatures from the 1993 American League Central Division winners. His thought was it should have been left in Spruce Wood. Going into witness protection, you leave quickly, and you take only what you can carry. His son did not pack, it was him that did it. For a second when they arrived in Utah, he was happy to see the ball that his father gave him twice. He was able to get the ball past the Agents in charge of moving them. How they rifled through all of their belonging looking for any kind of evidence of their former past lives. It worked, and it made his kid happy. Then he took it and pawned it for thirty lousy dollars.

Later that night, the scary guy that the waitress was afraid of, was in his hotel laying on the bed watching television. He was watching an old show called Bonanza on one of those channels that play old classic shows. He loved the old west, and this took his mind off his upcoming job. He was awaiting the cash to be deposited into one of his offshore accounts. He laid on the bed shirtless with a perfect six pack stomach. His bald head, which was starting to grow some small stubble, would have to be shaved again before he gets his next kill in. He could feel the breeze of the AC running its course to keep the room at a perfect 60 degrees, which he liked and had to have. It looked like he was all in on the show. But his mind was thinking of multiple things. He was calculating the next payday. He was thinking about how he would go about killing the compulsive gambler. An image of his childhood would play over and over in his head. How his dad stripped the fur off a rabbit. How he skinned the rabbit alive. Then he snapped off the head of the rabbit as it clung for dear life or in shock. Then how he would burn the fur off the skull. How he watched his twisted father clean the skull like he was mining for some diamonds. Then his mind went to how his father got mad at him. The time he tried to stick his face to the metal grating of the flaming grill in the back yard of their old house. He did not get his face, as he did make sure to grab his arm instead, but he burnt his elbow. To this day, he still had the burn marks of the grating under his left elbow and was looking at it while it was high noon on the program. He hated that bastard… he snapped out of his daydream and back to the show.

Chapter Twenty-Six

"I'M ON THE HIGHWAY TO HELL," blasted on the radio of the old Cavalier as it scooted down the highway at 65 mph. Jack Young, who was and went by, John Malone only years ago, was behind the wheel tapping his fingers to the steering wheel and singing to AC/DC. It was the wee hours of the morning, and he had just made it into the state of Idaho. Nobody was on the road, and he was not getting any good radio stations in the middle of nowhere. Luckily, he still had some reliable tapes that came with the car when he purchased it a few years back. That night he worked half a shift at the warehouse. He was driving the forklift unloading and loading trucks for the first four hours. He had the forklift driving down to a science as he could move pallets of truck parts up and down, in and out of truck trailers in his sleep. His mind was not on his job the whole night. It started with the dream he had in the morning. Everything felt so real. Seeing the love of his life, Cassidy, right there inches away. He could have sworn he woke up with the smell of her shampoo in his nose. That fragrance of wildflowers he could never forget. The way she fell asleep in his lap on the swing. The way he stroked her long hair. The way she breathed in a deep slumber. A few times letting out a cute soft snore. More of a purr like a cat would do in one of its many slumbers of day. He recalled the conversation about him and her being together forever and playing the game of baseball, another love he wanted to do forever.

That morning at the cages he went through many buckets of baseballs. The swing was perfect on almost of all of them. It was crisp and the ball launched off the sweet spot of the bat on many of the fastest pitches coming from one of the machines at the cages. He did some soul searching at the cages. He found a greasy spoon after the cages and sat down to have some eggs. After that, he made a phone call. He sat in the car waiting for the person to answer, and he did on the 4th ring.

"Hello, Rusty Mulligan here."

Jack told him he wanted to come up and try out for the Tacoma Twisters.

Rusty said, "the sooner the better."

Jack told Big Red he could be up there in the next few days. The conversation went very well. Big Red said if the coach liked the try out, that they would get him on the roster ASAP. The team still had about two months of the season left on the schedule. Big Red also informed Jack that he had a keen eye for legit talent and has seen him play most of the games this season.

"Play like you have, and you will definitely make the team."

Jack Young sincerely smiled for the first time since the days of Spruce Wood. He knew right when he clicked end on the cell phone, this was the right call. It was his calling, and he had to do it. He knew he faced a few challenges and some bumps in the road with his family and his job driving the forklift. It did not matter. He was going to get up to Tacoma and try out for the Twisters.

That afternoon he went home and packed a suitcase with just the essentials what he would need. His mom was at work. His sister was probably at basketball practice. His other sister was away at college. The homestead these days in Utah, with his father leaving, was like a ghost town. It was not like those days where everyone would be at home eating supper together. Even watching a movie on the weekend together which they did almost every week religiously. He packed his suitcase and was in and out like a bank robber as he left a note. He went to the gas station and gassed up his ride. It was an old car and did not look like much but was dependable as he maintained it very well. He then went to the bank and withdrew a few hundred dollars. He could use his bank card wherever. His bank was all over the states. He still wanted to have some cash just in case. After the bank he went to the supermarket. Loaded up a cooler with drinks, fruit and some sandwiches. He also had a bag of snack food for the long ride to Tacoma. According to maps on his phone, it would be a 16-hour drive from Utah to Tacoma. He would be traveling close to 1000 miles.

He would have skipped his shift at work, but on that night, he was getting paid. He did the first four-hour shift and then received his paycheck. The check he'd deposit in an ATM at some point to have enough funds, as he did not know if he would return to Utah if this tryout went south. He told a few co-workers he was going to take a quick drive over to Burger King. They all assumed he'd hit a drive thru and come back to the warehouse. Instead, he drove off into the night to begin a whole new life yet again. He had the trip mapped out and found the first major highway closest to work and took the exit. He made a promise to himself he would call his mother in the morning, as he assumed she was working the night shift but was unsure. He then looked at the visor image of the lovely Cassidy, and he promised himself he would meet up again with her at some point in this lifetime. He drove with all the windows down as it was a gorgeous night out in the middle of nowhere. Lots of stars lit up the skies. He changed over the tape to the other side to hear some "Back in Black," another one of his favorite songs that reminded him of the Chicago White Sox uniforms. He looked out in front of him and could have sworn he saw a shooting star or something. He was not sure but made a wish just in case, as he drove on into the night.

Chapter Twenty-Seven

The man formerly known as Arthur Malone was like a fish out of water and desperate. Where did it go wrong for Arthur Malone? It had to have started with when his son confessed to the murder of the Sheriff in his own hometown. His son saw a biker walk into Murphy's and at point blank range kill one of his oldest and dearest friends. Freddie Cook and Arthur practically grew up in the sand box together. Spruce Wood is the type of town where families plant their roots and never leave. Many of those families go back generations. Freddie Cook was happily married. The man was a womanizer who loved to dip his chip in many dips. Just loved women in general, and that was his major problem. He found himself in situations where he could shack up with a gal for a one-night stand that lasts for years with the same girl. Casual sex... he once told Arthur. Arthur always told Fred you have to stop doing that, you're married. Fred loved his wife, Erica. Fred had the addiction for the pussy like a junkie needed his stash.

Arthur thought he gave that addiction up. He could not believe his addiction got dangerous and resulted in him getting involved with a biker's old lady. To get involved with an Outlaw with a background as a killing machine from the military. Fred had all the Venomous Vipers' files. Most of them. They kept track of anything they could get on the biker gang. Even if it was something as small as littering. Even though, Fred crossed a threshold and started sleeping with a whore who was probably on drugs. Perhaps she was trying to get out from under the biker group and thought Fred was the Sheriff, so the ticket to a new life. If only Arthur knew, he would think over and over for years. He could have helped Fred. Perhaps prevented this nightmare. At the time, his son was unsure whether to do the right thing and testify. Arthur, not thinking and regretting what he had done, convinced his son to stand up and put this killer behind bars where he belonged. He was not thinking how his whole life would take a sudden turn. A turn that would pretty much ruin the whole family's bond and love. His wife Valerie told him repeatedly that he should not confess. Arthur did not listen. Then the unthinkable happened. The authorities gathered up the Malone family like the Nazis hauled away like the Jews in World War II. The Malone family was not going to the gas chamber. Perhaps it was a slow death sentence because after the name change from Malone to Young, everyone in the family is dying of a slow death. Without even getting to say goodbye to Fred Cook, his best friend. The Malone family was taken out of their home by the authorities. They were put up in a safe house in Chicago. Three weeks was all they had to learn their new identity. Three weeks they had to learn about each other over again from habits to hobbies and of course personality traits. Then his son finally testified against that dirtbag outlaw. He was not there to see this sociopath threaten to find his son and kill him and his family, which was him. Then to a place of not their choosing, they were shipped off like packages and wound up in Utah. They had new jobs which were not even close to their old careers. Arthur Malone was a car salesman at a Chevy dealership now. His new peers and co-workers only knew him as Justin Young.

Justin Young now found himself out of money. It was late morning, and he still was in Las Vegas, but off the strip. He found himself stirring his third coffee of the morning at a diner called Lucy's Fork & Spoon. Your typical old-fashioned diner with a long counter and stools. Then booths along the dirty windows, most likely from the dust that blows in time to time. He only had enough money to spring for the bottomless mug of coffee and a bagel. He had no more money for a place to stay, so he had to sleep in his car. He now was staring into his phone looking at his few contacts he had. Inside, he immediately ruled out some of the guys at work, especially his boss. He had walked off the job in the middle of a deal selling an Impala to a couple. He only had a quarter tank of gas and that would not get him back to Utah. Besides, he did not want to go back to the arguing with his wife. Even in his thoughts, his own kids hated him. Which one would forward some scratch his way? He really thought if he could get a hold of a few bucks he might be ok. He could win and get enough money to leave Vegas. Deep down he knew if he won enough money to drive out of town, he'd want to win more money to stay another night.

It had worked for months. He was able to live in Las Vegas for almost a whole year at a cheap motel he paid for by the week. He did not have to work. His day was all about handicapping and betting on sports. He was living the life of Reilly going to the sports book, watching the games, and winning all kinds of cash. He was eating like a king having steak dinners. He even had some lobster and crab at some high-level classy places. He did not want it to come to an end.

He glanced up and looked around the diner, seeing it pretty emptied. The morning rush was done. It left an older man reading the newspaper at the counter sipping on a mug of coffee too. His waitress was wrapping up silverware with the napkin ring. The cook, who looked like he could be a he or she. He thought a butch dike. He/she was cleaning off the grill to get it ready for the lunch hour.

Justin finished his third cup and left a few bills on the table, as he hated to screw the waitress on the tip. Leaving 30 cents will probably be talked about after he leaves. Perhaps they would understand as he was one step away from being a hobo. He looked at himself in the reflection of the windows when he stood up. He had a full growth beard going which was unkept. He had bags under his eyes with of course blood shot eyes. He smelled as if he had not showered or rolled a stick of deodorant under his arms in days. The coffee breath was fighting back the dragon breath. His dark blue polo shirt, which had the logo of the dealership he quit months back, was wrinkled like an old prune. He had gray cargo shorts with all the pockets which looked ok. The sandals exposing his discolored toes and plenty of hair sticking out between the toes sent out an odor. He walked out without looking at anybody. He looked like he had lost weight as whiskey was most of his meals. His salt and pepper hair was totally salty now. It was probably thinning more and in need of a comb job. The sun made his eyes squint when he pushed through the glass doors. He felt the heat hit his body in an instant coming out of the AC'd diner. No one said boo to him as he walked out. They might have forgotten about him or just did not care like most people in Justin's life felt about him.

The parking lot was emptied except a few cars that probably belonged to the ugly dyke and the fat waitress. The diner was at the end of town, so it faced an empty desert. It was located on a corner of businesses on one side, and nothing across the street except the wind blowing sand. If you really looked far out, you might see a cactus or two. Justin suddenly had an idea for how to get some money. He had two ideas actually, and he smirked as a dark sedan drove right by him. He did not see who was inside, as it passed by. He crossed the back of the parking lot and saw his car all by its lonesome. He had a ten-year-old Chevy Cruise. He made a funny to his family and called it his Tom Cruise mobile, like the actor. In Spruce Wood, that joke would have had everyone on the ground in a deep chuckle. In Utah, that joke meant he was looked at like he had two heads. He pressed the button on the remote on the key chain that flipped the locks. He needed to charge his phone to find a place he could go to get him some cash. He would also try his son. It had been a long time. He would be the logical choice, and the only one that would actually wire some money to his dear ole dad.

He got inside the silver Cruise which was in pretty good condition despite needing a bath. This despite all of his stuff in the back seat, which made it look like he lived in it.

He told himself as he buckled his seat belt, "I'll take the car over to that car dealership in town. They will give me cash for it, and then I will be back in business."

The person in the dark sedan slowly drove away from the diner as he was looking at his rearview mirror like something was going on behind him. It was very quiet around this area especially during this time of the day. 'BINGO,' the man thought as he found what he was looking for.

A fire ball explosion was seen lighting up the sky and heard by many. Some of the parked cars on the street came to life. Alarms started blaring from the vibrations and how loud it was. People stepped out of their businesses to look towards the diner. In back of the building, the parking lot was filled with smoke and some high flames. Inside the diner, the waitress slid under the booth when the loud explosion occurred. The dyke cook jumped out of her skin and burned her hand on the grill as she was in the middle of cleaning. She poked her head out the back door after feeling the building shake and the noise as parts of the Cruiser rattled off the brick building of the diner. Just a minute before, Justin had plugged his phone in. He was ecstatic about his idea for how to get back in the game. He put the key in the ignition and his life flashed by in an instant as he immediately was charred by flames.

The Eastern European drove on as he picked up some speed. Not too much. Just what the speed limit said. He turned up his book on tape through this fancy gizmo that played through the car speakers. He loved reading and learning about the Nazis.

"One down, and three to go."

Chapter Twenty-Eight

It has been a few days since Shawna Young and Brad Doxby hooked up. In Shawna's mind, she thought the night went well. Her visions of the night meant she thought it could lead to something long term. She felt comfortable with Brad Doxby, and like he listened to her. Every gal feels that way about Brad Doxby after a one-night stand. He had a way of making women think he was totally different than the other men. Was it his charm? Perhaps being three sheets to the wind could make anybody look and sound better. Brad Doxby had that look and could adapt to any women on any level. It was not just about pick up lines. He could probably write a book on the subject. He was a decent looking guy. Definitely not eye candy where women would immediately flock to him. Just looking at any girl, he could strike up a conversation and immediately the girl would be interested. In Shawna's case he just planted the seed like a farmer. Asked her about what classes she was in. Maybe a compliment on something only another woman would notice. Most men would miss it even if it had a bullseye logo on it.

Shawna thought she would hear from Brad as it had been a few days. She knew most men had that famous 3 days or more policy after a hook-up to not look desperate. Shawna mind was fuzzy about a few key parts. She sent him a few texts. Even left a voice message. She thought she'd make the first move, and that maybe in his mind he would like the women for once to do the chasing. She did not know if the people of Utah thought the same way as her approach, but she did not care. She never got any response back from him. She questioned whether she had the right phone number.

"Stop mind-fucking yourself," she yelled out to herself as she scrolled down her call list thinking she may have missed him.

Then she'd shake her head and remind herself that she heard his voice on the voice mail. Then her brain started having flash backs of the conversation, in between getting sweaty like some animals going at it all night. While they passed the joint back and forth between the both of them. The way she spilled her guts as if she had food poison and dumped all her insides in the toilet. Her face was flushed. She felt a cold shiver down her spinal cord like something bad was going to happen.

"Shake it off, you dumb bitch," she said to her reflection in the mirror.

She threw some water on her face. After all, he may be sick or something. He might be in bed not wanting to see or talk to anybody. Maybe he lost his phone; that could have happened. Right now he was probably ransacking his place looking for his phone so he could call. She decided to retrace her steps from that night and find Brad's apartment. Knock on the door and he will answer. This will give her a chance to have a quick cigarette on the way to completely calm her nerves.

Everything about the walk came back to her in an instant. She smoked her cigarette while she recalled the path they took to get to his apartment from the bar. Shawna was wearing jeans and black boots that fit under the pant legs. She had a pink V-neck shirt that was tight and showed off her cleavage very well. You could dive in and get lost in those puppies. It was a tight shirt which made them look well-stacked and distracted people. People looked at them first instead of her make-up free face. Her auburn hair was tied in a ponytail as she walked, inhaling one of her Salem Lights with her black purse dangling off her shoulder.

It was a beautiful summer day, and you could see the mountains off in the distance that made a very nice picture if you cared about such things. She found the apartment building, which was kind of an eyesore. Just a tall square brick building with a crème brick color. Looked like weeds growing along the sides. She came up to the door and did not have to buzz the apartment, as the wooden door was open with a wooden shiv keeping the door propped open. Somebody could be moving in or moving out, but that did not matter. She climbed the stairs as she remembered the elevator did not work. The stairs were dark and musky. She felt her underarms perspiring, as she climbed the steps quickly. She found the floor and walked the hallway which smelled of spoiled food. It was dark and musky. She found the door and gave it a tap. She waited a few minutes and then gave it a louder knock, not quite a Police Officer knock but a degree lower. Then she heard a door open behind her. She could smell some cigarette smoke oozing out as she turned around. She saw the chain on the door, that was open only a crack. She could see a few puffs of smoke spiraling towards the hallway ceiling. She had to look down as she saw a little old lady.

"Brad is not home, Miss. He has not been home for the last two days."

Only her eyes could be seen, which made her look like an owl. Then she saw an orange glow in her mouth which explained the raspy voice. She did not give Shawna a chance to answer her before she shut the door as she heard the lock twist. She decided to leave the same way she had come.

As she descended the concrete stairs, her biggest question that she asked no one in particular was, "Where the hell did he go?"

She thought he had to be at work as more conversation from the night came flooding back in her mind. She walked through the back parking lot just to see if his car was there. It was gone, so the lady was probably right. The lost phone had to be the only explanation as she hightailed to the Pelican to see if he was at work. She was not sure the Pelican was open this early, but she would find out when she got there. It was probably about a mile walk. Which did not bother her as her exercise was all about walking and smoking. Her long muscular legs could handle it and get her there pretty quickly.

The Pelican was in the middle of the downtown area. The front had a Pelican neon sign, with many trees in the front which surrounded a wrought iron fence. The fence surrounded the beer garden which was decorated in a Hawaiian style. Many tiki torches surrounded all the chairs and tables. It was too early for them to be lit as she went along the alley first to see if his car was parked by the dumpster. The brick building of the Pelican had vines growing on the side which hid the original logo of the Pelican that was painted on the bricks decades ago. It was fading, but you could still see most of the bird. She saw the green dumpsters with the leprechaun on them. Lucky Leprechaun disposal to be exact. Behind them no car was parked there like when they left that night. Where he went down on him. Where she swallowed for him.

"What the fuck?" she whispered to herself.

She walked back to the front door and decided to go in and ask. A crazy thought entered her head as she felt like a pregnant girl looking to expose this information to a guy from a one-night stand, which she hoped it was not. She was not pregnant. She was on the pill because this guy was not her first rodeo. She pulled the glass door open, which also had the Pelican logo on it, and walked into the bar. Inside the bar was just opening. All the chairs were still on top of the tables that went all the way down along one side. She recalls the third table they sat at while chatting that night. The bar was one of the longest bars many people had ever seen. It was made out of glass block windows, and the glass top held water with live fish swimming inside it. Behind the bar were shelves loaded with all kinds of bottles of booze. Shelves lined up along the wall all the way down in front of mirrors on the walls. They had old fashioned post lights on top of the mirrors that gave them all that dim low lighting. All the stools had backs on them and were made of leather. She approached the bar and was noticed by the bartender; one she didn't recognize and who seemed to be stocking some beers in the cooler.

"Sorry, we are not open yet."

He looked like the guy from Laverne and Shirley who they called Squiggy. He was a short young guy in his early 20's with a lemon-shaped head. His hair was jet black and greased like Squiggy's . It was darker black the closer you got to him, and he had a small curl right in the middle of his freckled forehead. He was wearing a white shirt, a green vest, dark pants and gym shoes.

"Oh, I know, I was wondering if Brad was here."

She put her purse on the bar and stood there hoping this guy knew where he was because it was getting very frustrating. Then she finally got closure of this situation she found herself in. It was like a gut-wrenching blow of someone from Alien or some animal just reaching their big paws right through her chest. Ripping her beating heart out of her and showing it to her.

"Oh, he just quit and said he was moving to Vegas."

The bartender was up close delivering this blow of terrible news.

Her head went straight down and eyeballed a multicolored tropical fish swimming inside the top of the bar. If you asked her if she saw it, she would not be able to tell you what color the fish was. Her legs got wobbly, and she felt like she was going to faint. She thought about how she told this joker her whole life story.

"Are you OK? Please sit down and I'll fix you something to ease your nerves."

She felt like a puppet as a puppet master moved her body and sat her up on the bar stool.

"OK, thanks," she squeaked.

While she did not know what her next move would be. While the bartender made her a cranberry and vodka, his signature drink. Outside the Pelican bar, a dark sedan with tinted windows pulled up with the engine running still.

Chapter Twenty-Nine

Way out in the country, probably a few miles away from the old Venomous Vipers Club House, in Drumleen, it was a beautiful summer day in a Southern Illinois quarry surrounded by a forest preserve. There was fresh country air. On this summer day, the sun was out and not many clouds lurked in the blue skies. Fresh water ran down the well-sculptured rock elevations of the quarry. Birds were singing and the weather was perfect.

"BOOM," echoed throughout the forest.

Seconds later, another boom sounded as birds flattered their wings escaping the ruckus that was going on in the forest. Some might think it was a car backfiring. Some might think it was a hunter looking to take out a deer. They liked to hang out and drink from the stream that led to the water-filled quarry. These sounds were too far away from the road to be heard. Each boom sometimes was followed with a tin can rattling.

A young woman was in her stance. She had her hands gripped around the handle of a berretta pistol with most likely a 15-bullet magazine. Like at the shooting range, she had the earmuffs covering her ears. Her dark jet-black hair was braided into a long ponytail. She was wearing safety goggles. She wore a thin layer of vortex style gloves on her hands as she pulled the trigger. It was a hair trigger as the bullet shot out in the blink of an eye. It destroyed an aluminum Old Style beer can that did the hokey pokey and fell to the ground.

Once a week, Cassidy Sorensen came out to the rock quarry and practiced firing her gun. She would line up cans and use them as target practice. She would bring a small bag of empty cans from home. Lots of times she found a small pile of cans in certain areas leftover from high school kids coming up to drink beer by the quarry. She came up very early in the morning to have the place to herself. She did not want to risk putting a bullet in a human being, especially somebody in high school. She herself had been out of high school for only a few years herself, so she knew what time most likely they would come out. Besides drinking on the weekends, some would come out to make out with each other. She had come out and made out with John, which seemed to be such a long time ago. She fired another shot which just missed a PBR tall boy can and sailed left as the bullet burrowed into an oak tree.

She's wearing jean shorts that show off her nice tan legs with a pair of tennis shoes. She wears an old White Sox Bo Jackson black tee shirt with his name and number on the back. The one brief stint with the Sox and he was still her favorite player of all time. She lined up all the cans in height order. Placing them on low tree branches. Some cans on rocks and tree stumps. She fired from all different kinds of distances. She fired another round, and the bullet nicked the PBR sending it twirling from the stump of the tree. She was working up a sweat as this was her third magazine of the morning. She did not just simply stand and shoot either. She did some different stuff. She would move like the Police SWAT teams that were about to kick open the door. At times she thought about joining the police force. She was attending a junior college and had done most of her general ed classes.

She had no school today, so this was a good day to go to the quarry and practice her shooting. She could not go to your typical range because the gun was not registered. She was still living with her parents. She certainly knew her parents would put the kibosh on having a gun inside their home. Like most parents would say, their house their rules. Besides, she did not have the money to buy a gun like she had. She ended up stealing it from the guy in the Venomous Vipers. Like he'd miss it with the serial numbers filed off. Plus, he had too many pistols in his house. How would he ever know? She set up a P.O. box in a different name to order bullets. She used her uncle's name. She was smart as she learned how to fire a gun from the U-tube videos on the interwebs. She learned the police stances from them too. However, she could say if the conversation ever took place, she liked to watch many police movies and shows. Shooting a gun once a week cleared her head. It relaxed her. If she ever came to the point where she was firing the gun, the person being fired upon would probably think she did not know how to fire a gun with her innocent young-looking face. They would learn the hard way when taking a bullet perfectly in-between the eyes.

Chapter Thirty

"BARDHANA, YOU LITTLE BASTARD! WHAT DID I TELL YOU ABOUT DIGGING THROUGH ME BELONGINGS?"

CRACK… The slap snapped the guy sitting in the car out of a daydream. He looked like he was in some kind of trance. Beads of sweat were forming on the man's albino bald head. The car was running, and the AC was on. The temperature in the car was a perfect 65 degrees, which he needed. More like he made sure wherever he stayed or whatever car he drove in, the temperature had to be exactly 65 degrees. He was a stickler when it came to being precise. Even if the temp read one degree below or one degree above, it was not a pretty sight. He had his laptop open. He had plugged in a few addresses for his possible next destinations. He pressed the tab to begin the download for the fastest route while he kept an eye on the Pelican bar across the street while his sedan idled as smooth soft jazz sounds came out of the stereo. The stereo volume also had to be precise. However, different situations called for different settings.

He then opened the console in the middle of the front seats and pulled out a folded bright white handkerchief. It looked like it was brand new, as he wiped his face and the scalp of his bald head. He then started thinking more about that day when he was only twelve years old. He had found something in his father's bedroom chest. It was a notebook with all kinds of names in it. It had dates, times, and whereabouts. He was flipping through it which even explained the death of all these people on the pages. He did not understand as he got smacked from behind. It was his father who had caught him peeking in this book. He quickly dropped the book as the back of his hand knocked the daylights out of him. It left a mark on his face for two weeks. He remembered his jaw was not quite the same for a few weeks. The worst part was the ringing in his ears. He was proud that he did not cry as back then he was just skin and bones.

He remembers getting yelled at right then and there. Then something occurred downstairs in the house he grew up in. Then the sound got louder as something made a crashing sound. His father, who was a big guy back then, took him by the shirt. He picked him up off the ground and threw him in a closet. Closed the door. Then minutes later he heard gunshots. He heard lots of yelling. He heard words he probably was not meant to hear until he was an adult. He remembers being so frightened he crawled out of the closet and grabbed that notebook. More commotion, so he crawled back in the closet with the notebook. More gunshots went off as it seemed like the sound was getting closer. He stashed the notebook in a shoe box under a pair of dress shoes his father wore. He was thinking he would be killed. He was thinking if this notebook was saved and hidden, he might get out of his doghouse. More yelling and more bullets flying. More things crashing and breaking. He just went into a fetal position in the dark closet covering his ears until it was all over.

The temps that day were not 65 degrees. The man in the car still had his eyes trained on the front door. He did not think the place was even open this early, so what the hell was she doing inside? He had to make his move soon. It was very quiet with not many people lurking around. He only wanted to kill the girl. He had no problem killing others in the way. They were like collateral damage. He checked the clip in his gun. He checked the silencer. It was screwed on tight. Everything was in working condition as he opened the door to his car and felt the heat, like a slap to his face similar to the day he got hit by his father. It was not the first time. But it was the last time he ever laid a finger on the boy.

The man that looked like Squiggy was in his 5th year at Utah State. His name was James. He changed his major, and that's why he remained at school. He was on track to be there another two years. He did not mind because he liked to work at the Pelican, where they paid him well. Girls loved his drinks and not him. He was nice to everyone. James was a vulture. Anything not picked away clean by the customers. Anything that had a set of tits and drunkenly unable to figure out how to get a cab or even get back to the dorm, James came in like Batman to save the day. He would get them home. Sometimes he would be able to get in their room. Sometimes he'd get lucky. He earned the girl's trust and once they were alone, he'd be trying to cram his tongue down their throat. His hands were like Dr. Octopus; if one hand could not get a feel of tit, the other would be knocking at the door.

"How was that drink?" He stood behind the bar drying off a glass that was in the suds of water behind the bar.

Shawna Young was on her third drink of the day. She was not tasting anything in the drink as she gulped it down. She was like a person who just saw water for the first time in days after being out in a hot desert. James' drinks were numbing the pain in her mind. She was able to relax and get her mind back on track regarding what to do next.

"It's delicious."

James was working his angle. Less like a bartender and more like a drug dealer, using the drinks like a dealer would push his or her product. He took the glass he had dried off with the towel, and he began to make another drink, this time much stronger. His vodka pour was far past the four-second pour time.

Laughing, he said, "It's a simple cranberry and vodka with the James additives in it to make it the most wonderful drink around."

Shawn was thinking maybe Brad would not tell anybody. It was only a one-night stand. She was thinking he probably didn't even remember anything. She questioned herself about whether it was such a wonderful night or whether it was two horn-dogs going at it. Two drunken horn-dogs. She laughed inside her head as she was feeling better now. She wondered if James was going to charge her for these drinks. That's when she heard the door open.

James heard it too and continued to make the drink. He gave an automatic response over his shoulder.

"Sorry, we are not open yet."

Nobody said a word as all they heard was a click. Then he turned around to hear Shawna's head nosedive into the bar top. The last thing she saw was that colorful fish looking at her eye to eye. The man in the black ski mask, dressed in all black and even wearing black gloves, fired another shot that hit right in the "Squiggy" part of the hair on his forehead. He dropped the red drink on the floor and crumbled to the floor behind the bar. The man in the mask walked out the door he came in, and even turned the lock on the joint while he closed the front door. Nobody was in the area to see him take the mask off. He walked off back to the running, but locked, car. He flipped the button on the hand remote to unlock automatic locks, got in the car, and drove off.

Chapter Thirty-One

Everything went smoothly for Jack Young on his ride to Tacoma, Washington. He was really impressed with the drive. Out in the country, tall trees lined up on both sides of the highway he took. Between the trees and over the bridge, he saw fresh clean waterways that were so breathtakingly gorgeous. Then all the different greens everywhere you looked from trees to the different grasses and ground cover. Utah had a great view of the mountains. Washington State had huge mountains with plenty of different greens blended in on the rock formations. This made any picture you took, a postcard. The state reminded him of the Old Country. He has never been there but has seen all the pictures from his relatives going over to the old country of Ireland.

He stopped at an old Texaco station off the highway for his second fill-up of the trip. It was good to stretch the legs and give the car some fuel. He made a few calls and took a leak in the bathroom, the tasks he needed to complete. He looked up to see that the rock formation across from the station had a stream winding through it. Fresh mountain water you can drink. The air he was breathing seemed so fresh. He parked the car near the pump. The gas station had four pumps covered by a small square roof overhang. They had a separate square brick building with snacks and drinks inside with a public bathroom he was going to use. The big Texaco sign was posted on a big white pole that could not even quite get halfway up the mountain. The gas station was right in front of a slope of the mountain which has a semicircle brick wall to prevent boulders or rock falls coming down hitting the brick building of the station.

He slid his bank card in the pump, put the nozzle inside the gas tank, and gas flowed in. He took out his phone, looked at his contacts, and dialed his mom again. First time, she did not answer the phone. He did not leave a voice message. This time if she did not answer, he intended to leave a message. He did not know if she was working a 12-hour shift or at home sleeping. She worked some odd hours at times. Everything was odd about everyone's schedule who lived in that big Utah home. It started to ring. He thought it was as if you were home, nobody else was around. Having the house to yourself was good. However, this arrangement we had was like roommates instead of family. It was on the fifth ring when he noticed he had the gas station to himself. He noticed a few cars, going towards Tacoma the way he was going to be going after this pit stop, would fly by. Not many people on the road as it was a dreary sort of day with the fog lifting. He finally heard his mother's voice message. It was so bland that is sounded like terrorists or kidnappers were forcing her to read that simple message.

"Hi, this is Darlene. Leave a message."

"Mom, this is Jack, your son. I wanted to let you know I'm heading out of town for a while. I have something important to do."

He paused and took the nozzle out of the gas tank. He put the nozzle back in the square pump as the screen asked if he would like a receipt. He quickly hit no. Then he continued.

"Mom, no worries. It's a baseball try out for a minor league ball club," and he paused again. "It's out of state, so I'll call you when I get there."

He said a quick 'I love you' and hung up.

He was about to put his phone back in his pocket when it started ringing. He did not look at the number and just said hello as he thought it was probably his mother.

"Hello."

"Hey Jack, this is your good friend, Big Red Rusty Mulligan."

Jack thought to himself, 'I've only talked to you a few times and we are friends.'

"Hello, Mr. Mulligan, sir."

"Call me Rusty."

"OK, Rusty."

It sounded odd to him as he never can get used to calling elders he doesn't quite know, by their first name. It was just that he was brought up very old school and used Mr. or Mrs., or Sir or Ma'am.

Rusty Mulligan asked Jack how far away he was from the stadium. Asked him how the drive had been. Then told him the team was putting him up in a hotel tonight. He said his try out had been moved to tomorrow instead of this afternoon. Rusty told him to meet him in the restaurant/bar at the Howard Johnson Hotel, and he'd give Jack all the details about the try out and what to expect. It sounded OK to Jack as they said their goodbyes, and Jack placed his phone back in his pocket. He went into the gas station and used the bathroom. He ended up buying a few bottles of water because he did not like using someone's bathroom without purchasing something. He did not need the water, but he would drink it at some point. He then walked back out to his car and drove the rest of the way to Tacoma.

Chapter Thirty-Two

DANVILLE, ILLINOIS

It's been a whole week and the vision of one of his friends remained in Blade Runner's mind. The man who had ridden a bike for the Venomous Vipers for decades, whom they called Hot Sauce. Both Hot Sauce and Blade Runner were friends for years as they once rode in the same charter. Both went their separate ways. Both found themselves in the same prison. Hot Sauce was from another charter in another state. Blade Runner was in prison for killing the Sheriff, the man that had done things with his old lady in bed. To tape these things. Things she did in bed that he did not know she could do. Plus, they convicted Blade Runner for the murder of the FBI agent, Terry Long, who died on Venomous Viper property.

Hot Sauce came in two years after Blade Runner shot the Sheriff. Hot Sauce was down at Southern Illinois University visiting his daughter. He got the tour around campus and spent the whole day with her. Hot Sauce was so proud of her as her grades were high and she wanted to be a doctor. Everything went well and Hot Sauce rode up with another friend from the Venomous Vipers. They went to the bar that night. The other member was in the bathroom as Hot Sauce sat at the bar drinking his tenth beer with a whisky chaser. Both members of the Venomous Vipers had their jackets on to advertise to the whole world what kind of people they actually were. But this particular day and into the night, it was a celebration seeing his daughter of whom he was so proud. Neither member of the Venomous Vipers was chasing after any tail. They were not causing problems in the neighborhood. It was two chums sitting at the bar having a good time drinking beer. People in the bar, Stu's Tap and Grill, judged these guys like judging a book by its cover. After a few drinks, everyone was liking both of them as they actually bought everyone sitting at the bar a few drinks. Stu's Tap was a decent-sized bar that had a few tables occupied by other patrons. The bar extended to a bigger room of billiards tables. None of those patrons knew what was going on. They were all getting along around the bar like they had been friends forever.

A football player who was playing pool most of the night probably had drunk a truck's worth of beer. He was a big lineman who the team called Ox. Ox was not liking them. This was a kick to the nuts to him. Seeing this element in his watering hole. As soon as the one guy went to the bathroom, Ox, with no reason, walked up the bar. He took one of the pool sticks and hit Hot Sauce right in the back of the head. It broke the stick. Hot Sauce took the hit as he sat on the bar stool and did not move or flinch. He took another sip out of his mug of beer and chased that down with a shot of whisky. Seems like everything stopped right then and there. Not a sound, just turned heads. Perhaps the music even stopped. Ox holding half of the pool stick looked on in shock when the guy did not fall to the ground. The other member of the Venomous Viper was taking a shit, so he was going to be awhile. They call the man Hot Sauce because in an instant, like a drip of sauce hitting your tongue, it starts to burn. You may start to sweat. Your first instinct might be to dose it with water. I guess you could say Hot Sauce dosed the burn, the gash on his head, with a shot and sip of beer. He unleashed an anger that turned the big Ox white like Casper the Friendly Ghost. Hot Sauce was able to throw the big man through the window of Stu's Tap. After the body and all the glass landed at the same time on the sidewalk, Hot Sauce finished the man by picking up pieces of broken glass and slicing that man's throat. Blood gushed on the sidewalk like a geyser. You could still go by there today and see the stain Ox left. Hot Sauce was picked up right away. They say he went to the bar and enjoyed one more beer and one more shot while everyone filed out of Stu's like there was a fire.

It was a week ago that Hot Sauce was on work detail and jumped by multiple skin heads because something was quite wrong with the coke they got. It was a bad batch. Ended up killing one of the bald Nazis. Those skin heads cornered Hot Sauce, who did not have a chance to defend himself, and grabbed him immediately slicing his throat. You could say what comes around goes around. But besides that, all the skin heads took turns and stabbed him over 200 times. It made a bloody mess out of his body as they eventually carried him out of the laundry room in a body bag.

It's been a week and finally Blade Runner would have his revenge. He walked into a supply room as they had one of the leaders of the skin heads tied up and gagged in this room. He was naked as a jay bird. The skinheads, from the beginning, were the group that the Venomous Vipers could not get along with. The Venomous Vipers were proud to get along with all the gang bangers. They were proud to get along with other biker gangs, especially in prison. Venomous Vipers were smart not to step on other groups' territories. They found strategic spots for their hired dealers to sell their coke on corners that were not occupied by other groups that would want to spill blood. Sure, blood spilled. Drugs and money lead to violence. But paying someone off to go away. Violence came into play if another group was causing problems. Their top guys would be wiped out one by one until they thought about leaving that area. But the skinheads for years have been up the Venomous Vipers' asses like a nasty rash or evil dingle berry tied on to their hairy bum.

The skinhead's hands were tied around a pole in the supply room. His hateful eyes glaring at the entrance of Blade Runner. They closed the steel door with the small window as a black guy stood at the door on look out. That was not necessary as the guards on duty that day, the right men to be paid off, were elsewhere. Blade Runner was dressed in all orange. His sleeves rolled up exposing his dragon tats which looked like they could come alive at any point and burn the porcelain Nazi skinhead. His muscular body filled with hate. Swastikas and German crosses mostly. Some skulls and crossbones in black and gray ink covered his whiteboard of a body. A Mexican gang banger dressed in orange also handed Blade Runner a knife with shark teeth on the blade itself. The skinhead had a rag in his mouth and shook his head as the eyes looked on that shiny blade in full mode panic. The other guy, another biker from another group & another charter, also was dressed in Orange as that was the color of the day. He just punched the skinhead right in the kidney with his beefy mitt.

He looked like a boxer as he said, "SHUTUP SKIN JOB."

The skinhead grimaced in pain. Blade Runner cleaned the knife off which had nothing on the blade. He wiped it on his dragon tats like the fire from the tat would heat up the blade in some crazy way. He looked at him the same way he looked at the Sheriff before he blew his head off.

"You know why you're here?"

Some distorted mumbling behind the rag.

"You are going to pay for what your group did."

He got up in his face the way a manager would do to an umpire.

Then he took the blade and started carving up the skinhead Nazi like a Turkey on Thanksgiving. "Anybody for white meat?"

Blade Runner held up a big piece of skin with the German cross on it.

It was part of the skinhead's shoulder. The Skinhead grimaced and angry growls came out from under the rag. Blood ran down his left shoulder dripping on the floor. Then the boxer/biker gave the skinhead another punch, this time in the other kidney. They were in a supply room filled with boxes on the shelves of toilet paper, paper towels, and pretty much all paper products. The black guy watching the door looked at the tattooed skin that had just fallen to the floor through the window. He thanked God that was not him. Blade Runner continued as he worked on the other shoulder and scraped off another tat, this time of a skull. That skin dropped to the floor. Blade Runner continued and took off tats on the man's leg. He then worked the chest carving him up with precise cuts taking the skin off in thin layers making this skinhead pass out in-between cuts. Then to awaken in anger, shaking his head as he looked at what once was albino skin turning into a pinkish hued skin, with blood seeping out of his body.

Last, but not least, the skinhead still alive and able to see the grand finale, he cut his dick off. His shaft and his balls fell to the ground like a piece from a Mr. Potato Head toy. Blade Runner gave the knife to the Mexican whose job was to get rid of it. The other bike gave the skinhead one more punch for the road. They all walked out as the black man opened the door and they turned off the light in the room. They left the skinhead bleeding like an animal inside a slaughterhouse. The skinhead passed out. Then he bled out and eventually died. A week later, all the evidence pointed to Blade Runner, but he did not care because he was never getting out. What… another life sentence after a life sentence. What are they going to do with him? No death penalty in this state, so oh well, their loss is his gain.

Chapter Thirty-Three

VEGAS

It was a Las Vegas police station that was investigating the car bombing which took place at the diner. The station was on the outskirts of the main drag or strip, as some people referred to the main action of gambling and the shows taking place under the lights. Like any major city, they had multiple police stations designed to protect a section of the town of Las Vegas. Off the main strip, not much really took place. It was the Mayberry section of town. The Police station was in an old three-story brick building that once upon a time housed a hardware lumber store like a Menards or Home Depot. It was more like a True Value or Ace, but a tad bigger and still smaller than a Home Depot. The side of the building paint was peeling as you could still see the logo of some handy man with a toolbox carrying some lumber. They did not have enough money to give the building a makeover. Much of the budget was spent on rat traps they had to deal with when they moved in. Not all of the building was even being used. The detective squad was on the main floor when you walked in and saw the receptionist. The Walmart greeter job, which they would joke about between officers.

The detective squad room was out in the open. Desks shuffled all over the place in no special pattern. They had metal desks each with a computer monitor, phone, and lots of paperwork stacked up in the boxes marked "IN" and "OUT." On the brick walls, they had white boards and bulletin boards surrounding the desks. They had high ceilings with the open look of a warehouse which exposed metal ducts and piping used for lighting and electrical needs. It was not a Police station, but more like a warehouse for storage. They had jail cells on the bottom level, the basement of the warehouse, into which they put good money constructing cinder block walls and bars so nobody could bust out and escape into the night.

The squad room was half-filled with people at their desks. The atmosphere was one of quiet conversation that was louder due to the openness and clitter clatter of the keyboards from people looking up information on a particular case. Detective Kenneth Davenport was talking on the phone with a cup of coffee, half-drunk, and a pastry, half-eaten. He was listening on the phone more than speaking, as he saw one of the computer geeks approaching his desk. He wanted some information off a burnt up charred phone. He was still putting the pieces together with the VIN number of the car that was scorched from the explosion.

Detective Davenport hung up the phone as Samuel, the computer geek from India with the British accent, spoke. "Good news, Detective. I was able to get something which hopefully you can use."

Detective Davenport is a middle-aged black guy who looked at the brown man in his early 20's. "What you got for me, Sammy?"

Samuel pulled up one of those cushioned office chairs with the wheels on them and sat down placing a white index card on the desk. He looked at Detective Davenport with a thick mustache like a mop, bristles perfectly groomed. He sipped his coffee and looked down at the card with two numbers on it. The dress code was casual as Samuel was wearing khaki dress shorts exposing his hairy legs with a pair of bamboo moccasins. He wore a colored polo shirt, navy blue. He pointed at the numbers on the index card as the Detective noticed the hairs coming out of his knuckles.

"Only thing I could muster up was these two phone contacts, but I could not get the names of the people. The phone was badly damaged."

The Detective looked at the index card, and then at the brown man's face who was cleanly shaven and had a square type of head on a long neck. His nose was square, his eyes were like a horse's eyes, and he had horse gums with big teeth. He had dark black hair jelled perfectly in the middle, like a boy scout.

"Sammy, my man, this will work fine."

The detective put his hand up as they high fived each other. The detective's hand was way bigger than the computer techs.

"Thank you, Detective," as Samuel got to his feet and continued. "Anything else you need help on?"

The Detective stood up wearing a navy blue polo shirt with the Las Vegas logo on the right peck of the shirt. He had on Khaki pants with a black belt that holstered his gun and badge in front, cuffs in the back. He towered over Sammy as he looked down.

"Tell me one more thing, Sammy. I was just speaking to Gary. He said they have a case over at the Motel with a beheading and another victim dead lying on the bed. Did you know anything about that case?"

Detective Davenport was in great shape; tall and the shirt was tight on him showing off his well sculptured body. His face was young as he took care of himself with a healthy diet and exercise. He had a medium sized nose with dark eyes and was clean shaven. Had the 5 o'clock shadow going on his head as he liked to shave that to get the Michael Jordan look, his favorite player of all-time.

"I've only heard about that one. Lopez is helping on that one. I'll probably get involved as soon as they finish gathering up all the facts and bagging all the evidence. I'll let you know what we get."

"Alright Sammy. Sounds good, my man. Let me know if it's just some kind of fluke that these two incidents are the same," as the Detective tapped him on the back and sat back down in his chair.

He took another swig of coffee to finish the mug. Then stuffed the rest of the pastry in his mouth as he typed in the VIN number of the car. Presto, Justin Young's picture came up on the scene.

"I'll be damned. I think we might have the victim."

He took the phone and dialed the first contact.

It went straight to a voice message of a middle-aged lady. Then that was followed by a robot voice saying her mailbox was filled. Then he dialed the other contact Samuel provided from the phone. He tapped the number, and it started to ring.

On the third ring some guy said, "Hello."

Detective Davenport said, "To whom am I speaking to?"

"My Name is Detective Henderson of the Utah Police. Who am I speaking to?"

The pelican bar was surrounded by flashing lights.

'This case just got really interesting,' Detective Davenport thought.

Chapter Thirty-Four

CHERRY HEIGHTS, UTAH

It has been a while for the middle-aged woman, Darlene Young. She's on top while her hair whips into the air, sweat beads off her forehead while she thrusts rhythmically over and over as she finds the man very deep inside her. The feeling she has not felt in years. It had to have gone back to when she went by Valerie Malone. The man with olive skin lies on his back holding her thighs with his hands guiding her up and down. The man had some dirt under his fingernails from his daily duties until this occurred suddenly. He admires her handful breasts, white and creamy looking, the nipples now red as he suckled on them just moments ago. He brings her down all the way to get more manhood deeper into her body and then thrusts into her faster as he guides her up and down as she has already come once. Liquid exploded out of her like a sprinkler, which had never before happened. Her loud moans echoed throughout the house as her hair whipped around some more. Her eyes closed and she could feel the ceiling fan whipping from above sending a cool breeze onto her perspiring back. Her whole body was letting out stuff, so logjammed since the last time she had any satisfaction.

Outside the Young household, a dark green Ford F-150 truck, with some rust patches on the body, was parked between the neighbors and the Young residence. On the door of the truck were some magnetic signs with a logo of a lawn mower that said Juan's Landscaping in black bold lettering. The bed of the truck was filled with grass clippings. The truck was connected to an enclosed black box trailer. The trailer was filled with lawn equipment as the back door was down, creating a ramp to get mowers up and down. It was a sunny day, and no mower sounds were heard. The neighbor across the street attended to her mail from the box along the street. She did not notice anything out of the ordinary. She took her handful of junk mail and walked back to her home. She did not see a dark sedan parked a few houses away, under one of the many weeping willow trees along the streets. Even one of the other neighbors pulling out of the driveway did not notice the sedan or the unattended lawn mower at the back gate. Motor off and gate open, with only one path of grass that was cut before suddenly, everything came to a halt. The man was too busy talking on his cellphone as he was late to a meeting at work as he left the newly developed suburb.

This was not Juan's first ever rodeo. He has enjoyed a few nooners in his lawn cutting days over the years. The man was dark, handsome, and his landscaping business kept the young Mexican Stallion in shape in his middle 20's. He was a simple man that just liked his tacos, a few cold cervezas, and a soccer match. He sent money back home to his family. He was not married or tied down by anyone. He had a few senoritas here in the states and back at home in Mexico. In the winters he would be with those ones, and in spring and summer he knew a few in Utah. Something about white women he loved. They had a certain taste that he loved. Especially the ones who were married. They just wanted him, and it was a 'wham bam thank you mam' type of relationship. The husband's away at work, so the mice will play; he always thought of that saying. He knew what a glass of lemonade or an offer for some iced tea was all about. About an hour ago, he was offered a glass of sweet tea, Darlene called it, and told him to come on in. This has been going on for weeks. The innocent waves. The smile after the wave. He had the feeling he was being watched as in 'I'm hot for your body' watching. Right when he walked in, she was all over him like a cougar that swallowed a bottle of blue pills. Even though he knew it was the opposite way. Clothes flew off right when he walked through those glass patio doors. Kissing was heated from the get-go. He had his pants off and his buttoned shirt was ripped open, exposing his six-pack of olive skin and rippling muscle. Her shorts were immediately thrown to the ground, and he was in her and on top of her on the kitchen table. Then it escalated to the bathroom and into the shower, as they both were naked and stuck together like glue as water rinsed them off. She wrapped her arms around his shoulders, and he pinned her up against the tile of the shower, inserting it in her. He banged her against the wall as the shower washed them off in-between thrusts. The moaning and yelping echoed through the house. The heated passion between them both turned into animal-style lust.

The back door remained open. The Albanian man entered from the back door all dressed in black. He looked at the floor of the kitchen to see clothes on the floor with a bowl of fruit scattered all over the marble cream-colored floor. He noticed the gray button-down short-sleeve shirt and the name Juan on the patch over the pocket.

He chuckled, "This is going to be too easy."

It was like Hansel and Gretel following the crumbs as he went right to the stairs and found a black bra on the first step. He heard a vibration from a phone that was on the table in the foyer by the front door. The Albanian, wearing black gloves, looked at the number and noticed the Vegas area code. He shut the phone off sliding it in his back pocket as he might need it. He knew his job was not done after her, the target. He could hear the moans coming from upstairs. He made his way up the carpet steps that had some kind of floral pattern to them. He noticed it was thick carpet. He loved these newly built houses because most of the time, the stairs did not creak when you walked up them. He slowly made his way up the stairs. He thought this would not be the first time he has killed someone with their pants down. He noticed a family portrait on the wall halfway up, and noticed the dad and the sister, two targets eliminated already. He patted the picture, kissed his gloved hand, and tapped the frame as he walked up with his gun that had a silencer on the end of it. He found his way to the top of the stairs and he could go either right or left. He followed the noise and went left. He saw the bathroom straight ahead, as he followed the hallway to a set of doors.

Juan was really liking the energy she brought to the table. He thought like a tiger ravenous for flesh. The thought of two people getting out of prison was the way this was playing out. Because she wanted more and more, as she wet the sheets with her bodily fluids that continued to erupt. He now was behind her thrusting in and out like a jackhammer doggie-style. His hips were absolutely pounding her, as she was panting and breathing heavily.

"Oh my God, don't stop," she yelled.

Sweat was flying from both of their bodies as the covers on the bed had been completely torn off the queen mattress. He was thinking 'this woman has worn me out today in a good way.' He might not be able to finish off all his jobs today. He knew he would eat well because his tummy was rumbling. Ten to twelve tacos might be enough to recharge his batteries. He continued thrusting as she moaned with pleasure, and he felt it coming any second. That's when the door opened. A pow followed by another pow as the first bullet hit Juan right in the back of his head. He fell forward still in her, as he came right before his brain flew out his forehead from the bullet. Darlene felt the weight of Juan on top of her as her knees gave out. She did not know what happened, but she saw a figure of a body walking in from the doorway. Only for a second did she look, and in that instant the bullet hit right between her eyes. Her body collapsed with Juan still in her.

Chapter Thirty-Five

CRACK....

"Rusty, where did you find this guy?"

They watched another ball get crushed as it orbited over the deepest part of center field above the row of spruce trees.

"How many is that now that have gone over the fence?"

The fat GM asked. He hadn't even gotten a response from his Chief Scout.

"Chet, that is the tenth mammoth shot. But who is counting?"

He had his eating pants on as his gut rested over the seats in front of him. They watched Jack Young swing the bat.

Chet Duncan, GM and half owner of the Tacoma Twisters, had fat pasty white reddish cheeks. He was chomping down on an unlit cigar, half smoked. He had three chins as the sweat on his nose was making his glasses slide down his nose. It was a cool day, but any excitement made Chet a sticky sweaty person. He looked at Big Red while wiping the sweat off his forehead and adjusted his wool Irish lid on top of his head. He had a few strands of light brownish hair coming out of the hat. Most of his brown hair had been taken over by gray fog, which he tried hiding tucking the rest under the lid.

"Rusty, you have found a gem. I have to sign this kid! How come no one else has? What is wrong with him? There has to be something wrong with talent like this, hoss." He adjusted his glasses and slid them back up his nose. "Where did he come from, or did you answer that already? Speak to me, friend."

CRACK...

This time Jack Young crushed a breaking ball, lifted it practically off the ground and golfed it down the right field line. Some of the Tacoma Twisters players were in the outfield shagging balls, looking on these balls crushed like they were watching fireworks poof on the Fourth of July.

"He says he never played ball on a high school or college team."

Rusty seemed to always be wearing something that said Tacoma Twisters on it. He had a huge tarp-sized wind breaker that had the team logo on it. Chet was dressed in a very loud style of suit. It was a blue and white plaid jacket and pants.

"I find that hard to believe, but who gives a shit where you get the cow from as long as the milk comes out and is cheap. I don't care anyway. I've seen enough to work out a deal and get this kid in the lineup starting tomorrow with the Dragons."

"He has not even done any fielding drills."

Both of them sat behind the dugout on the left field line in the stands with a seat in between them as their big butts were really jammed in those typical ballpark seats.

"Rusty, we go way back, hoss. I know you would not bring me half of a player." He let out a hearty chuckle.

"His fielding is actually amazing at first base. He has a glove that sucks up anything and most importantly, you know Chet I like the key details. He can turn the double play with the best of them."

"Well, there you go, hoss. SOLD to the man in the checkered suit," as he chomped on his cigar. "Now go on and tell the boy to unpack his things. He is staying for a while."

A big smile went across Rusty's face as he was excited for the kid. He loved finding players for the Tacoma Twisters. He got money for doing it. He loved his job finding players, traveling to all sorts of states, and watching the game he loved. He had a good feeling about this kid. A feeling this kid can go to the Bigs. Rusty found one guy years ago who had a cup of coffee for the Angels, but he did not last after a few games and never found his way back. Jack was different... a totally different feel.

"Will do, Chet, will do."

"OK, let me get my big fat ass up and see if Marcie can get me a contract printed up for him to sign."

Chet eased out of the chair, and his thighs brushed against the aisle walking out. Rusty watched from his seat as Jack got one right off the sweet part of the bat, a screamer line drive that shot through the gap and hit off the chicken wing restaurant sign on the outfield fence with a clank.

Chapter Thirty-Six

MISSOURI

Anaconda was away from the club for the weekend. He was out of town right over the border of Illinois, to a small town in Missouri. Bakersville, Missouri was where the big man grew up. His parents still lived in the small community. His plans were to shack up at the Gung Ho Lodge, which was on the edge of town. His parents had moved into trailer park housing and sold the bungalow where the big fella grew up. Besides seeing his parents, he had big plans with his woman from Spruce Wood. She was known to him only as Raven. Since he went and introduced himself as Anaconda, her thoughts were if he were a snake, why couldn't she be a bird. Raven, who is known as Cassidy in her community of Spruce Wood, Illinois, texted him that she would be there.

Her text said, "Be prepared for me to absolutely fuck you so hard you'll have no further brain activity to remember it."

He has not remembered even one time he and she did it. He saw signs of it the next day, but he could not recall any highlights. It's been about a half dozen times. Each time they would be out painting the town red. Then come back to the Motel, and he remembers starting things with her. Kissing. He remembers her breasts as she teased him with them. Then his mind draws a total blank. Did he just see her boobs in a dream? Then his rational thinking would kick in. No way would that explain the next day. His thought process was not sharp like it used to be. He was a demolition expert. He was in the Army. It was a very long time ago. He knew about all sorts of explosive devices. He was part of the bomb squad to disable them. He was also great at setting explosives in the key places to make things blow up the right way. A few times a tad too close to the explosive, that sent a ringing through his ears after it went off. Lots of headaches. Lots of meds. Lots of drugs. Lots of alcohol to numb the pain.

He figured that was why he could not remember anything he'd done with Raven after nights of partying. This weekend was about big time fucking without any drugs or medicine, especially alcohol. He will remember so he can have an image on another night when he's in bed by himself to recall and perhaps relive. He was very excited when she said yes to his invite. Said she'd happily stay the whole weekend and really get to know each other. Those words he saw texted on the screen made him hard. Made him excited to have maybe finally something with this girl, perhaps exchange real names. Maybe she wanted to meet his parents. She even agreed to rent the room, so all's he needed to do was drive there. She would wait and be ready to attack him when he walked through the door.

The Gung Ho Motel was originally owned by a war veteran. He died and his family sold it to some Arabian guy who uses it as a tax write-off. The place is a hole in the wall dump. Nothing has changed as it still has the old 1970's décor. The only cool thing and probably the only thing you would keep, was the sign outside while you bulldozed the building. It had an Army jeep high in the sky with a grunt driving dressed in fatigues, with the sign in green light bulbs that lit up the words, 'Gung Ho Motel.' They used to have old guns on display in the lobby. Now they have pictures of animals. The building itself is a one level concrete L-shaped building with peeling green paint. The doors were in camouflage greens. Also peeling. Used to have little infantry metal army guy knockers above the peep holes in their glory days. The office was in front of the short L-shaped part. The driveway followed along the building as you parked your cars right in front of the door of your room.

Anaconda's motorcycle roared down the driveway. He could feel the pavement had lots of cracks and holes that vibrated his hog. He slowed it down a tad and guided the big hog to a stop. Then he backed it up to room 16. This motel had no windows looking out to the parking lot. It was like solitary confinement, a room with only a king-sized bed, a TV on top of a dresser, and a small closet. Then a small bathroom attached. The text not too long ago said she was there, and that the door was open. He was excited as he took off his helmet that had the cool spike sticking out of the top. It also had a killer snake painting wrapped around the helmet itself. He strutted to the door with his big arms extended from the broad shoulders of a body builder. He could still smell the scent of his aftershave, Cherry Dragon. He sensed he might have put on too much.

He opened the door, and the light was on. He looked at the bed and saw millions of flower petals all over the mattress. The smell of mold mixed with flower petal and the aftershave lotion made him want to sneeze as he closed the door. The television had an X-rated movie on. He saw two girls on one guy action that made him officially ready for the night to get started.

"Raven, where are you at, cinnamon bun?"

He called her that because it was his favorite pastry. He took his Venomous Viper sleeveless leather coat off and placed it on the floor. His magnum six shooter cannon now was exposed as he heard the shower in the bathroom on. No reply, but that is ok because shower sex is great. He walked towards the door and took off his plain black tee shirt that revealed his body tattoo of a snake, an anaconda to be exact, wrapped around him. He threw the shirt on the bed. He thought he heard sirens in the distance. He walked to the bathroom door displaying his other tattoos of barbed wire and skulls like almost all bikers have. He even had a few military tats with the American flag. He also had some burnt flesh, most likely from working with explosives and getting burned a few times over the years. He opened the bathroom door. The light was on as steam was felt on his face. He could hear the shower running. He quickly took off his boots and threw his pants and skivvies back into the room with the bed, closing the door.

"HEY, BABY CAKES."

Outside the Gung Ho in the Wags restaurant parking lot next door, Raven sat in her car. Raven, who really was Cassidy, had her jet-black hair in a ponytail. She was dressed like a cat burglar, all in black. She sat in the front seat of her Chevy Malibu. Her car was facing the Motel. She just watched Anaconda park his bike. Then watched him enter the Motel room. She had her phone in her lap. She was waiting on two things. First, an angry text back from Anaconda wondering where she was. She thought she might get a concerned text wondering where she was. Wondering if she was ok. It was the phone call she had placed. She heard them. Then she saw the squad cars screeching down the Gung Ho Motel driveway with their lights flashing. They held off on the sound because it was the call that made the Police come very quickly. It was the call that had them running out of their car and charging for room 16. It was the call that had them with their guns in their hands ready to pull the trigger with any slight movement they did not like.

They charged through the camouflage door, breaking the old door off its hinges. Cassidy never got that text from Anaconda, as she glanced down at her cell phone. Then she heard gun shots. From her view of the closed Wags, she could see flashes of light in the room. If Anaconda was not killed, he was going to be up the creek without a paddle when they find a brick of cocaine. She left some items to make things worse just in case the brick was not enough in their world. It would seem like he was looking to sell, which would get him some major hard time. With his record, it might lock him up for good. If he were killed, that would be the cherry on the sundae. He served his purpose in her multiple step plan she had in place. She pressed the button on her window, and the glass rolled down. She then with both hands reached out the window and snapped the phone in half, before rolling the window back up. Put the car in reverse and backed out of the spot. Then she put the car in drive and was heading off back to Spruce Wood after a job well done. She was glad that was done. She was eager to get to the next stage in her grand plan. She put the radio on, and they were playing "Girls Just Want to Have Fun." She sang the lyrics as she was having some fun for once.

Chapter Thirty-Seven

"Jack, we are glad to have you in our little home," said the heavy-set lady in her late 50's.

"Thank you, ma'am, and thank you for having me in your lovely home."

Jack Young followed her down the stairs. He could see her gray hair was receding on the back of her head, looking like a patch of missing grass.

"Bernice, you call me Bernice and call Mr. Garvey, Henry. Even though you have to speak up so he can hear you."

She flipped on a switch that lit up a really nice, finished basement. It had a couch and a few chairs in front of a good-sized television.

Henry, Jack met briefly when he walked through the front door. He was quickly introduced by Bernice and shown to his living quarters. That's what she called it as he went through the main level of the brick Georgian, and down a staircase to a nice basement where everything looked new.

"Your room is right through here."

She opened a door that led into a hallway from the TV part of the basement. She flipped on the switch and the room was small, but had a brand-new bed, dresser, nightstand, and a small closet. Jack nodded his head, to show it was OK.

"The bathroom which has a shower," she pointed at a door across from his room, "is right there with some fresh towels."

He walked in the room and put his duffel bag down alongside the bed.

"This is nice."

"Why don't you get yourself settled and then come up and have dinner with us. I'm making my famous American stew loaded with potatoes and dumplings to give you that extra energy. You've got to smack one out of the park tomorrow against that North Dakota squad, who we do not like."

"Sounds good, I just need to call my family really quick, get freshened up, and I'll head up."

"Ok Sweetie, now say it… Berrrrnice."

Bernice reminded him of one of his aunts he had back in Spruce Wood. He'd get his cheeks squeezed and be called sweetie a half dozen times, over a few hours span.

"Yes, Bernice."

She chuckled as she waddled off, "That's my sweetie pie. See you in a few minutes."

Everything was going relatively quickly for him today, he thought as he sat on the bed. After the tryout, he signed the deal with the team. He was told he and the team would be heading on the road tomorrow to North Dakota. The contract he signed meant he was not going to be paid a whole lot. Driving the forklift at the warehouse pays way more. He would get free room and board. That's where the Garvey family come into play. Many of these Independent leagues, the teams have fans that volunteer their house for the players. The fans would get some deal with season tickets and other small perks. Mostly being involved in the team was their thrill by helping to take in a player or two each year during the season. It was a day off for Tacoma during the tryout. He met a few of the players that were there getting in some extra practice. He met the owner and the manager. He'd meet the rest of the staff and players tomorrow when they headed out of town for a three-game series.

He felt excited about the opportunity to start playing professionally, even though this is how it happened. He pictured going away to college playing for years and then getting drafted. He obviously has taken a different path. First thing he did was take out the picture of him and Cassidy at the carnival, the same one that was behind the visor. He placed it on the nightstand in the room as he sat there wanting to call her to tell her the great news about his dream coming together. After a moment or two of thinking just about her, he dialed up his mom again. This was the third time he tried her and this time it just went straight to voice message. He thought about calling Shawna, but she was always too busy every time he tried calling her. He'd leave a message or even shoot a text and not hear back from her until a few weeks had gone by. She had some excuse and apologized. He tried his younger sister. Pulled up her contact and hit send. He heard her pick up on the second ring.

"Hello, Big Brother. How are you?"

"I'm fine, Little Sister. How are you?"

They tried to always talk to each other like this, without actually using their first names.

They have had moments when this conversation took place in Utah. Nothing has remained the same since they moved west from Spruce Wood.

"Doing well at basketball practice, and about to take the court."

He could hear a whistle in the background, and the coach yelling, "Let's go."

"Sorry, I'll be brief. Have you talked to mom?"

"She had a double shift, I believe."

She was guessing on that as she had stayed over at her best friend's house, had gone home once, and she was not there.

"OK, I won't hold you. I'll try her later then."

He could hear the coach in the background scream something like, "Today, gals."

"Sorry, big brother. Have to go, I'll call you a bit later."

She then ended the connection. He did not even get a chance to say goodbye. He did not even get to tell her the good news he had. He looked at the picture and whispered.

"Oh God, I miss you so much."

He felt like he was going to tear up. He got to his feet, went to the bathroom to throw some water on his face, and looked in the mirror. He gave his reflection a half-assed smile. He was excited. Then thought he should call his dad. As he toweled his face off with a fluffy green towel, he thought 'he'd be looking to get some kind of loan from me to gamble it away.' Shook his head and thought this was not how he pictured any of his dream coming together. He shut off the light and headed up to the main floor to eat some of this American stew from Auntie Bernice. He smiled again, shaking his head.

Chapter Thirty-Eight

Outside Thomas Jefferson High School, the dark sedan circled the block once again. The Albanian nightmare for the Malone family, known now as the Young family, has just found his next target. Thomas Jefferson High School was not that big of a school. It looked like the size of a grammar school rather than a high school. The whole school campus was about two blocks long. It was summer and the school was pretty much emptied. They had some janitors doing their off-season work to get the school prepped for the fall. Give the school a deep clean. Tackle the list of stuff that needed to be fixed by the time the fall arrived. Only thing going besides the work of two custodians was the Women's Basketball team practicing in the gymnasium. The guy in the dark sedan thought he was going to have to take down his next target outside. Other ideas included following his subject to her next location. Then another idea emerged as he saw the janitors coming out a service door to throw away garbage in the dumpster. He noticed this door was propped open because they probably had multiple trips back and forth to the dumpster. That door would be his ticket inside, he felt as he found a nice spot to park. It was a nice spot for a clean getaway as when he went around the first time, he noticed it. The car remained idle as he prepared himself for the assault on Thomas Jefferson High School.

Inside, the girls' basketball team was starting with their warm ups. Gretchen Long turned off her phone after answering it and talking with her brother. She put it in her gym bag that was along the court, off to the side. The girls did have a locker room off to the side of the gym. They were in the middle of remodeling it. After about ten minutes of stretching exercises, the head coach blew into their whistle and told the team to line up for lay ups. The girls immediately split up into groups. One group on each side. One side had the ball while the other side got the rebound after the layup. Then she passed the ball back to the line that originally had the ball. The rebounder would then line up in the shooter line. While the shooter went across to the line that was rebounding. They did this to get everyone warmed up.

The Albanian hitman used to go by Bardhana Hoxha. He has changed his identity over 100 times since he dabbled in his God complex and ending people's lives. He was dressed in black as he walked quickly over to the dumpster in back of the school. He hid behind it, waiting for the janitor to come back out. He did not know how many people were in the school, and he hoped he could get his target for sure. Sometimes in his head, he did not mind collateral damage along the way. He knew they were innocent bystanders and had nothing to do with why he was hired in the first place. The main thing was the target and the escape. If he could take out a few others for kicks, it was a good day at the office. As he crouched down by the dumpster waiting patiently, he could see the door was being propped open by a plain old brick. As he dug deep into a black duffel bag, he pulled out his black ski mask and put it on his bald head without pulling it all the way down. He put black gloves on and rolled down his sleeves. It was a nice day out. Too hot for long sleeves and long pants. but this did not bother him.

He was pulling out his Glock and making sure he had a full clip of bullets inside. He clicked it back in. Tightened up his silencer. Then he flashed back to that notebook he had hidden in the shoe box, way back when his father busted him looking at it. That was the last time he saw his old man alive. He was walked out of the house as the Police told him to close his eyes. He saw his father dead after being shot multiple times, that day. Then he noticed his father took many officers with him at his childhood residence, which at the time had witnessed multiple homicides.

He then heard a man whistling and the footsteps coming closer to the propped open service door. He quickly pulled his mask down. Then the door swung open as he saw the janitor's steel toe boots and his dirty pair of jeans crouching low behind the dumpster. He looked up and saw he was carrying a few boxes that were covering his eyesight. The janitor lifted the boxes over the dumpster as he was facing the side just about touching. As he let go of the boxes, they made a noise as it dropped a foot landing on something. Right at that moment, the Albanian popped up and with a slide, kicked off the janitor's leg, knocking him off balance. The janitor, in his early 30's, was really an actor. During the day he worked for the school, but at night his dream was on the stage. Freaked out at the moment his feet were touched thinking it was some kind of animal. He tried to grab onto the edge of the dumpster. Instead, his head actually rammed into the ledge of the dumpster causing him to black out as he hit his head again on the pavement. The slide klick move the Albanian pulled on this guy, showed the special agility this guy had. As he was able to pop up right after the kick knocked this janitor out. Then the Albanian hit man, without even thinking, put the blade of his knife right through the guy's neck. He pulled the knife out like a magician making a rabbit appear; it was that fast. It was like cutting butter as it went in. He pulled it out as blood dripped a few drops on the sidewalk, and it was back in its holder on the side of his belt. He quickly picked up the janitor, tossed him in the dumpster, and threw in some cardboard to cover him up a little. Took a quick look around and saw nobody in the area. The location was perfect in a secluded spot, especially with the dumpsters blocking the door. He then opened the door, peeked in to see nobody, and made his way into the school.

Thomas Jefferson High School was home of the Wild Cats. The sophomore women's basketball team was now practicing the three-person weave across the court. The lesbian head coach, who was definitely in that butch category, looked to be on the border of man or women. Her voice was border line between man and woman as well. She was wearing all gray with white socks and gym shoes. She had her whistle around the neck of her sweat suit. She was flat chested with short hair, almost like Moe from the Three Stooges in style. You could say she was a woman by looking at her sparkly fruit earrings on her earlobes. She had a 'Stache going above her lip that brought you to question what gender this person was. She was a very good coach as her record for the school over a decade speaks for itself. She blew into her whistle that sent as shrill shriek echoing throughout the school. The women were lined up in threes. One in the middle and two at the ends of the wooden court. The object was not to dribble the basketball down the full length of the court. Just crisp passes all the way down until they get to the end where one of the ends would go towards the basket with an easy layup.

These were just typical fundamentals that were mostly run in grammar school teams. However, the Coach of the Wild Cats was big on small details. She practiced the fundamentals of the game every week. Some practices without even shooting at the basket. Her teams made few mistakes and hardly turned over the ball. Their passes were crisp. They had multiple ball handlers which prevented teams with easy steals. Gretchen Young was in the middle as the whistle blew. She passed it to her best friend, Molly, who was running down the court. Molly caught the pass and she then passed it to the other girl on the opposite end. Then it came back to Gretchen, who then made a nice pass to Molly breaking towards the basket. She put it off the board and in, as they were very successful with the drill. Another three girls lined up and they did the same thing.

Upstairs in the equipment room of the gym, the Albanian hitman made his way there through the school. He eliminated the other janitor on the way with a head shot from his Glock that put a bullet right between his eyes. He was quickly pulled into the room they were remodeling and stashed behind dry wall. He made his way to the gym and saw the girls'

95

basketball team practicing. He gave a quick peak into the gym from the door window. He counted in his head all the people he could see. Which was the players, and he thought some ugly guy as the coach. He saw some stairs and he sneaked up them, not even making a sound.

Chapter Thirty-Nine

Cassidy drove back over the Illinois border. Her first plan of the day's work was setting up Anaconda. She would know shortly from her Police scanner if Anaconda was arrested or shot to death. Lot of loud chatter was going on over the scanner. She turned off the stereo in the car and listened carefully to what they were saying. She wanted to do one more thing before she went back to Spruce Wood. According to all the information she was able to get from Anaconda's phone, the Venomous Viper's new clubhouse was only miles away from the Missouri border. She had downloaded the route to her phone. She did not need the phone since she had it down in her memory like a branding iron. From her multiple conversations, Venomous Vipers had eyes and ears almost everywhere. She knew the location of the new hideout, but it was hidden, so no authorities would be able to pinpoint their location. It was like the Venomous Vipers created their own bat cave. She was traveling now off the main highway down a two lane road with woods on both sides of the street. She slowed down as the street had no lights, just the headlights from her car. She slowed down and rolled to a complete stop as her foot stayed on the brake and she did not put the car in park. She quickly pressed the button for her flashers to start blinking as she looked at the route she had downloaded on her phone.

"It has to be right around here. What the fuck? I see nothing."

It was true, just a thick tree line on both sides of the street was all she could see. Then she heard chatter on the Police scanner, that they had one Police Officer down. They needed paramedics ASAP for a few officers that were hit with a bullet and needed medical assistance. Then she heard the scene was under control and the suspect was dead.

As she looked at the route on her phone, she said to herself, "I never got to meet his parents. Shame on me."

A few minutes went by as some more Police chatter came through. Nothing that interested her as the Paramedics were now two minutes out. She had her seat belt still on, gave the forest on both sides a look, and pressed the button on her flashers while tapping the steering wheel in frustration. She slowly pulled away when she heard the roar of a few bikes pop on to the road out of nowhere. Three big hogs following each other in a single line coming out a narrow, what looked to be for walking, path of some kind. She drove with caution but did not slow down to look and stare. All three raced by her car as the headlights gleamed off her face, three separate times seconds apart. She looked at her mileage on the dashboard and only one click rolled next to mileage. She'd remember that and she would adjust that to the numbers she had from the beginning. Now she had figured out where their hideout was exactly. The hideout they wanted no one to find. She had the lucky coordinates which is the key to finding their club house in the middle of the woods. It will be another day and another time, as she was 2-2 today. Both operations had worked to perfection. She turned on some music and headed back to Spruce Wood.

Chapter Forty

The basketball practice continued on. It was the off-season, so Coach Jenny Lindenhurst allowed her gals to have some fun after running basically fundamental drills the whole time. She switched it up and had two girls become captains. They'd break down into two teams and scrimmage each other for the last half hour of the practice. The gals, like most people in sports, like to play the game instead of running boring old drills over and over. During the season, Coach Lindenhurst rarely ever had the girls scrimmage each other. It was all about the drills. The game plan. Making sure every one of them were in prime-time game condition. In summer, she would get involved, as she watched her girls play hard, have some fun, and compete. She had the whistle and if they were going to keep track of the score, she was going to call fouls and she better not see any double dribble or travelling as that made her very angry.

As the game played on, up by the score board there was a small sliding wooden window. It was an equipment room and if the score board needed to be worked on, it was in reach from this window. None of the gals noticed the wooden window slid open a crack. It was one of those sliding windows like in a speakeasy, but much bigger.

As the gals went up and down the court, their shoes squeaked on the wooden court. Then a blast from Coach Lindenhurst's whistle would stop the action momentarily. None of them noticed the dark room that held some extra equipment for the school, basically for the gym classes. A silencer on the end of the rifle was not sticking out, just blending in. They had no chance of seeing an eyeball peeking through the scope of that same rifle. The Albanian man had the rifle assembled from behind his back in less than 20 seconds. He had it mounted on a shelf, and he had the target perfectly set on the person he came for. He could pull the trigger any second and get a perfect head shot that would end her life. He moved the scope around, and he saw all the girls' stuff alongside the stainless-steel bleachers. He knew all of them had their cellphones packed away during this practice. He knew texts from people from the outside would be waiting, for them to respond after their practice. Some had games and music ready for download. Some had their whole world on that thing. He thought he'd kill his first target and whoever was stupidly unlucky & running towards their phones, he would shoot. Just like shooting ducks in a barrel.

He continued to view the whole gym while adjusting his specs on the scope. He thought about how he came back to that notebook he found which was his father's. The one he had hidden in a shoe box under a pair of his father's shoes. He hid the notebook because his old childhood home started to get shot up. His father was who they wanted. His father was the reason they came in blasting. Finding that notebook was the last time his father and he ever talked, even though it was him being scolded as a little laddie. Seeing all those bodies after hearing multiple gunshots, took that notebook right out of his head. Decades later, the notebook was found again by him. It was still under the pair of shoes never to be worn again, in the shoe box. It was his uncle's house that held his dad's stuff. Asked him if he wanted any of it. Or else he was going to donate it. He looked through his dad's old stuff. Then when he saw the shoebox, it jogged his memory back to when he hid the notebook during those dark times during his childhood. He then took the notebook and read every page, cover to cover. He was intrigued with it back in the day when he was just a young whipper snapper. It was his father's log of every person he had killed. The way he killed each person. Finding that note once and hiding it. The Police never found it. Then, it comes back decades later, still in the same spot, which was a sign from God. It was then he knew what he wanted to do.

He followed in his dad's footsteps. He joined the military right out of High School. Because the military trained you to become a sniper. Plus, how to fight. He soaked in all the combat moves, even learned stuff on his own, and built a hit man that nobody would want to mess with. A hitman who was so precise and so perfect as to get the kill and leave no trace. He turned himself into that man after he fought for his country. He followed in his father's ways. Even though his father was no longer around, he wanted to make him proud. He wanted to have more kills than his father. His father did have his own code of things. He was all about killing the target or the enemy, such as the authorities, trying to track you down. Sometimes the people that employ you want to wipe you out when you're done with a certain hit. His old man loved to kill whoever he was supposed to kill. It was the kind of high like a vampire sucking the blood out of your body. Bardhana Hoxha was a vampire-type feeding his hunger. The same way his father would cure his hunger and move on. Bardhana wanted to feast on the blood. He wanted to make a pig out of himself. Like a dog would continue to eat and eat, if food was present. Today, his target was Gretchen. But he wanted to wipe out all of them as he waited up in the equipment room, watching and salivating. Like a wolf seeking to attack the whole field of sheep.

Coach Lindenhurst blew the whistle, "OK GIRLS, ONE MINUTE UNTIL SPRINTS."

The scrimmage game was tied so all of them knew the next bucket wins. Molly Gretchen's best friend had the ball and dribbled it out of trouble with the other team doing a full court press. Two gals tried to trap her at the sideline. She bounced the ball in between the one girl's legs and darted right between the two defenders, grabbing the ball and getting it over the line. She dribbled the ball and looked for the open person since she got double teamed and saw Tracy all by herself in the corner. Molly made a nice pass that fed her into the corner. Tracy got the ball as she was in her three-point attack as a defender; she left Molly and came towards her. She saw the defender and broke towards the basket, as the defender tried to reroute her away from the basket. It was too late; she made a quick bounce pass to Gretchen who caught the ball and laid it in for the winning basket.

Clapping her hands in excitement, Molly screamed, "Way to go, girl!"

Coach blew the whistle with two quick blows which meant it was time to line up for sprints and call it a day. All 11 gals lined up behind the basket further away from the side Bardhana was on. It was like a shooting range for him though it was the perfect vantage point. He looked at his main target, Gretchen, who scored the winning basket as she was huffing and puffing with her hands on her knees. The dyke coach was off to the side where all the bags were. All 10 girls then caught their breath the best they could and spread out waiting for the whistle to blow from the Coach. It did with a solid blast. That was a sign like a starter pistol going off at the running of a race. The Albanian pressed the hair trigger and fired his first shot which was a head shot. Right when Gretchen was going to take off, her life was over. Her long legs gave out and a poof of red blood splattered out of her head. It seemed like they did not hear the shot because the girls were sprinting all the way down the court. He pulled the trigger again and took out a girl on the far end in full stride as she crashed into a row of metal chairs along the sideline, which made a loud clatter. That's when the dyke coach, in his book, saw two girls down. Make that three. Gretchen's best friend Molly went down right before getting to the other side. Others were turning back as they touched the ground with their hands and headed all the way back to the other side to see three bodies down. It was suicide sprints they were doing.

"EVERYONE TAKE COVER! GET OUT OF HERE," the coach screamed at the top of her lungs.

Another shot came out as a girl stopped in her tracks looking down at Molly, reaching down as the bullet perfectly hit the back of her head as she fell face down. A few girls hugged the wall frozen in time. Those girls were out of the sniper's sight. Another shot, this one not a head shot, right in the stomach of the girl that had the assist. She fell down holding her stomach, as blood trickled through her white hands. She could hardly breathe through her tears that came down.

Coach Lindenhurst was by one of the exits yelling and waving her hands at a few girls hugging the wall, "COME ON, COME ON!"

She had the door open and ushered four girls out as another shot took out another and then another as Bardhana took 6 out of 10. The rest fled out the door the Coach had open waiting for all of them to exit. She was watching one girl running towards them, but a bullet caught her in the side of the head. She looked at the gym one last time to see her court littered with her players, most likely all of them dead.

With everyone gone and no one else in his sights, it was time to go. He broke down the rifle and packed it away in his duffel bag. He thought the good thing about survivors was he could hear their scary tale about how an evil sniper shot up the school and killed many of their friends. He knew he was not going to be recognized as he put his ski mask over his face. He took out his Glock which already had a full clip in. He opened the door and took a quick peak but saw nobody. His thoughts were that all the remaining survivors would head for a classroom and lock themselves into a room. He thought none of them grabbed their cellphone. He figured no way the dyke coach would carry a cellphone while she worked. She looked like a rule stickler. He went down the same way he had come, slithering down the steps unheard and carefully looking to cap anybody in his way.

He was now at the bottom of the stairs. He had the duffel back at his side. The strap around his neck while the bag itself was along the right side of his body. He had his gun in his hand, with his back against the wall right under some advertising for the fall formal. He could see the gym door he peeked in earlier. He knows the survivors ran through that door to escape his target practice. He peaked down the long wall and saw nothing. It was surprisingly quiet. They could have gone down the long hallway. If they followed it all the way to the other side of the building, they'd come to the door he came through. He was going to go the same way as he made his way through the hallway.

On both sides of the hallways, lockers ran for all the students. In between rows of lockers on each side, stood empty classrooms. He walked briskly holding his gun out and peeking in classrooms as he walked by. The main hallway ran into other hallways that branched out throughout the school. If it were him, he would have run to one of the side exits, if the doors were open, and left the building. Perhaps they were in one classroom hiding under a desk with the door barricaded. He was keen on finding out as he crisscrossed the hallway a few times holding his gun until he came to another hall intersecting with the one he was in. He stopped and looked down at the intersecting hallway to see a ghost town of just more lockers and classrooms. He saw another stairway to his right going up to the third floor. He ran across the hallway as now he was coming up on the room where he killed the second janitor. It was where he stowed away the body behind the dry wall not used yet. He passed the door, looked, and saw it still the way he left things, quiet.

He continued as he passed another hallway that was off to the left, with nothing to the right. He passed by another poster for the fall formal. He noticed some "Just Say No to Drugs" posters as well on the way out. He could see the door was still propped open. He looked on the floor of the hallway to see some chards of glass which he had not noticed before. He did not think anything of it, as now the way out was coming up. He was about to push the door to exit the school when something caught his eye at the last second. It came from an open door and before he could react, it hit him right in the shoulder.

"WHAT THE FUCK?" he muttered with his accent.

The object tore through his shoulder as now he could see it being retracted by the person with a whistle. The blade of the axe ripped through his black shirt and his flesh, as some droplets of blood splattered up like a sneeze. The pain was horrendous when the lesbian Coach with the not very big breasts, swung the axe again. This time he tried to stop her with the hand he was holding the gun with, but the axe knocked the gun to the floor and took out another piece of flesh. This time above the glove, while the gun clanked against the floor. She then was going for the third swing, but this time he was ready. He used both hands and grabbed her hands before she came down.

"YOU BITCH," now leaked out of his mouth as they both were in a tussle for the axe.

She was pretty strong for a woman as she heard "bitch" and pushed him while both of them had their hands around the handle of the fire ax. The same fire ax he missed when he passed it by in the hallway. Now that explains the chards of glass he had seen.

"Give up you cunt," as his eyes bulged out of the ski mask.

They were the eyes of the devil. The rage pumped up in Coach Lindenhurst at that moment, and she looked like the mad killer. She pushed him like a tackling dummy into the lockers as his feet tripped up. The duffel bag slammed against the lockers, knocking him off balance on the shiny waxed floor that was taken care of by those janitors who remained close by.

His feet came out from under him as the bag hit the floor. Followed by him as he still had his hands extended on the ax. Coach Lindenhurst still had her hands on the axe as her momentum followed him and she fell right on top of the hitman. Her knee hitting perfectly at his family jewels and her body coming down hard on his chest. The axe broke away from both of their grips and slid away from the two laying on the floor out of reach. She then stuck her fingers in his eyes trying to gauge his eyeballs out.

"You dirty cunt."

He tried to shift his body to shake her off. As he grabbed her arms, it looked like they were having kinky sex in the hallway.

She pressed one of his eyeballs hard and cut it with her fingernail. He felt pain in a few sections of his body form; this total interference he thought was originally a good plan.

"FUCK YOU, DIRT BAG" as spittle flew from her mouth.

She was working his eyeball until it liquefied. He started punching her in the side as one of her ribs broke, but she stayed on top of him with her knees pressed into his chest.

He felt a sharp pain like a knife in his head. His one eye went dark. His good eye was hazy and cloudy as he used all his strength and might to grab her muscular body.

He tossed her off him by saying, "GET THE HELL OFF ME YOU SMELLY DYKE," as she landed right next to the ax.

He sat up and could see his eyeball hanging on by a thread. He tried to push it back in. His head still had a sharp pain, and his vision was blurry. His lower regions felt like he was going to pass out from being kneed in the balls. Meanwhile the Coach stood up, saw the axe, and grabbed it. He couldn't see because his back was towards her as he tried to deal with his eyeball.

"YOU ARE DEAD BITCH!" He yelled with a shriek while obviously in pain.

She felt her side be in pain with one arm. She had the axe in the other arm. She had adrenaline shooting in her veins and said nothing as her face turned the red of a fire hydrant. She did a wind up with the ax like those strong men swinging the sledgehammer at a carnival to send the thing up the post to see how far you got. It was all in slow motion as she hit the blade right in the middle of the hitman's head. She split it like a log just as his eyeball popped out onto the floor. She let go of the axe as the body collapsed from a sitting up position onto his back. The axe stuck out of his neck with his face split perfectly in the middle. Blood percolated up like lava in a volcano as she stumbled out the back door to be surrounded by what was left of the girls' basketball team. On a day she will never forget. A day she showed courage to fight this trained killer to save the rest of her gals' lives. She would never be the same as this day would haunt her in her dreams. No meds could combat the pain she went through, or the visions she saw like a soldier coming back from war.

Chapter Forty-One

"I couldn't believe the daughter jumped in my bed that night."

"What did you do," a big redneck asked the question while he dug his dirty fingernails into a bag of Redman chew.

The Tacoma Twisters were on their way to North Dakota to play the Fargo Ice Breakers in a three-game set. Jack Young, and his new team the Twisters, ventured off early that morning. Earlier than the roosters or any military guy that did multiple things before six AM. The morning hours on the team bus, a used, semi-modern grey hound style, were quiet. The wee hours and late in the morning, it was quiet while most were sleeping. Jack Young got some nods of sleep, but he was excited. He thought about Cassidy of course. He thought this dream of playing professional ball would have her by his side every step of the way. He wondered what she was doing right at this moment. Probably sleeping like every other person on this bus. He noticed many were listening to music, with headphones on, dreaming of the big show. He was excited and thought this was the best time he had had since the family moved to Utah. Then thought, well this excitement is actually in the state of Washington. Now it would be in the state of Montana. Jack was able to get a few winks of sleep as the wheels on the bus went round and round. That song was stuck in his head from one of the guys singing that getting on the big gray bus with tinted windows. They all stopped at a greasy spoon for lunch, where Jack finally was able to meet more of the guys. The coach tried a few times earlier that morning when everyone arrived.

"This is Jack Young."

Everyone mumbled something or some did not respond at all, as sleepiness was still in their eyes. They might not have had a huge breakfast like he had that morning from his room mom. That's what they called these fans that brought the players in. She was waking him up like he was her son.

"She wanted me bad as she pulled down my shorts while I was sleeping. She started sucking me off and I swear I almost kicked her in the head with my knee."

Spencer responded to the redneck's questions, who went by Billy Jo.

Some of the guys in the back of the bus were amazed by Spencer's story and jealous at the same time. They gave a laugh after Spencer chuckled himself. Jack thought to himself that he was not sure if Spencer was a good ball player, but every team has a guy that can tell stories, either true or false. Even that person that always had most of the team in stitches as Spencer had the small group on the edge of their seats really enjoying his story and he was getting some laughs at the same time.

"Man, I would have to piss like a racehorse if someone woke me up in bed."

Billy Joe said it with a grin as his smile revealed a few missing teeth.

"Jacky, old Billy Bob here," reaching across the aisle and tapping Jack on the shoulder to make sure he would hear the end of this wild night.

"Only this old hoss can think about draining the pickle instead of creamy filling like she's got."

He chuckled and got some laughs all around the group, even from Billy Joe, his face bright red and laughing.

"Billy Joe, you need to stop sleeping with your dad's farm animals and think about trying an actual woman who doesn't say moo or oink."

Then Billy Joe responded, making fun of himself, "But ole Betsy was my mama's prized piglet!"

Everyone laughed at that as others turned around in the middle of the bus, wondering what those guys in the back were laughing at.

They welcomed Jack on this team instantly, as he felt like he had known these guys for years. It was pretty easy with a good group of guys. They reminded him of some of the guys on the old high school team. He then thought about his best friend, Jake, and wondered what he had been doing in the years since he left his hometown of Spruce Wood. Jack told him about the house mom he had. They all knew her very well. No time for yourself in that house, as she'll be catering to your needs every minute you spend there at her house. Billy Joe added she would probably wipe your tail after taking a deuce in the toilet. Old Billy Joe was all about the potty, fart, and private part jokes. They all did agree she was very impressive in the kitchen. The meals she made were awesome.

Hours through Montana, more stories were exchanged with that group in the back of the bus, as the bus drove down the highway. The AC inside of the bus was on full power. Outside the sun was bright and bringing the heat as the bus traveled down the two-way highway at the speed limit, in the middle of nowhere. The guys caught a few more nods of sleep as the journey of his first game of pro baseball would be tomorrow. His first road game as well. He got in a card game in the back of the bus. He felt like he was a part of the team already, before even playing one game. His head was clear for the first time in years. He wasn't thinking about Cassidy. Nor was he thinking about all his friends and people he knew in that small town he grew up in. The madman he witnessed, that killed the Sheriff, did not cross his mind. His family in Utah, he did not think about. He talked to his youngest sister for less than a minute. He still did not tell any of them he had left and was going to play baseball since he had made the team. Not telling them was on his mind, one of many thoughts he had racing through his head. But at this moment, he had a nice hand in the poker game. He was enjoying himself as he laughed and smiled for the first time this much in years. The bus rolled on as the driver had the road to himself. He had dinner thoughts on his mind, as the plan was they would be in North Dakota for dinner and to gas up before they made the drive to Fargo where the hotel waited for everyone. The driver was thinking meatloaf with mashed potatoes. He was retired and a bus driver part time for a charter in Tacoma. Loved driving the team for the road games. Found himself going to quite a few games when they were at home. He was a fan. The sun was bright, but he was prepared as his frames he wore shaded up when the sun hit them. Transformed like Optimus Prime he thought, as he was a movie buff and of course a baseball fan. His face was like a well-oiled catcher's mitt. He was approaching seventy years of age and had a mop of white hair on his head like Albert Einstein's nest. He was mouthing the words to an old Rolling Stones tune.

"What in the Moses?" He eyeballed his side mirror.

The bus was the only vehicle on the road it had seemed for the last two hours. In the distance, he saw a vehicle approaching at a fast pace. Then he noticed lights flashing like a Police car. His thought process wondered where they could be going as they were a few hours out from a decent sized town or sign of civilization. They probably had some people living off this highway in a remote cabin out in the wilderness. Loners or Unabomber type. The bus speedometer was just a tad over 65 and cruising past open prairies with forests of tall trees beyond that on both sides. It seemed like it did not take long as now everyone on the bus could hear the sirens approaching. Some still sat with their eyes closed on the bus with headphones on listening to music. It was a two-way highway, so driver Gabe Walters pulled closer to the side of the road and brought the bus down to 60 MPH. It was a navy-blue undercover sedan with strobe lights in the inside of the car flashing as the car had caught up to the bus. It stayed there for a while as now it was completely in the blind spot in Gabe's vision as he tried to look for the car through the side mirrors. Some of the players tried to see to see what was going on out the side windows. The bus did not have any back windows to see out of due to the restrooms.

Gabe kept the bus going at 60 as he continued to peek out both mirrors. Still no cars except him and this undercover. He got closer to the side of the road in hopes the undercover sedan would just race along side of him and pass up the bus. Like he predicted the future that suddenly happened, as the undercover car was in the other lane right on the side of the bus. No oncoming traffic so he stayed on the side of him. Gabe brought the bus down to 55 in hopes these cops would just race past them and all could get on with our business. Then finally the cop car was neck and neck with the bus. Jack sat in seats along the window facing the prairie, not in the oncoming lane of the highway. He tried to rubber neck to see what the hell was going on. He heard the sirens as he suddenly felt queasy in his tummy. Gabe brought it down another 5 mph as he looked out the side window and saw the car's window roll down. A guy that looked to him like a G-man, popped his head out the window wearing a dark suit and mouthing to pull over, flashing his badge. Gabe, who had never even had a parking ticket, slowed down while the undercover car with tinted windows raced in front of the bus that eased its way to a stop. Gabe could see that the back plates on the sedan were definitely feds, as he knew that somehow. Probably from all the movies he has watched. He heard many of the guys on the team whispering to themselves, as some people woke up from their deep slumber.

"Are we here?"

Over all the chatter, the coach asked, "Why are we stopping, Gabe?"

"Not Sure."

Gabe pulled the bus to the side of the road right behind the undercover car as the bus made a hiss when it came to a complete stop.

More chatter behind Gabe as he pulled the lever to open up the side doors. They flung open, and he felt some heat coming in from the Montana weather. People started to stand up in the aisle looking on and wondering what the heck these guys wanted.

Gabe could feel the coach on his shoulder ask the million dollar question, "What the hell do these guys want?"

The car door opened up at the same time as two men dressed in dark suits, both wearing shades, stepped out of the car. The sirens still flashed as they kept their car running. Both of them were over six feet tall with their side arms holster and their badges on their belt. Both guys, to Gabe, could have played football, as they were built solidly. Both were Boy Scouts with their clean-shaven faces and short hair parted off to the side perfectly. They made it to the side door as the coach shushed everyone behind him. Gabe was about to ask what this was all about. Until the first Fed showed his badge to no one in particular as he stepped on to the first step of the bus. He moved his head as if to scan everyone like Terminators did in that series he thought of, as he kept the dark glasses on.

"My name is Agent Matteson and behind me is Agent Thorton."

Agent Thorton gazed at the side of the bus. Could he see into those tinted windows on the side of the bus? Gabe wondered.

"WHAT DO YOU GUYS WANT? WE ARE ON OUR WAY TO FARGO, NORTH DAKOTA," the coach yelled over the talking behind him.

Agent Matteson had those thin lips and a pointy nose as his dark glasses still hugged his eyes. "Sorry coach, we need to see Jack Young right now."

He looked right at the coach and then eyed the driver.

Jack Young sat in the back and did not hear his name mentioned by the agent. His head started to ache. He felt beads of sweat forming down the back of his neck even though he was under an air conditioner vent.

"What's this about? Why do you need to talk to him?"

The coach had quieted down and asked this in his raspy voice, clearing his throat at the end. The coach was over 50 but looked older after still smoking a pack of cigarettes a day. His bald head had poofs of his hair standing up in a half circle, probably from traveling all day. Or it could be he was nervous about his new player he did not know much about. Agent Matteson responded all business and only business-like.

"Sorry Coach, but that is classified information. Is he on the bus?"

"OK, OK," as he told the one of the pitchers next to him to go get Jack and bring him up there right away.

The player quickly listened to his coach like a dog and yelled ,"Clear the aisle coming through. Jack Young, you are wanted up front."

"What the hell is going on Jackie Boy" as Billy Boy chimed in watching Jack's face turn white as a ghost.

"Not sure," Jack whispered as he stood up and he felt his legs were not going to hold him up as if they were pure jello.

This was one of worst feelings ever in his life as it was the walk of shame. Everyone sat down making way for Jack Young walking down the aisle of the bus. Everyone remained quiet and all speculated as to what he did, as no one really knew him. His ghostly white face looked at the well-dressed man in black, seeing the shiny badge in his hand.

"JACK YOUNG?"

"Yes," Jack whimpered as his hands shook.

"LISTEN AGENT WHOEVER YOUR NAME IS," the coach spoke loudly. He was looking up at this government agent he disliked, as he hated them all in general.

"Agent Matteson, sir."

"Well Agent, what did he do? You can't just come in."

"Sorry Coach, this is an emergency matter. I'm not required to explain anything to you so settle down or I will be bringing you in as well."

He showed the badge to Jack, "Jack, you're coming with us. My name is Agent Matteson, and this is Agent Thorton.

The Coach knew he was beat. He put a hand on Jack's should, as he could feel his body was scared.

"Go with him son, you will be OK."

Everyone on the bus was quiet. Agent Matteson ushered Jack down the stairs into the hands of Agent Thorton and those two walked off to the car.

"Sorry, coach. He will be OK. We just need to get him to safety. Something happened to his family and that's all I can say."

He walked back down the stairs as Gabe could see the other agent put Jack in the back of the car.

They all watched both agents get back in the car and drive off. They did a U-turn in front of the parked bus and high tailed it off into the direction they came. Gabe closed the doors as everyone was asking what the hell just happened here.

Chapter Forty-Two

DANVILLE, ILLINOIS

In Danville, Illinois, just a bit away from the prison. An overturned bus filled with inmates, sat in flames off the main road. Smoke filled the skies for miles. Inmates screaming and being burned alive. The driver and two prison guards burned as part of this human BBQ, but they were shot and killed before the fire was set. Miles away from the scene, Blade Runner was in the back of the van exchanging his prison clothes for a pair of jeans and tee shirt. Plus, his leather vest that had his name in front. The Viper hugging the Harley on the back with the words, Venomous Vipers.

Chapter Forty-Three

Blocks away from the Tacoma Twister bus, Jack Young was told his family had been murdered. The two FBI agents broke the news to him in the car. He was told the new identity was now a thing of the past. Because obviously the witness protection list had somehow been compromised. Like his original name, John Malone was history. Like the whole Young family, the Jack Malone saga now has come to an end. Jack was told a new identity was in the works. Right now he was going to be headed for a safe house. Then he would be quickly taken to another location to live in a new community where he did not know anybody. He would be living there himself, as he would not even get a chance to say goodbye to his family who were killed within a few days. Totally wiped out.

Jack Young sat in the back seat staring out the window with a blank stare. Tears flowed down his eyes onto his cheeks. It seemed like only hours ago he had talked to his younger sister. As the Montana prairies and forest of trees he had already seen whipped by, the Agents cruised the speed limit perhaps five over without even talking to each other. Once in a while the radio would come to life like a police scanner. Pretty much silence the whole time. He did not know how he was found as he told no one he was going to be playing for the Tacoma Twisters. He did not give it to deep a thought as his family was gone, even his father in Vegas. The FBI probably can find anybody. Jack Young would find out later that Blade Runner had escaped. This was all because he helped put a bad guy behind bars. Being a good citizen had screwed up his life in so many ways.

Chapter Forty-Four

It was closing time at a pub named Kelly's Landing Strip in Derry, Ireland. It was in the wee hours of the night, and two patrons at the corner of the bar had half pints of Guinness. They clanked their two shot glasses with a clank as they were both pissed drunk. Irish music played on the jukebox, a slow playing fiddle song of one of the great musicians in the area. The place smelled of beer, stale smoke, sweat, and urine. They packed them in after a local Rugby tournament right across the country road. The two patrons, who sat on the wooden stools off in the corner of the little shoe box pub, played in the game earlier. Both wore striped button-down polo long sleeve shirts with grass stains all over. Both men were in their 30's, and one still had not washed some dirt off his face. It mostly blended in with his grizzly stubbly face. Some dried-up blood mixed in as well.

The pub was right across from a vacant field in the middle of nowhere surrounded by farms. The vacant field was where they played the Rugby games on Saturday. Kelly's was an older pub that had been around since the days of World War II. The Germans accidently bombed some of the town back in the 1940's. It was a white cobblestone building that looked like a shoe box on a corner facing the field. It had a gravel driveway that went around the building in a horseshoe pattern for parking. The green sign had Kelly's with an old World War Two plane and a shamrock on the tail. They had a wooden plank door and a small port hole window with a neon sign that said Harp. The P was burnt out, so it lit up HAR instead.

"Aww I told you your bloody wanker arse, you'd like this game better than the paddle game named after some infested insect."

The guy with the dirt on his stubble and blood dried on the tips of the gray in a red beard continued. He spoke in a deep Irish brogue and the more drinks he had, the deeper it got.

"I was getting better. I had a few googleys with the big paddle."

He had a five o'clock shadow and talked like he was from Canada or even some part of the states. He wore his hair long in a ponytail.

"I'd like to stick my paddle in her... a beautiful angel," the Irish guy in the red beard raised his glass and looked at the bar keep. She was a female who was washing the pint glasses. He then whispered to the Yank Canadian and said, "I'm going to fuck the shite out her tonight. So beautiful. Her name is Deedre." He stood up and put his arm around his friend.

The Canadian yank downed the rest of his Guinness and said to his friend, "I know. You've introduced me over a dozen times."

Deedre smiled, wearing jeans that tightened up her booty and made it very appealing in dim lighting. Many wanted to tap her ass. She was short and well-stacked on top. She had short brown hair parted in the middle and cropped right above her shoulders. She was wearing a tee shirt that said Kelly's Landing Strip right on her breasts. It was tight and the patrons could see a nicely formed rack in the V-neck shirt with some cleavage ready to pop out. She dried her hands, looked down at the two of them, and smiled with the rosy red cheeks on her porcelain doll skin. She was a cute girl overall. Her smile was contagious and just brought you in deeply. She headed to shut off the "Har" sign in the window.

"Finish them up, boys."

"Johnny, since you joined the squad we have won all of our matches undefeated, and you probably never experienced that over in the states playing that boring old game of baseball."

The guy in the red beard drained the rest of his beer in the pint glass and placed the beer on the varnished red oak wood that was the bar top before he stood up

"I have to drain the lizard. Do you want ta hold it, cousin?" as he went to the Lou.

"Not sure I'd be able to find it."

Johnny laughed and stood up, leaning against the bar. Out by the tables, Deedra was dumping ashtrays of cigarette butts. She showed what a sarcastic smart ass she was.

"That's very untrue. He is big down there, but he just has nothing inside his head."

From the bathroom was yelled, "I HEARD THAT!"

Johnny, who was originally John Malone and went by a few other names as well, just laughed. He had a nice buzz going, but he felt a little stiff and sore from playing rugby all afternoon. The soreness and stiffness hit him from sitting on a bar stool for like 8 hours drinking beer after the game. He thought about a few years ago and what happened in New Jersey. He thought about his old neighborhood back in Illinois. Most importantly, the girl. His best friend who he could never get out of his head, the love of his life. What was she doing? God, he missed her so much. Then a tear came down his cheek as he stood there by himself alone in Kelly's. His cousin was still in the Lou and Deedre was putting the finishing touches on the kitchen counters. He flashed back to a pet store in New Jersey.

YEARS BEFORE IN NEW JERSEY

In New Jersey, John Malone and his Utah name, Jack ----- were gone. His new name in New Jersey was Steven Brown, which meant he felt like Charlie Brown from the Peanuts looking for the true meaning of life. New Jersey took time to totally get used to. That day he was in the back of a pet store where he worked, loading big bags of dry dog food into a wheelbarrow to take it up front by the display. That was when they walked into Angie's Pets Shop which carried live animals, accessories, and food. He somehow had gotten involved in a relationship with his boss. On that Saturday afternoon, an hour till close, he heard a few motorcycles roaring their engines as they sounded like they had parked in front of the store. It stopped him in his tracks and just seeing or hearing them gave him the willies. It seemed like time froze for Steven Brown that day. He was not sure how long it was, but his boss girlfriend came in at the speed of light.

"Stevie, quickly go out the back door. They are here for you, but I'll get rid of them."

He stood there for a very long time it seemed. His jaw dropped. Panic took over his body and mind, like a person having a panic attack and not knowing how to stop it.

"GO NOW," as she slapped his face which was a loud crack to bring him back to earth.

He darted out the door, as he thought he heard the chime to the glass door in front of the store.

110

Chapter Forty-Five

It was close to noon the next day. John Malone was up with a cup of coffee in the kitchen of his cousin's house. The cup looked like one of those handmade ceramic soup bowls with a handle on the side. Steam was rising from the top of the marlin blue mug. It was something to get used to in Ireland, that they never had the heat on during the day. As a result, he always felt a cold chill in his bones. He sat at the table looking out into the breathtaking backyard, with all kinds of wildflowers and trimmed hedges with dark green grass. His cousin owned the nice cobblestone two-story home in Letter Kenny, Northern Ireland. His cousin and Johnny were the same age and only had seen each other half a dozen times in their lives until Johnny crossed the pond two years ago. A few family trips from both sides meant they'd meet from when they were little, to their teens, and then in their adult years. He stood up and went to the counter for some more coffee as he heard some movement above him.

His cousin had brought home his girlfriend, the bartender Deedre, and he heard the bed frame rattle and hum against the wall that separated his bedroom from his cousin. He thought that girl could moan, as his cousin knew the right spots because he thought he dreamed about her moaning in some twisted sick dream he would not speak of. Then he heard creaking down the stairs from upstairs, as his cousin appeared in the kitchen doorway shirtless.

"GOOD MORNING COUSIN JOHNNY! HOW DID YOU SLEEP?"

He was wired, and definitely not hung over, as he had energy to burn. He walked across the ceramic marble floor of the kitchen with his bare feet, wearing just green and gray checkered pajama bottoms. He went for the coffee right away like he needed some.

"Slept good," Johnny lied, as his eyelids were heavy, and his body was sore from the games of Rugby yesterday. "I made a full pot if Deedre wants some."

"I thought really hard on what you told me yesterday," as his cousin poured his own cup of coffee his mug which was canary yellow.

Johnny knew he rambled on about a lot of stuff last night with his cousin, Liam. John Malone's mind was still fuzzy from after the Rugby games, as drinks were had. They started drinking before the rugby game, plus during and right after, until they closed the bar. He knew the basic plot of the night, but he did not think he revealed anything. Especially to his cousin, who is quite a mad man, but a brother and he had loyalty for the cause and family blood.

"About letting that guy get by you in the second game."

A loud chuckle came from his cousin who was lacing his coffee with half a bowl of sugar. His red hair was sticking up like an out-of-control forest fire. The beard was all curly and scraggly on one side, while the other side was patted down from sleeping on his side. His eyes were bright blue and wide open. His nose looked like it had been broken a few times and stuck out in the hair. As he sat down, he was slim and trimmed with muscle mass, as if he needed that to support the head of all that hair.

"Johnny, that was not my man. We will dive right back in the game, in a bloody second."

As he sipped the coffee, Johnny noticed one of the many tattoos on his body. This one on his hairless chest with a noose around the Queen of England.

"I'm talking about what happened in the states."

Johnny told his extended family in Ireland half the truth. They knew the family was all killed, but they never knew the cause of the whole thing. When they left for Utah, way in the beginning, they had to cut ties with everyone, including the extended family. Years went by and calls were placed, but the family from Ireland got no answers. They got no notice that the family had moved. The authorities in the states, when they looked into it to see what happened to the Malone family, got no answers. People were pretty pissed off. They still were, as Johnny felt things were not right. But his cousin Liam was different. He did not have the old way of Irish thinking of just sweeping things under the rug. He lived for the day. The present day. After a few beers with his cousin, Johnny and Liam were tight as ever, just like when they left off.

"The motorcycle gang, I'm talking about, and what they did to your bloody family."

Liam walked over to the cabinet and opened it up, looking inside and moving some boxes.

"Maybe boobs up there, when she awakes at some point, can make us something. Well, might not have anything to make, which brings up another problem."

He spoke quickly and had an energizer battery in him as he kept going and going, Johnny thought. Johnny felt a little nerve wrecked and tried to remember if he just opened up and all his guts came out with the secrets. There were a lot of them he might have told his cousin. Things he didn't tell his boss in New Jersey about. Not all of them, but some. Did he tell his cousin all? How could he? The man cannot sit for more than five minutes, as he already walked out of the room. He'd headed to wake up Deedra because he was hungry and wanted eggs and sausage. Johnny remembered a night back in New Jersey.

JERSEY - TOWN OF WILDWOOD

Witness Protection put John Malone in the town of Wildwood, New Jersey. Hearing the town's name, he thought back to the soda he and his friends drank from the local Garden Drug store. Cans of Wildwood that came in multiple flavors. Wildwood, the town, was right on the ocean and had a nice beach to go with the town. That night, he was experiencing something he never had before with a woman. His boss at the pet store, was Katie, and she was much older than him. She was 15 years older. In her mid-30's while he was just a pup in his early 20's. She lived in the townhouse next to his. That night they finished work and got Chinese takeout. Lang Lee had the best chop suey in the area. They went to her place. They ate at a table with dim lighting and a bottle of wine. He never cared for wine, but she brought a whole new world to his. He remembered they always spent hours after-hours just talking. Just like the days with Cassidy.

On this night, they found their way into the bedroom. One moment they were talking about random things at the store, like always. Then they looked each other in the eyes while sitting right next to each other. Seconds later, she was like a cat killing a mouse and pounced on him. The chair was too old and rickety to hold them, and they locked lips. Even tongues as she wrapped around him like a Cobra snake; cracks were heard as they both landed on the floor and the chair legs just caved in. He remembers he actually accidentally bit her lip and they both laughed. She had a nice laugh with a smile that exposed her dimples. Then his eyes looked at her round face with her bright blue eyes, which looked like glaciers in the pure blue water of Antarctica. That's when she unbuttoned her work shirt and underneath revealed a pink rose bra, as he could see her nipple pressing through. She was on top of him as she dived in their lips interlocked again. That followed by the tongues softly sword fighting in their mouths. It was like, "1-2-3, I declare a thumb war," but just with tongues. The kissing was heating up as the tongues sloshed through the mouths. At one point, she caught his tongue between her teeth as they danced around some more and the lip smacking increased. Their bodies were compressed together. He felt himself get hard. She felt him get hard when her hand slid right over his pants. He felt his button of his pants come undone as he got even harder, if that was even possible. She slid her hand down his pants as he was pinned down and the tongues were still working it like a Richard Simmons workout video. Her hand just brushed up against his penis like a gentle petting, as he was ready to blow.

112

"COME ON," she whispered into his ear and stood up grabbing his hand and pulling him up on his feet.

Shelby was Katie's last name and she stood close to 6'ft, at 5'11 tall which is tall for a gal. Katie had a high-octane engine. She was skinny with high energy. She could eat like a drunken sailor but not gain an ounce. She was toned but not muscular working out wise. Owning her business, she was always on the move. Especially dealing with animals. She ushered John Malone, known as Steven to her, out of the dining area across the living room. The broken pieces of the chair still littered the throw rug under the dining room table. They passed through the living room with Steven holding up his pants so they would not trip as he held her hand and was being guided like a kite on a windy day. She practically threw him on the bed, and then undressed in front of him as his feet still touched the ground. His back was on the floral comforter as he looked at her, and he could not resist. Her long dark hair flowed down past her shoulders. She had a pretty face with bright eyes and a smile that showed off her perfectly white teeth. Her eyes had that sexy look with the nice dark eyebrows that stood out in the dim lighting, from the aquarium housing a turtle. She looked like a jungle cat ready to mate as she tossed her bra on the wooden floor of the room. It was like she was doing a strip tease as she slowly unbuttoned her pants and brought them down to reveal these skimpy pink undies she had on. She stood up and he got the view of her breasts. Perfect handful squeeze types with round pinkish nipples, perfect circles. She leaped into bed on top of him. In seconds, he had breasts in his face. It was one of the few moments he had that he did not think of anything from his past.

In the first few minutes, he came instantly. She did not make him feel ashamed. The one thing he would get to experience about an older woman who did not look like she was in her middle 30's. Only a few wrinkles under the eyes, if you really got close up. She was not a girl that got around. But she had experience, which he did not, just a few things with Cassidy. It was more exploring each other's bodies than anything. This night, Steven Brown, originally John Malone, would experience different positions he may have only seen in movies. Perhaps looking through some dirty magazines when he was younger after playing baseball. This felt better to him than when he hit the ball into the stands. Baseball was forever his passion. Thank God he was young and did not need the blue pill. He was like the energizer bunny, and he had come at least 5 times throughout the marathon of sweating up the sheets. Maybe he had not satisfied her sexually. She was moaning like an animal in heat, so he imagined a job well done. They laid in the bed at the end, half asleep and sticking to each other. The sheets on the bed were completely off.

Sometime later, in the morning, they held each other close while in the cuddling stage. He opened up to her. He remembers it just all coming out like a pipe had burst. He felt a closeness to her like Cassidy. It could have just been he had this hanging over him way too long. That night he just up-chucked all the thoughts he had ever held in. Told Katie the whole story. His whole life story. He remembers tears over all the events that took place, streaming down his cheeks. She listened while never interrupting. Never judging. That night he grew a bond with her. He even thought this relationship could be his future. Maybe he now had to walk down this road. Forget about Cassidy. Forget about his hometown of Spruce Wood. Would he, or could he, get past the game? Giving up what now looked like a pipe dream playing baseball. Would a pet store in Jersey be his life now? Kate would be his life. Something deep down was saying no way in hell baseball, or even Cassidy, would be tossed away. The love was strong. But, at that moment he questioned himself.

Chapter Forty-Six

"YOU'RE CHOKING ME," the man on the ground shouted as his windpipe was closing in and he gasped for air.

"You will breathe again when you answer my question," a stone-cold female voice said, as the heal of her boot was dug in on side of his neck with her Glock pointed down at his head.

An elderly lady in other room was ushered too another room quickly after the female and male detectives burst through the door with their guns blazing.

"Again. Where are the guns?" She put more pressure down on his windpipe.

"Warrant," he was able to gasp out.

She heard the lady yelling something in Polish at her partner from a room that was probably the kitchen. The door was off the hinges and lay on the ground with splinters pointing out like a porcupine defending itself from an attacker. The night was cool and a breeze followed the detectives in. Some neighbors living across from the bungalow home were looking out their doors while some squad cars pulled up with patrolmen getting out. The sirens were loud and strobe lights were flashing. Detective Cassidy Owens dropped the warrant she had dug out of her flap jacket. It slowly descended down and landed right on the dirty red carpet of the living room in eyesight of the biker who had been followed to his mom's house.

"Read it and weep, you savage."

Her voice was angered, but not loud for the whole block to hear. As she heard patrolmen approaching, she released her foot from his neck.

The guy on the floor was sucking in air like a fish out of water. She glanced at the door as the footsteps were getting closer. She still had the gun pointed to him on the ground. She lifted her leg and stuck her steal toe boot right into the side of the perp. It was very hard, so he squealed and coughed as the shriek of pain ran through his body. The patrolmen, two young kids, came in with their guns drawn. They looked nervous but relaxed after seeing the detectives had everything under control.

"Get this dirt bag out of here," she barked.

The two obedient patrol officers were like lap dogs, quickly holstering their guns. They moved quickly and had the guy in cuffs as they lifted him up off the ground. His head still looking at the ground, he tilted it to look up at the 6ft long legged Detective wearing jet black boots with blue jeans. She had a dark blue tee shirt with a darker colored flap jacket over her shirt. She holstered her gun on the black belt she wore around her waist. She bent down as the guy's head still hung down and his long hair covered his face. She grabbed the guy's greasy black hair and looked into his dark bloodshot eyes. He thought to himself, "Why is this broad so mad at me?" Her bright eyes looked like she was going to strap him to the chair and stick the needle in him, herself.

"You will rot in jail, and I hope they butt rape the hell out of you."

She showed nothing but her stone-cold face as she smiled behind the light red lipstick. Her long hair tied down in the ponytail as she let go of his hair.

"Take him away."

The patrol officers ushered a giant biker named Fredrick Molinski to their patrol car. She wiped her hand on one of the lazy boy chairs that were in the room facing the old tube television which was on with some old Mash rerun in mute. The biker, Molinski, thought she broke a rib as he had a hard time breathing and leaned on both young patrol officers. He was cuffed behind his back as he lumbered out in pain each step.

"She's crazy. I think I need a doctor," he whispered to young officers hoping she would not hear him.

One of the patrol officers wondered how the hell she had put a beat down on such a big massive specimen. The other just thought she was hot. Both officers walked Fredrick down the sidewalk and to the squad car. A few more officers headed inside Fredrick's mother's house. A few more looky-loos gathered across the street and watched their neighbor's son be put in the back of the police car. The neighbors knew Molinski, and most did not like him. His bike roaring in the wee hours waking up the block. The shouting matches he got in with his mother constantly. The happiest day was when he moved out.

"Seriously, fellas… a doctor," as they lowered him in the back seat. Glancing at his leather coat with the Venomous Vipers logo on the back.

The patrol officers ignored him and shut the door. Freddie Molinski's code name was BOOM BOOM as he was a scary guy who blew a guy's head off his shoulders with a stick of dynamite forced in his mouth. He may have seen his precious baby, his Harley motorcycle for the last time. It was parked along the side of the driveway as the squad car pulled away. The big guy's side was killing him. That bitch detective; it was not the first time he had a run in with her. She was a lethal warrior princess that took him to the ground in seconds and she was scary in his books.

Inside, Detective Cassidy Owens yelled out to every officer who entered the house and said, "People, we are looking for a black gym bag. So let's get on this and yell if you find it and come get me"

The officers jumped at her commands and started to search every nook and cranny of the house. Her partner had Mama Molinski calm and drinking tea at the kitchen table. Someone yelled out,

"Found it!"

Detective Cassidy had a gleam in her eye as she had become a regular thorn in the sides of the Venomous Vipers. In her head, it's just another one behind bars. She wanted them all banished from her presence. She opened up the bag and knew what they had found.

Chapter Forty-Seven

VENOMOUS VIPERS

In the middle of nowhere down in the open fields of southern Illinois. Along the Ohio River in Pulaski county, locally known as Little Egypt. Three rivers border the area: Mississippi, Missouri, and the Ohio. It was a meeting of the minds of the Venomous Vipers. A little pow wow between three different charters. The Southern Illinois charter President and former President arrived first around the noon hour, as they drove down a dirt road with towering trees on one side. An open barley field to the left, signaled them to kill their engines and park their hogs. Blade Runner, still a wanted fugitive, has been flying under the radar. Has not gone on many rides, but he was present for this meeting. Still had long greasy hair, but now more salt and pepper than the jet black it was before he went to jail. He reached in to grab a cigarette. He flipped the golden Zippo, smelling the lighter fluid as it ignited from a blue flame to orange. It was a beautiful day with not a cloud in the sky. Birds were chirping from a distance. The road that got them there was deserted. Not too many cars travel down the country two-lane road. The Shining was the new President of the Venomous Vipers, ever since Blade Runner went to the big house. Since Blade Runner was still wanted and not able to ride and be at places regularly, he could not lead their biker gang. They made him Co- VP, #2, and this had not sit well with Blade Runner all this time. The Shining still looked like a young FBI agent. Short blonde hair combed neatly as he took off his state trooper style sunglasses.

He looked at his military watch, with his shades now on top of his head, and said, "Looks like we made it here early."

They have made it to the meeting spot about a half hour early. Blade Runner pushed The Shining to get moving early due to a shift change by the highway patrol.

"Yep," Blade Runner said looking through a pair of round sunglasses as he sat on his hog looking off in the distance.

It was a clear day with not a cloud in the skies. It was a perfect day, not too hot and not too cold. Blade Runner inhaled another drag as the ash at the end lit up the cherry. He took it in and inhaled. He was wearing a black tee shirt with no sleeves with a no sleeve old jean jacket with the Venomous patch on the back. On the front, it still said President on the color-fading jacket. Maybe his first one he got when he joined. He blew smoke out of his mouth and nose. The Shining did not really care for Blade Runner since he escaped prison. The thoughts were, Blade Runner was holding a grudge after the first, and only, plan the club had for his escape did not work. No other plan was in motion. The Shining could sense the edginess as he stood up from his bike and felt around for his gun still holstered... still there.

"Should be a nice party tonight at the house ." Shining was making conversation looking over at Blade Runner's exposed tree trunk arms decorated with all sorts of colorful tats.

"Flea Bag is very good at rounding up the bitches. I can use my pipes cleaned."

Blade Runner spoke in a hoarse voice as he took one more drag of his cigarette and dropped to the ground at the side of his Harley Hog. It was one of the biggest bikes Harley made.

The Shining nodded his head in agreement about their biker friend, Fleabag. He was very good at doing that. He had ties to some very nice strip joints throughout Illinois. He loved rounding up college gals from SIU. Southern Illinois was a party school and those gals loved to party. They did a lot of kinky shit that made most of the club members love the young tail.

The Shinning had a long-sleeved black shirt with a death metal band on the front, with a name Blade Runner had never heard of called the Crimson Crypt Keepers. Which had a skeleton biting a nipple off a big breasted lady. Blade Runner had never heard of the band.

"I need to drain the lizard," and he walked off to the tree.

Blade Runner stood up as he stretched as his knees crackled getting off the bike. They both heard a motorcycle in the distance. "I hear someone coming," as his stream came out soaking the side of the tree as the roar of the engine was very close.

A puddle of urine formed on the ground as it ran off the tree bark like a waterfall. The engine was louder, and they could both see a motorcycle turning the corner. One guy who they both recognized. It was a guy from their own club nicknamed Electric Eel. The Shining zipped up his jeans and buttoned his fly. He wondered why the Electric Eel came all the way out here in the boonies for a charter meeting. One which he was not to be a part of. POW......

The gun shot echoed over the noise of the bike. The Shining collapsed as his knees folded and he fell face forward with his hands on his crotch. He never heard the footsteps of Blade Runner who brought his cannon Magnum six shooter which was smoking on the barrel. Electric Eel parked the bike right by the dead President biker with a gaping hole in the back of his cranium. Then a van turned in on the road with a few other guys. Blade Runner and the guys will have their former President buried in no time, and the Venous Vipers will have a celebration of getting rid of themselves a President. One who in their opinion, did a bad job for their charter. They never had a meeting with other charters that day. It was a day they had to reshuffle the top of the deck and get rid of the joker.

Chapter Forty-Eight

CASSIDY'S INTERROGATION

Freddie Molinski, AKA Boom Boom, a club member of the Venomous Vipers, felt like he was holding his own. On the night he was taken into custody by that bitch detective and her hapless side kick, he felt he was like Charlie Sheen and winning. He even had wondered if he really was winning. He found himself thrown back into the same interrogation room the next morning. He thought those two asshole detectives came at him with all they had. He did not bend. He did not break. In the wee hours of the morning, they tried to stump him up more than once. This was not Boom Boom's first rodeo with the law. He did not care for a lawyer to represent him. He liked to fight his own battles. They had him on weapons charges. They had him on drug charges. They found his bag of tricks with guns and a brick of heroin inside the black duffel bag. She threw the bag on the table and got in his face. He looked down her shirt to see her cleavage. He even knew what pissed off that bitch more. He will be ok serving jail time for the weapons and drugs. Right now though, he just denied everything like the way that car salesperson President did in the 90's about the blow job he had gotten from the help, as he liked to say. Or was it that he denied inhaling? His mind went back to Monica something with a Polish last name like him. She had those lips too, probably, and his train of thought was ruined when she, the she-devil, walked into the room.

"Good Morning, Boom Boom," tossing a file folder on the stainless steel metal table in the middle of the windowless room.

"I'll take steak, eggs, and an OJ," he demanded as he looked at her standing tall looking down at him. One hand cuffed to a half circle bar in the middle of the scratchy surface of the steel table.

She had on black boots with high heel platforms to make her taller. She had on dark pants with a dark short sleeved tee shirt, this time a lighter gray color with the State Police logo in a circle right in the middle of the shirt. Her hair tied back like when she came through his mother's door. She just gave him a smirk. "Oh Freddie, you're making things worse for yourself," as she reached up in the corner of the room and unplugged the camera.

Was this supposed to make him shake in his boots? Even though they had him dressed in the standard orange state pajamas with no laces style slippers on his feet. He did not bother to look at her as his hair was long and covered his bearded face. Right now he looked like Cousin It, looking at the table following the scratches like some kind of trail that led to something. She sat down on the other side, on a metal style folding chair. The same kind he sat on. She could smell him across the table, the man was in need of a shower. Smelled of bad body odor and sweat. She said nothing but opened the file and restacked the contents in it. He looked up as he brushed the hair from the front of his face and growled.

"You got nothing from me yesterday. I ain't telling you Jack today, Missy."

He put his head down and saw that someone had carved their initials in the table indicating, "Brad was here."

"OK Freddie, I'm deeply disappointed in you for not cooperating with me." She said it like she was his mother, although Cassidy Owens was way younger than this biker.

His mind had thoughts of just slamming her down on the table and fucking that bitchy attitude out of her. She was hot in his mind. But that mouth… he wanted to slap her silly. It would not be the first gal he belted in anger.

"FEED ME BITCH," as he looked up spittle flew out of his mouth, "eggs scrambled, steak pink in the middle… I like pink in the middle." He stuck out his fat tongue and dribbled a few drops of saliva on the table.

"OK, is that the way you want to play this game?" She reached in her pocket, pulled out a phone, and hit a button while speaking into it. "You ready on your side?"

She nodded her head, then pressed a button and looked at the screen. Then slid the phone over to him on the other side of the table. Freddie's heart skipped a beat, and his eyes opened up wide looking down on the screen of the phone.

In a stern tone, "Now will you tell us where your club house is?"

She grabbed the phone as she stood up, his face was white as a ghost. His eyes were popping out of his sockets. He choked out a few words as his forehead wrinkled in with the eyebrows squiggly in a perfectly anger face.

"You can't get away with this. That is my mom."

"Freddie, Freddie, you should ask around about me." She put the phone back in the back pocket of her pants as she paced on the worn-out gray tile floor.

"YOU'RE BLUFFING BITCH," trying to yank the cuff off his hand or break the metal ring bolted on the table with no success and leaving a red mark around his wrist.

"No Freddie, I'm not bluffing. Did you see her face?"

He just stared at her as she stood there in her tracks and stared back deep into his soul.

"I will slice that woman's throat in a heartbeat, and no one will know except me and you," she whispered.

She was very convincing as she got the location of their hideout. She had went over there in the morning and set up a ruse with his mother pretending to be beaten up with some simple Halloween costume blood kit. She made a threat to her about her son which worked, as they both thought she was going to kill the other one.

Chapter Forty-Nine

IRELAND

Johnny found himself in another pub that day with his cousin, and his cousin's girl Deedra. Liam had someone to meet who was going to benefit Johnny's life at a pub in Letterkenny, Ireland called O'Malley's Pub. This was located in their small downtown area of the little village in Northern Ireland. Not the North part of Ireland ran by the Brits. Liam promised them both that O'Malley's makes a great breakfast as well. Johnny thought they would be eating pickled boiled eggs out of a jar with a pint of Guinness and a chaser of Paddy whiskey. Johnny has been down this same road with his cousin. Since living in Ireland, Johnny was building quite a tolerance if that even was a remotely good thing. It was Sunday in a hole in the wall pub with dim lighting. The wooden bar took up most of the space inside, which had almost every seat taken up as we arrived. They had wooden booths with pew style seating along the other side of the wall. Walking in between the booths and bar was not much space, so if it became crowded, you'd be crammed inside like a sardine in a can. They found three stools right in the middle of the bar. They sat down on the leather padded bar stools, as a fat guy with rosy red cheeks on pale white skin asked what they wanted. Before that, he knew Liam as he was a regular. The guy was in his 60's with buzz cut hair and clean shaven wearing a white colored shirt and brown pants with a dirty apron around his waist covering his belly.

"What brings you in today?" He paid no attention to Johnny or Deedra as they were just people watching a soccer game on a television up in the right-hand corner of the bar.

"I'm here to see Aaron and get some breakfast," Liam said as he extended his hand out to shake the barkeep's hand.

The old guy extended his hand over the dark stained cedar wood. He had soft mitts from washing pint glasses most of his life as he been in the bar business since he was taller than the bar. He was the owner, Joe 0'Malley. "Good to see your friend Aaron at his table. A round of Guinness and three breakfast plates, then," as he looked at everyone.

"That will work well. I been telling these guys all morning that your wife Maura makes the best eggs in town," as he slapped his cousin Johnny on the back. He nodded as did Deedra.

The barkeep served up the best Guinness he had in Ireland, so far, in Johnny's opinion. Liam took his pint and said he had a meeting of the minds down at the other end of the bar with some guy named Aaron. Deedra took a quick swig of her Guinness and vacated her stool to hit the loo and saw a gal she knew. Johnny sipped his Guinness, watching the soccer game along with most eyes around the bar trained on the screen. The bar smelled of breakfast sausage, coffee, and stale cigarette smoke still in the air from the night before. He was wondering what Liam was meeting Aaron about.

Then his mind went back to running out of that pet store. How he was so scared and got out of town. Found a train that brought him to New York. He had some cash he withdrew from the ATM before the train took off. He did not want to use his ATM card or his cell phone. He found a cheap place in Brooklyn to rent for a few days thinking the coast would be clear. He hoped she was ok. He tried to call Katie from a pay phone a few times. Then he saw on the news how a pet store owner in New Jersey was killed in her own store. Suspects were still at large. Those pricks drowned her in one of the fish aquarium tanks until she lost consciousness for good. The thought of her head underwater being held by some guy with tats on his hand around her neck. The fish scared out of their gills, retreating to a cave behind a plant or something. To see the bubbles popping up out of her mouth screaming under water. While another biker probably held her legs as she was upside down talking her head off asking where Johnny went. She never gave up the location because she did not know where he went. Johnny then thought when she finally ran out of air, they just dropped her. The tank probably fell on her as glass cut her neck when the aquarium crashed to the ground. As fish bounced around on the floor as they now could not breathe. While all the other pets witnessed the horror that took place. Dogs barked. Birds flapped their wings in panic. As two ugly and bottom of the barrel type of people walked out, even putting the closed sign up as they left her dead.

Another person dead because he testified years ago after seeing the president kill the sheriff in the restaurant after the baseball game. His hometown. He does not even remember if they won that game back then. It was so pointless as that might have been the last happy moment he really had. Now that was just a blank with all the bloodshed of the people he loved who had been taken away by the Venomous Vipers.

Chapter Fifty

ELECTRIC EEL

Electric Eel was once upon a time ago, a Frogman for the United States Navy. He was a Navy Seal and went on all kinds of special missions. He swam through some of the murkiest waters in the world to complete these missions. He got his name when he bit the head off an electric eel right after he surfaced from the deep waters of a canal. He may have been able to cut that thing with his knife. That night he was so angry. He took the scuba regulator out of his mouth and saw one of these slithering by like some kind of snake in the jungle. He reached it, grabbed it with his hand, and looked it right in the eyes before he bit the head off the creature.

"This should weigh down enough where those nasty carp could pick his eyeballs off him clean," said Electric Eel. He had a big heavy duty chain wrapped around The Shining's body. He kneeled down, proceeding to put a master lock on to connect the links.

Blade Runner watched while smoking a cigarette with a smirk of satisfaction as he looked down at the hole he created in Shining's cranium by blasting from behind. "We don't need him resurfacing anytime soon," said the President of the biker club.

Blade Runner relived the blast of his gun that the bullet dug a hole through the former President's head. He thought he could have sworn he saw some brain matter fly out like when you sneeze and cannot get the Kleenex on it right away. The way the snot splattered, it was like how the brain chips flew out of his head as the body fell and made a thud he quite enjoyed.

"Do you want the feet or the shoulders?" Electric Eel asked as he got up from fastening the chain he snaked around the dead body.

"I take the feet," as he tossed the cigarette, reached into his back pocket and put on his gloves.

Electric Eel started in the Venomous Vipers with the Blade Runner. He was very loyal, especially to the Blade Runner. He was about the same age as Blade Runner. His head was cleanly shaved off like the Michael Jordon look. He loved using his big blade to shave his head. He used that blade for almost everything. He wore thin frames around his squinty eyes with light features. A medium nose and thin lips with a nice salt and pepper goatee shaved nice and neat. He stood close to 6'ft tall, medium build. He was in good shape but had a spare tire. He had one side of his body all tattoos of different tribal stuff and one side was a blank canvas, as he called it. Wore a long-sleeved shirt on one side, exposing his arm on the other side. He loved chains around his black tee shirt promoting some craft beer he liked. Had those skeleton rings on both hands. He had a belt filled with gadgets and compartments like he was Batman.

"Ready," Electric Eel said as both lifted the body and carried him over the ridge.

"You ready to say wash the dishes, dry the dishes, then sling him over the ridge, dishes?" Electric Eel chuckled to himself out loud, as he was the only one that liked that.

"How about on three and drop the fucker over?"

"That will work as well."

They dropped the body of the former President of the Venomous Vipers off the ridge as he fell 30 feet, give or take, and made a splash like a cannon ball in a pool. He sunk immediately and they both watched with interest. They heard a falcon-type of bird squawking above them as it may have seen some food, In its mind, it was being wasted for those things that live in the waters. It flew on like nothing else to see here. Both of them walked back to the bikes and drove off heading back to their hide out.

Chapter Fifty-One

RECON MISSION

After high school, Cassidy did two years of junior college and took all the general education classes. She thought she was on with her life and just was not sure what she wanted to do. She did well in school. In high school she ran cross country and track. She played softball. At junior college, she did not think she could stomach playing softball. She still ran track and cross country. She was not bad at it either, which earned her a scholarship at Western Michigan. That's where she went. One day driving, she saw a police squad car pull over a biker which set off a fire inside herself that meant her vendetta was back, and it was back for good. She got through Western Michigan like gang busters and got a Criminal Justice degree with better grades than she had at junior college or high school. She kept in great shape running cross country and doing track. When she got through, she took the test for the state police. She easily passed and then did Police Academy with a breeze as she was motivated and dedicated to law and order.

She started off in a squad car. With only one year under her belt, she was making headlines. She was being noticed as she saved someone off the side of the highway when their car caught on fire from a multiple vehicle accident. In another incident, she was able to take out a hit-and-run driver in hot pursuit when she ran the guy off the road after catching up to him. His car was totaled, and he survived but did not escape. The elderly lady he hit, while on drugs, was killed. Her biggest thing she did was stop a bank robbery in progress. She saved lives that day. Gunned down two bad guys at the same time and got the third guy in custody. The FBI wanted her after that. She stayed with the State Police and quickly moved up in the ranks. Now she found herself parking her personal car a few blocks away from the Venomous Vipers compound. The new compound she found out about after Freddie Molinski. She looked in the rearview mirror, dressed in all black. She cut the engine as the sun was settling in the West out in the boonies. She started to rub black out stuff that baseball players use under their eyes as a camouflage for her face. Her hair was in a ponytail. She was prepared for war, but in her mind, she just wanted to see where the place was located. She thought about her threat she made to Freddie. That if he told his lawyer that he told her about the whereabouts of the hide out, Cassidy would torch his mother's place with her in it. Cassidy thought he might not tell them anything, so he does not go down as one of those bikers for the Venomous Vipers that actually cracked. That was a no-no. If you ratted any stuff about any of your brothers or any secrets of the club, the group would skin you alive. Boom Boom was there at a few of those. He was there for one where he set the boom boom off. Dynamite in the mouth of a trader. The guy's head exploded like a pumpkin, as seeds went all over the empty field. Instead of pumpkin guts, it was brain matter splattering all over as a crowd of bikers. Bikers cheering him on like it was some kind of entertainment on a Friday night.

She had prepared for this moment for a few years. She got out of her personal car, which was a newer model of Chevy Malibu. She had the car parked off the road in a driveway. One used mostly for police vehicles to make 3-point turns. Most people did not even know it existed, so it made a great place for speed traps. Her car was not exposed on the road to the few cars that did pass by. She grabbed a black duffle bag from the back seat and placed it on the ground by the trunk, which she had popped open with her key chain remote. Inside, she opened up a case that contained a rifle. She quickly assembled it, including the scope and strap connected to the rifle. She placed that on her shoulders. Then she lifted up the black bag and placed that over both shoulders on her back. Closed the trunk as she knew she had quite a walk ahead of her. More like a hike, as she'd be climbing some heavy terrain to get to the Vipers' hide out.

She was eager to use the rifle. She has been practicing for a long time on it. She learned to use it at the gun range as she was hitting moving targets from a great distance away. Tonight it would be mostly recon as the sun was going down. She stopped, dug into her duffle bag, and pulled out a set of night vision googles. She had saved up for, and purchased, all this stuff herself. She had gone about a half mile so far, and she could feel the sweat forming under the flap jacket. She had been preparing for this mission for a full year. The night was cool and calm. The sun had completely gone down as the moon was lighting up the heavily wooded area. She guzzled some water, put the goggles on, and reset everything as she continued her hike for another two miles or more and finally found what she was looking for.

The terrain started out mountainous, and then turned into flat land that had different levels. Cassidy wondered how the hell did they come and go, and then answered her own question after seeing the road they made along the terrain. It was interesting because they made paths and roads that tree branches covered, so this place would be hidden from any satellite footage. It was out in the middle of nowhere as if they all had cabins like the Unabomber. She found the road when she was walking and heard the engine of the motorcycle roar by as it came out of nowhere and scared the shit out of her. Freddie warned her they had security guards that would walk the roads at night. After the motorcycle zoomed by her, she came out of the trees to cross the road and scale some more rocky terrain. She walked through more heavy woods; sticks would crackle as they snapped from her boots, but she was doing really well at maneuvering around to limit the twig snapping. She was getting used to the sounds of the animals. The hoot of the owl made her spine chill. She finally then came to the edge of the cliff, and she hit paydirt. She followed the noise of the music. She looked down, as she laid down in the ground cover hoping it was not poison oak or some kind of plant to make her itch and break out in a rash.

She looked through the scope and saw two huge bonfires in an area where they had cleared out the trees. They were surrounded by trees still, but they had two stainless steel half-soup-can buildings that were set up in military bases. Rounded ribbed metal in a half circle. They did have cabins. They had electricity. They even had some tents out. She saw some lighting beyond that area higher up in the terrain, so the Venomous Bikers had built them self an undetected compound-style city that was the perfect hideout. She could not believe her eyes as she realized they were having a kegger. They had naked bimbos dancing to loud heavy metal music, and she was soaking it all in. She knew she would have to come back another time. She would take some photos. She would see if the compound had any weaknesses. Her brain was racing with so many thoughts. She felt angry as she had a fire in the pit of her stomach. She felt like just picking one asshole off at a time using her rifle and taking head shots with a bullet right between each of their eyes. Her finger played with the trigger. She took a deep breath to calm herself down and think of the intel. Come back with a plan. She found the place, which is a huge win. Years previously, she found their old compound. She never got the courage to do what she was doing tonight. That was before she became a state trooper. That was before Western Michigan. Then she heard a sound coming from behind her. Probably just an animal as she lay still thinking there was no way anyone would notice her. Another sound like a twig-breaking footsteps.

"Shit," she whispered to no one. She sat up, looked behind her, and lost consciousness.

Chapter Fifty-Two

COMING TO AMERICA

Johnny Malone laid in bed that night wide awake. He could not shut down his brain, as his mind was racing. The events of the day did a 360 turn on him after just going out for a simple breakfast. The meeting his cousin had was about Johnny. It was all about Johnny's past. About redemption. The return to his hometown to slay the dragon that made everything a living hell.

"We are going to the states," Liam had said after he returned to the bar.

He said it when Deedra was chitchatting with an old girlfriend down at the other end of the bar. Johnny asked what his cousin was talking about. "I'll tell you later when the lady is not present," Liam said as the three of them ate their meal at O'Malley's pub.

It was not until they got back to Liam's house that Johnny found out about who his cousin was talking to. Found out a secret he did not know about his cousin. Liam was a part of the IRA organization. Which did make sense based on some of his tattoos. Around the household, he noticed a few books about the British/Irish conflict which has taken place in Northern Ireland for decades. The older guy that Johnny only had seen from behind sitting along the side of the bar, way in the back of the establishment, was higher up in the IRA organization.

"I can't tell you all the specifics, but we are going after those reptile bikers," he said. Johnny remembers sitting with him at the same kitchen table they had coffee at late that morning together.

Instead of coffee this go around, they had a bottle of whiskey at the table with two glasses. It was Paddy, which was pretty strong as he still had the taste in his mouth laying there looking up at the ceiling of his cousin's spare bedroom. It was the wee hours of the morning as he heard rain pelting down on the roof top of the home. He was on the third floor of his cousin's house, where he earned money blowing up cars and being what some would call a terrorist. Some would call him a freedom fighter.

"What are the two of us going to do against a whole biker outlaw club?" Johnny remembered asking this, as he thought the whole idea was absolutely looney.

His cousin was stone sober, which was hard to believe after what he had drunk over the last two days. The IRA had some soldiers in the states. The IRA supplied most of those biker gangs in the states with arms. The IRA needed money for their fight and cause. Both packed their bags after that meeting. Johnny argued, but after a few hours Liam had talked sense into his cousin. It was just a short meeting Johnny remembered with the guy at O'Malley's, and a plan was hatched as they had a boat they would be on sometime in the morning crossing the pond to the states.

Chapter Fifty-Three

CASSIDY TIED UP

It felt like a lifetime for Detective Owens as she was hanging on for her dear life. She regained consciousness, waking up to her worst nightmare. Anybody's worst nightmare. She was tied to a chair in a dark room with a gag in her mouth. She thought it was a dark room, but she wasn't sure since she had a bag over her head. Her head was pounding after getting whacked in the head by somebody. It happened too fast to remember what she saw, that knocked her out or who did the whacking. Her mouth was dry. Her body was overheated with sweat coming out of all her pores. She could feel her leg on some kind of metal chair. Where the fuck were her pants? Felt like her shoes were missing. Her arms were hog tied behind the chair like some animal. Her feet were tied to the legs of the chair. She tried to shake the bag off her head, like a dog trying to get the water off their fur from a bath. This just made her dizzy. Time was passing, but she did not know how long she had been unconscious. Was she still at the Venomous Vipers hide out? She tried to listen but could not hear anything. She had to remain calm.

"Be calm Cass, be calm," she whispered to no one except herself.

She somehow remembered her scuba diving training. The controlled breathing part of going underwater. Nice easy breaths. No panicking. She took deep breaths. Then she heard what must have been the door squeak open followed by steps. Her heart started racing, and her breathing was getting quicker. More sweat poured out of her body. She had never felt this scared since John Malone and his family disappeared after the night the shooting took place after the big game. Working her way through the State Police, she had never felt this scared. She had never found herself in this kind of situation. She immediately went on the attack trying to yell something out of her gag. To the person walking in, it was just mumbling under a bag.

She suddenly felt the bag over her head slide across her face and over her eyes. The lightness blinded her instantly. She felt a breeze through the open door as she shivered from it like stepping out of the shower and opening the door, not fully dried from a hot steaming shower. She tried to adjust her eyes as she saw a shadow figure in front of her.

"Detective Owens, you have been a thorn in my people's side for a long time." A deep dark hoarse voice added, "too long actually."

She saw it was day, as light came through the room as she adjusted her eyesight. She recognized immediately who was doing the talking. It was himself, the bastard that caused her whole life to change, Blade Runner and the leader of the Southern Illinois charter.

Chapter Fifty-Four

CHICAGO

"Miller." The agent picked up on the second verse of the Imperial March from Star Wars.

"You are not going to believe who is coming state side," Agent Hawkins, on the other end, said.

Agent Miller was driving, doing some much needed errands on his day off, as he was just pulling out of Jiffy Quick Dry cleaners. "Is it good intel?" He turned down the radio as he had been rocking out to some Metallica on the local radio station in Chicago, called the Loop.

"Our guy Bucky is undercover with those Irish pricks, and you'll never guess what they have planned."

"What are they up to?" Miller changed lanes and was heading to the grocery store, but he knew better with calls like this. He was going home to get ready. Get ready for what, is the Million dollar question as he turned on to side street.

"Something is going down with the IRA and the Venomous Vipers biker gang." Agent Hawkins was calling from the downtown FBI Chicago office.

Agent Miller pressed the brakes on his Escalade really hard to make the SUV jerk as if something came in front of the vehicle. "Did you say Venomous Vipers?" His voice changed as his face turned ghostly white as he got a glimpse of himself in the rearview mirror.

"Have you heard of them?" Agent Hawkins asked in a concerned voice.

Miller said nothing as he thought about that day of the big game. The day the team made the playoffs. How most of the town was packed into Murphy's talking about the big win. Eating burgers and drinking cola by the pitcher. Then the shooting. That damn biker gang that caused his hometown so much trouble. Cost him his best friend who went missing after that. How he testified and the authorities took his entire family and moved them away in the middle of the night. He remembers looking for his old friend when he made it into the bureau that first week on the job. The records were not there as if they disappeared completely into society. He then recalls having that conversation with his friend's gal Cassidy when she became a detective for the State Police. Meeting her in the city while having a cup of coffee to break the news he could not find John or the Malone family. Thoughts of her not believing him entered his mind after she left that little coffee place.

"Are you there? Hello," he heard inside his ear as he pulled the Escalade into his driveway.

"Yeah, I heard you," Miller finally responded.

"You're going home, Jake".

Jake Miller knew he was going home. The town of Spruce Wood, which he has not been to in over ten years. He did not have any ties to the city as the family has all left. Agent Jake Miller would still know people there. "Hawkins, get me everything you know about the Venous Vipers. Find out which agent has been investigating the local thug group. Let's assemble a tag team so we can strike them all and hope to stop this small war before it escalates."

"On It."

Agent Miller had his garage door opening as he quickly walked through to get into the house as he talked through the earpiece. "I know a Detective at the State Police who were investigating these thugs. I'll call her to see what she knows, and I'll see you in ten minutes." He ended the call before Agent Hawkins even said OK.

Agent Miller had no time to run down memory road as he quickly got his stuff he would need for this mission. He knew the IRA would bring an arsenal of weapons. The thug biker gang does not play by any rules and has a stockpile of weapons. Jake knew he certainly could not bring a knife to a gun fight.

Chapter Fifty-Five

ON THE MISSOURI BORDER

John Malone and his cousin walked into a huge barn that looked like it was falling apart on the outside, into some kind of war room. The inside of the barn was completely gutted out. No hay in the loft. No farm animals. It was like a secret militia headquarters with about 8 to 10 commandos dressed in fatigues. They were busy gearing up for a small-time war it looked like as they were walking in. Tables of weapons. Guys clicking cartridges which looked to be some kind of AK-47's. Johnny could not believe the reception his cousin Liam got when he walked inside the barn. All his brothers or soldiers or group of extremists acted like he was Norm walking into the bar. Johnny was still dazed and confused about his cousin being a member of the IRA for over a decade. Not just small potatoes of this organization, but a soldier that has moved up the ranks and was a big deal. The kills he had were like those of soldiers who fought in major wars in war-torn countries. Liam has done most of his killings in his own backyard. Liam O'Donnell was a wanted terrorist around the world. His cousin showed his fake passport to him on the long boat ride across the pond, which was really the Atlantic Ocean. Johnny did not know if he was getting seasick, or just queasy from listening to stories of his cousin doing some terrible things. He was family and he was on a mission to get his cousin's life back and perhaps his dreams back at the same time.

Inside the barn, the comrades of Liam O'Donnell put down their arms and all yelled, "LIAM," like it was a bar.

They even had a makeshift bar in the corner of the barn which had a spotless concrete floor throughout the structure of the barn. Johnny stayed behind his cousin as he walked through a bro-hug line as each member chest-bumped him. Inside the barn was a lot to soak in, like the private plane that took them from the east coast to landing in a farm field on the border of Missouri and Illinois. To be picked up in a Lincoln Town Car and driven ten minutes to this barn that was off to the side of this house in the middle of nowhere. "THIS IS MY COUSIN JOHNNY," Liam called out over the chatter and some Irish rock music that was going on.

Johnny had always been shy, and he felt hands patting him on the back as he nodded his head and shook a few hands. Johnny felt like he was in some kind of movie he'd stay up late and watch on WGN the "Superstation" on the weekend. It seemed like another world ago timewise. "Take a seat over there for a minute and let me catch up with the guys," his cousin said.

Johnny looked around and saw some seats at the folding tables in the middle of the barn being used for the guns and the loading of the ammunition. One of the comrades tapped him on the shoulder. "Follow me," the guy, who sounded like he was from the Midwest, said.

Johnny followed him, looked around and saw a table with computers and monitors showing footage from security cameras. He noticed one screen had a picture of the plane they took. They had an easel holding up a huge bulletin board that had the map of the area of everything on both sides of the Missouri and Illinois border. The guy led Johnny to the bar as he walked behind it and asked, "Do you want anything to drink?" He opened up one of those fridges that let you see the contents inside.

Johnny noticed plenty of beer which took up most of the shelves with water and soda.

"I'll take a water," he said as his throat was a little dry.

"Take a seat." He pointed to one of the many bar stools with leather padded cushions with stainless steel legs and no backs. He grabbed a water and placed it on top of a wooden bar made from wooden pallets.

The guy had a mop of curly blondish hair with Spock ears pointing through the curls. His face was rat-like with the perfect amount of mousey facial hair coming in lightly with dark brown freckles on his face. "My name is Chris." He closed the fridge and had a bottle of water in his hand standing behind the bar.

"Johnny," he mumbled.

Chris wore a black shirt that was tight on the body with long sleeves showing, fatigue pants, leather boots and was of medium height with a slender build. "If you need anything, give me a shout out," as he walked out from behind the bar and headed back to his co-workers.

Inside, the barn looked like it was remodeled with unfinished wood throughout the walls. They entered through a service door because as Johnny now noticed, they covered up the big barn door. As Johnny swiveled on the bar stool, he looked at the other side of the barn. In the corner there were rows and rows of ATVs. Johnny's cousin was checking out all the weapons as he clipped in a cartridge on an AK-47 and admired it like it was one of his tools of the trade. The commanders separated as some went over by the computers and hit some buttons causing monitors to come to life. Johnny chugged his water and got his nerves in control as he bit his lip after he quenched his thirst.

He would find out these guys were just a cell of the IRA, a militia that worked with the IRA on missions in the states. That answered the question in his head as half of them had no Irish accent. He wished this were all over. He thought about how this is the closest he has been to his hometown since he testified that day. He thought about the town. He mostly wondered if Cassidy still lived in the town and what was she doing in her life. His family crossed his mind, but he pushed it out of his mind very quickly. Would he see the Blade Runner? Liam had taught him to shoot a handgun as they shot at milk bottles in Derry. Liam shot close to one of the cows perfectly without hitting him to get them to "moo." That moment of him mooing at the cow loudly through the pasture seemed like a lifetime ago. He drank his water and then just stared at all the different beers they had in the fridge behind the bar. He thought about what was about to go down. As a vision of shooting Blade Runner crossed his mind.

Chapter Fifty-Six

Cassidy opened her eyes as if she were having a nightmare and her heart leapt out of her chest. Her head was pounding, her left leg was throbbing, and her throat was dry. She did not know how long she had passed out for. Now she was lying on the ground and felt like the side of her face was on some dirt still located in the dark room. She winced in pain as she tried to move, but she was still hog tied with her arms behind her back as she lay on her side. She blew the air out of her face hoping she could see anything, but it was dark. She did not even know if it was day or night. She calmed her breathing to slow her heat rate down. She tried to recall her thoughts as she battled the pounding headache, a kind that makes you nauseous as she felt acid rising up from her stomach. She remembers the President of the Venomous Vipers paying her a visit after she was hit in the head. Blade Runner then brought in one of his guys they called Jaws. She didn't ask, but Blade Runner gave Cassidy an explanation for why they call this ugly mother fucker Jaws. The words from the Prez, "He's a man-eating shark ,or a women, but you seem to have balls on you like a man so be prepared"

The Venomous Viper named Shark walked in and did not look like a biker. Medium build and height. Looked more like a computer expert than a ferocious eating sea creature. Early 30's with short blonde messy hair like he did not comb it or shower when he got up. Had an American flag bandana he used as a head band. Clean shaven with wire thin flames and had the joker 's smile with too many teeth popping out of his mouth. Cassidy's first opinion in her head was that he's a guy that had mommy issues. Jaws did not speak as a hammer that seemed brand new as it sparkled from the dim light bulb in this dark shed with the door closed, appeared, like he had it nestled in the back of his waist band of his jeans. Just like how some would put their gun there to hide the fact they had a weapon on them. He quickly swung the hammer landing on the big toe of her left foot striking the nail of her bare feet because these reptile bikers took her shoes. The pain shot through her body like electroshock treatment to an extreme level.

"Now tell me Madam Detective. Who else knows the whereabouts of the club house location?" He spoke like he was a professor at an Ivy League school.

"Fuck you," hissed Cassidy in a whisper.

The Shark-man paced the inside of the shed looking at her while holding the hammer in one hand and stroking his incoming peach fuzz with his thumb and finger like he was in deep thought. The Shark has devoured many people when it came to getting information. Torturing was his livelihood as he knew all the pressure points a body could take. He loved deforming the human body with all kinds of methods by using all kinds of tools. He slowly walked around her like she was blood in the water with the hammer in one hand. Then taking his other hand and stroking Cassidy's side of the face with the back of his fingers. She moved her head and felt her stomach turn at the idea of this sleaze touching her.

"Such a pretty face. It will be a shame if I ruin it." He continued to circle his prey, this time using the hammer to stroke the other side of her face as she felt the coldness of the steel head of the tool.

"I'm going to kill you when I get out of here," she stayed relatively calm, cool, and collected even though her big toe was in pain and turning purplish. The nail lay on the dirty surface of the flooring inside the shed.

"Really?" He smiled as teeth popped out like the fangs of a vampire.

Suddenly things got vicious as he swung the hammer more than once and attacked the rest of her left foot. He then moved up the same leg taking swings at the ankle, the knee, and the hip as bones snapped in pain. She shrieked as finally Cassidy fell off the chair, hit her head, and passed out. The leg was completely shattered as if it was in a highway wreck in a car that took the brunt of the big crash. The hammer had skin tissue on the tip with crimson blood dripping off it and onto the dirt inside this little shed of darkness.

"This is my version of the Hammerhead Shark. Such an interesting creature. Don't you think?" As he wiped the hammer on his jeans, he loved the idea of a torturer leaving some kind of memory.

Before she closed her eyes, he hung up a face shield and some kind of rain suit. Then he injected her with a syringe on the side of her neck with some kind of substance to knock her out. "Sleep tight my beauty," as he pulled the syringe out of her.

Then walked out saying, "The next time I come in Princess, we are going to have a bloody good ole time," as he opened the door.

Cassidy's eyes flickered from the light and then shut as she was out cold. She dreamed of her times with John. She thought about the swing falling asleep in his arms on that Summer night. Thought about all the good times they had. About how both families liked each other. It was a storybook ending where two high school sweethearts fall in love and live happily ever after. Then the night Blade Runner came in shooting the Sheriff. The sounds of the gunshots played in many dreams when she was in the bathroom that night. The streaks of panic about John being shot played in her head over and over when she shut the light off in the bathroom and locked the door. She woke up with the thought process of how she would escape and kill that guppy who called himself a shark.

Chapter Fifty-Seven

SPRUCE WOOD

The sun was setting in the west that evening as the fiery ball was calling it a day, leaving some rays shooting through the tree lines of Spruce Wood. It was supper time for most of the town as the locals camped out in front of the television sets eating their dinner. On Elm Street, a clearly Navy Blue undercover sedan pulled up on the residential block. A G-man stepped out of the car, shut the door and looked at the house which looked like no one was home. It was a red brick two-story house the G-man was looking at as he lumbered up the sidewalk between two trees on the parkway. The dark shadow continued up the driveway as he made his way to a walkway that led up to the front door as the sensor picked up movement. The sidewalk in front of the nice landscape which had flowering scrubs and nicely shaped Evergreens, lit up.

"So you're saying no one today has spoken to Cassidy Owens," clarified the six-foot 200 pound of meat as he hiked up the stairs.

Agent Jake Miller was back in his hometown where he had not been in over ten years. He hit the orange glowing bell and followed it up by whacking on the screen door which echoed through the street. Miller had his earpiece on his right ear and looked like he was talking to himself like some mental patient.

"This does not raise up any red flags? A Detective missing when a crucial operation is going down." He pounded on the door louder with a knock that could wake the dead.

Agent Miller ignored the door knocker as he looked around. It still had not fully soaked in, being in his hometown. The Miller family was only a few blocks from Cassidy's house, and her family and the Malone family's homes were not too far. It occurred to him that Cassidy did not move very far from her parents' house or his old friend, John Malone. Jake was wearing blue jeans with that standard navy blue tee shirt that had FBI in bold print on the back in yellow colors, on his tall stocky frame, standing over 6 feet tall. Jake was clean shaven and a chubby baby face with thinning hair and was only 30 years old. Jake had big arms with a spare tire over his waistline that had his gun, cuffs, and badge currently on the leather belt.

Only blocks away, another male walked the streets of Spruce Wood soaking it all in like he has not been here in a while or only had weeks to live. It was a nice evening with temperatures in the 70's. The tall lanky 6'0" guy stood in front of a brick bungalow, home to the former love of his life as he stopped and stared at the home. Memories came flooding back. It looked exactly the same as if he were there yesterday. John Malone had stepped out of the barn of warriors plotting and planning against the Venomous Vipers, earlier in the night. He wanted no part of it even though his cousin and this Militia cell for the IRA were doing this for him. But deep down, his blood boiled as he wanted to do what Blade Runner did to his loved ones. If he could time travel and just not be at the bar that day. If his father and mother would have grilled that night in their backyard while having Cassidy and her family over. What about that rotten Sheriff having an affair with a girl who had ties to some sociopath biker like Blade Runner? All he did was testify and try to do the right thing, which his parents had always told him to do when raising him. He stood there on the sidewalk just looking at the house wondering where the little garden alligator with the White Sox jersey on it was. It stood in the landscape for years being a marker and telling the locals that the Owens family were die-hard White Sox fans. He did not know if Cassidy still took up residence in this house. What about her parents and her sister?

Did they still live in this bungalow? He felt warm on his forehead. The pits needed another roll-on of deodorant, and his palms of his hands were sweaty.

"I have to know," he said to himself quietly as he started walking up the sidewalk towards the steps of the house. His steps were like walking on the moon in that space suit.

He even thought of the first moon landing, trying to remember the words. They were one gigantic step for man or something as his heart seemed to be beating out of his chest. He wanted to stop in his tracks but somehow kept going.

It might have been at the same time only blocks away from where two best friends grew up in the sand box. Two friends that rode their bikes up to Garden Drugs after returning pop bottles to the grocery store. Getting some candy and a pack of baseball cards. Chewing on that stale gum over-sugared and in between the pack of cards. Then playing the game of baseball all the way from the sand box through high school. Both friends left the town of Spruce Wood over a decade ago for different reasons. Both friends have returned to their town they grew up in on the same night. Both are looking for the same person, a girl named Cassidy, but for different reasons. Both found out at the same time Cassidy was not there to be found. Agent Jake Miller was told by a neighbor of Cassidy Owens, Stan Szydlo, who was adding seed in his feeders for his feathery friends, that she was not home. Still at work according to him. Then John Malone saw a sign under the address on the Bungalow home of where Cassidy grew up that said home of the Petersons. Which quickly turned back John Malone, as he went back to the car he borrowed. Agent Miller would return to his car. Both thought about driving by their own house, but time was of essence to the both of them. Minutes later, both of them pulled onto the main street that ran through the town of Spruce Wood. The main street which took them through the downtown of their hometown. Both Jake and John were driving opposite ways. Both of them were passing Garden Drugs which was still there. Both of them even eyeballed each other. Both best friends did not even recognize each other when both cars passed on that two-lane street, as they stopped at the stop sign. Both would get a little teary eyed thinking about Garden Drugs. Just driving through the town of Spruce Wood brought back multiple memories. Neither of them knew they would be running into each other in just a few hours. About 4 to 5 miles away from their hometown.

Chapter Fifty-Eight

WAR OF THE WORLDS

"They know where you are," were the words echoing in the head of the Venomous Viper leader, Blade Runner. "Who?" One of his hands was turning into a fist while the other pressed the cell phone to his ear.

"The authorities. Boom Boom cracked to the State Police," said the slimy lawyer who helps the Southern Illinois charter of Venomous Vipers in all these sticky legal situations.

The blood was now boiling in Blade Runner's body as he looked into the mirror seeing his face turn bright red. He tried to control his tone of anger on the phone. "When?"

"Not sure." The lawyer felt tightness in his throat as if Blade Runner were Darth Vader, making him choke through the phone.

Blade Runner threw the phone against the wall as the call disconnected leaving the lawyer saying, "Hello… you still there?" The lawyer drove off in his red Corvette as his night was done after his meeting with Boom Boom at the station, which took a really long time just to set up seeing his client.

The cell phone broke into a few pieces as another member of the Venomous Vipers, who went by Skin Job, asked, "You ok, boss?"

"Gather everyone into the club house and send me Shark immediately," he snarled.

"Right away." Skin Job was completely hairless and had that shiny bald albino head. He could have gone by Q-Ball. He hustled out of the gym where Blade Runner had been punching the bag the last 45 minutes.

Off to the west of the Venomous Viper compound, the FBI, led by Agent Jake Miller, has pinpointed the biker gang's compound. Miller used FBI reports the Bureau had gathered from their agents. Agent Miller also talked to Detective Cassidy Owens' partner. Plus, a huge lead was that the Highway Patrol found Cassidy's car, which was tucked away on one of those forest preserve dirt roads. The FBI were gathered on a farm, having been given the OK by the owner. They had multiple dark SUVs parked with a trailer which they would use as their command center. Inside, Agent Blake watched the technical support get all the monitors coming to life as they would also be using satellite footage from a drone and their arsenal in the air which was always at their disposal. "We need the assault plan updated to have a rescue included," Agent Miller said.

"Already done," Agent Hawken said.

Agent Derek Hawken was a black male in his late 50's, but he looked like he was in his early 40's. Agent Hawken has been in the Bureau for over 30 years and once played in the USFL for the Pittsburgh Maulers. He was built like a tank with hardly an ounce of fat or any wrinkle lines on the face that would prove he's been doing this job for 30 years.

"OK people, we are a go." Agent Miller said into everyone's earpieces once everything in the command center was up and running. The strike team outside the mobile trailer was gearing up, checking their gear and making sure the weapons were operational. Agent Miller wondered if Cassidy was still alive, as he paced nervously. The monitors showed what they were up against, a lot of shaded trees and slim pathways along a rock terrain.

"OK Cuz, this is how the ammo slides in and out." Liam was showing Johnny how to load the magazine of the semi-automatic pistol. Johnny had been getting a crash course on guns ever since he arrived in Ireland and hung out with his cousin. Johnny had it down as he inserted the magazine in and out like he had been using the weapon for years.

"Remember to aim and shoot. Just like that old Nintendo game, Hogan's Alley."

"I preferred Duck Hunt," joked Johnny. He was using humor to cope with the situation of going to war. He felt like he needed a container of Tums.

"Deedre makes an excellent Duck, by the way." Liam was cool as a cucumber, as this was not his first rodeo.

The Militia and the few IRA guys mixed in, were setting up their staging area on the East side of the Venomous Viper compound. The group parked about a mile up the road as they hiked it from there. They would have people with their engines running to drive on the abandoned farm field to be like the cavalry if needed, or the escape plan. They had a few guys that were going ride the ATVs up the dirt roads to stop any escaping thugs.

"ARE WE ALL LOCKED AND LOADED?" Liam shouted out to the group.

A few of them mumbled yeses as they did a last-minute weapon check. "OK, Johnny you stay right behind the entire way." Liam sounded like a General.

Johnny nodded nervously.

"Breathe cousin, breathe."

Johnny took a few deep breaths and was ready to go.

"Let's follow the exact plan and go in and kill all those filthy animals like we drew it up."

A few "Yeah's" and "Bloody rights" as a few of them raised their semi-automatic machine guns in the air like the Wolverines did, in the movie Red Dawn. All of them headed up the hill in a single-file line ready to spill blood.

"KILL THE GIRL." Blade Runner snarled at Shark, this time for not getting her to talk, seeing him while he made his way to the club house.

"On it." Shark quickly wiped off the spittle on his face that blew in from Blade Runner's snarl.

"We are at Defcon 3, so grab a weapon after you eliminate that bitch." Blade Runner lumbered off in quick strides.

Shark was smirking as he loved to torture his victims for a very long time. Sometimes keeping them alive for days. He knew what Defcon 3 was, so he'd be happy just to slice her throat and let her bleed out, he thought. He dashed his way to the shed.

The FBI started scaling the hill as they had two groups going up in a single file line. One group led by Agent Miller who had his earpiece on with his flap jacket carrying a M-16. Agent Miller was leading a group of FBI tag teams that were fully dressed in body armor with helmets complete with built-in communication systems inside and on the ear holes. Agent Hawken remained in the Mobile trailer. "Testing… testing… Do you copy?"

Hawken got two replies, from Agent Miller who had one team and Agent Donaldson who had the other team, as the radio came in crystal clear. Then Agent Hawken had a response from the helicopters, that they were ten minutes out. "Birds ten minutes out. I repeat, birds ten minutes out." Agent Hawken relayed the message.

"Copy that," was repeated twice in Agent Hawken's earpiece.

The monitors had body cameras on each man showing them lots of angles as the terrain was rocky. Then the radio cackled, "Switching on night vision goggles." On the dark side of the hill, all the body cameras now could see in the dark, relaying a nice feed back to the mobile command center at the farm.

Inside the dark shed, Cassidy was in pain she never imagined. She knew she had to be proactive. She was squirming around trying to loosen the zip ties strapped around her wrists. Then she heard footsteps. She could hear the lock clicking outside the door and actually see the shoes under the small crack of the door. Still gagged, she mumbled, "fuck," as she still tried to wriggle her wrists free. The doorknob turned.

"FELLOW VIPERS, WE ARE AT WAR. THE STATIES KNOW OUR LOCATION." This was shouted out inside the club house.

About 20 ex-military soldiers once upon a time ago would have had the clean-cut look. Now all looked like bikers or members from the band ZZ-Top with their long hair, long beards, and multiple tattoos of satanic rituals and F-the government. Then the logo of their branch of military they served under, which seemed like a lifetime ago. They still had the training inside them, as they worked together like they practiced every week. The club house, a bar, pool tables, jukebox, and couches suddenly turned into an Army Surplus store. Trap doors along the floorboards opened up and all kinds of weapons came out from the woodwork. The sides of the pool table's sections opened and instead of pool balls, they revealed a bunch of grenades. The walls behind pictures added ammo boxes and magazines. The top of the jukebox lifted open and multiple handguns came out from in between the CD'S of the Eagles and Rolling Stones. The entire club house worked like one unit, gathering and loading the weapons before heading outside to their assigned posts on all sides of the compound.

The door opened to the small 12 x 12 tool shed and a dark shadow entered. Cassidy saw the door open up a crack as a streak of light came into the shed. Cassidy quickly played dead and laid on the dirty ground playing possum. "The Princess is still in a deep slumber." Shark was wearing holey jeans and brown dirty boots. If Cassidy opened her eyes, she'd see them.

Shark took a step towards her as she lay in the fetal position on her right shoulder. The chair she once was tied to, was off to the other side of the shed on the ground where it was left when Cassidy was thrown to the ground when Shark left the last time. Shark slid the bowie knife he carried from the leather holder as he took another step. "Fe Fi Fo Fum, I will be smelling the blood of one dead State Police detective." Now he was over her and the knife was completely out.

He was about to bend down when Cassidy's good leg swept him right off his feet. It was hard enough that it knocked him off balance as he fell to the ground. Her eyes opened to see the door open fully, and the light blinded her for a second. Then she heard the knife land as Shark fumbled it, coming down with a hard thud to the ground. Shark grumbled something. Cassidy, with all the pain in her one leg, managed to scissor lock Shark's neck. He did not expect this as it came as a shock to his system. Adrenaline pumped in the blood of Cassidy because she compressed her legs tight around his neck and squeezed the life out of him. Then she was able to finish him off, snapping his neck. He lay lifeless as he mustered out at the end, "You bitch."

One of the FBI tag teams were making good time scaling the rocky terrain off to the west. Agent Miller's group had his guys on the top of the terrain and on level ground. The first group crouched down as they waited for the second group to get to level ground on higher ground. The FBI wanted to invade the biker compound with two teams. From two directions. At the same time. The other group had a much steeper climb as they were led by Agent Paul Casper, an ex-Navy Seal. Agent Casper's group did not notice a camera in the trees slowly moving while recording.

When Liam and his group reached the top of their terrain, the first guy from the local Militia, not IRA, looked over the top only to be greeted by a sniper bullet right in-between the eyes. It was the first shot fired in this altercation. The guy from the Militia was a redneck, named Vance Powers, who tumbled down the slope like a wet back of cement. His trucker hat, something with the NRA on it, flew off. "Holy shit," as the guy behind him caught him and placed him off to the side.

A streak of blood came trickling down the nose of the lifeless body as his eyes looked up in the dust of the night.

"Anybody see where that came from?" Somebody whispered.

"Keep your head down," yelled Liam as he thought he knew where the shot came from. He peeked over the terrain and saw a field of trees.

From one of the trees in the fields, in a deer stand, a sniper waited whose code name was Eyeball. A well-decorated sniper in his military days and a great hunter, saw Vance's head pop up and with quick trigger quick instincts, he squeezed the trigger from his sniper rifle and watched some hill rod fall back down the terrain. With his eyes still watching the edge, he radioed Blade Runner. "I got a sighting of one guy on the East side. He's been taken out. Waiting on more to come, out."

Blade Runner sat at the bar in the club house as all the televisions used for sports and women's mud wrestling were now used for the cause. It was the command center for the biker gang. Blade Runner had a laptop and typed in a few commands on a keyboard as he sat at the bar with a stiff drink. "OK, we have enemy combatants coming from both sides. Be ready." Blade runner played the keyboard like a piano player.

Agent Casper was almost at the top of his terrain when an explosion happened. Trees at the top flew off their stumps and came rolling down like a flaming wreckage taking half the FBI tag team with it. It was like an avalanche of flaming logs just mauling agents as they were trampled to death.

"NOOOO," Agent Miller shouted out as he watched this thing. Then he yelled to his team. "Let's go now," as they all hustled through the maze of the forest of trees. While they were running, "Team B has been eliminated. Repeat. Team B has been eliminated, not expecting survivors."

Team B's communication system went static. The body cameras also turned into static on the monitors as Agent Hawken can hear Agent Miller yelling into his ear. "Where are those choppers? We need them NOW!"

Cassidy managed to do a gymnastic move to get her hands in front of her on the ground, which would have been an instant 10 on the score card. She did it with the bad leg that was shattered in multiple spots. She moved like a snake on the ground, found the knife, and cut the zip ties off her wrists. She slithered with the knife to the body of the Venomous Viper called the Shark, took the blade, and stuck it in his neck to make sure he was dead. Maybe it was that conversation she had with John when they watched those horror movies. How the killer was always never dead on the first attack. Cassidy thought now he was, as the knife slid right in and out with a geyser of blood spitting out of the lifeless pile of heap. Before she could see the crimson blood dripping off the jagged edge that was meant for her throat, she heard footsteps. She just reacted and chucked the knife right at the opening. Bullseye! She got the blade into another Venomous Viper who fell towards her with the knife in the neck.

The guy, Defender, did not put his hands out in front of him. Instead, he went for the knife that was sticking in his Adam's apple, and he was dead when he landed. The blade went into his neck further. Now the shed was as crowded as the spinoff of *Three's Company, Three's a Crowd.*

Even so, she was hoping she could somehow walk out of here and over two bodies. She heard gunshots from a few directions.

"Listen, aim that bloody cannon right at that tree," Liam shouted.

The militia, mixed in with those IRA guys, lost two guys from the sniper in the tree. Johnny crouched down behind a boulder as his heart was racing. He felt sweat all over his body, even in places he never imagined, and on a cooler night. His gun was drawn as his cousin's troops were still being pinned down at the edge of the terrain by the sniper. Some dirt would sprinkle down their backs as bullets hit off the edge and pieces flew over the edge, hitting Johnny on the head. He was concerned that this plan was not off to a great start. Then through his ears he heard, "FIRE IT NOW," from his cousin Liam.

"EVERYONE GET READY TO CLIMB UP AND CHARGE" Liam shouted even louder.

Right when he said that, one of his cousin's IRA pals had the rocket launcher perfectly in the brush and targeting the deer stand. As the rocket whooshed out, quickly the tree exploded in a fire ball, including the deer stand. That's when everyone climbed over the edge and ran towards the explosion with their guns drawn, leaving two buddies on the side of the ledge of the rocky terrain.

Eyeball suddenly saw some underlying brush come to life through his scope. Eyeball had some potty mouth words come out as he dove off the tree, but the rocket came too quick and just turned the tree into toothpicks. As the flames burned his body in midair, screams echoed through the skies as his body fell from the sky and landed on the ground like a sack of spuds. Other bikers saw what happened. Then they saw what was coming in their direction as a firefight brewed with bullets whizzing all over in between the bikers and the militia. Blood spilled as both sides were taking on casualties.

On the other side of this Venomous Viper compound, Agent Miller and his group were weaving in and out through trees. Agent Miller led the assault and reacted very quickly as a biker named Genocide popped out from behind a tree. He got a bullet right in the head that knocked this hulk of a body off his feet as he died before he wrapped himself around the trunk of the tree. Then suddenly, bullets headed their way from other Vipers giving the FBI a welcoming party. "Take cover," Agent Miller hissed out through his headset.

Along one of the trails, one of the militia guys was moving along nicely in his ATV. It was a guy named Dale Snead, who could and should have been in Hollywood with his father and uncles as stuntmen on different sets of movies. Dale was great at racing cars, bikes, anything that had a motor. He was able to do all kinds of tricks as a starter when he was a kid, skateboarding or riding those DQ trails by his house with his BMX. It was called DQ because the trails were next to the ice cream parlor. The trails had cool hills and ramps that let you get high in the air going up those ramps at high speed. This go around riding his ATV, Dale did not pick up the stainless-steel thing coming out from the tree line. The biker, Black Ninja, swung the long blade and clearly cut the head off Dale's neck with one swipe. It was clean cut as the head came off and bounced on the ground like a ball before rolling into the ground cover. While the ATV drove on for another 50 feet, during which the trail took a curve and fell down the side of the hill. Black Ninja wiped his blade off and continued to prowl the trails for more victims as he put the sword back behind his back and disappeared. The engine of the ATV stopped and lay on its side with two of the wheels still spinning. Dale's body was still holding on to the bars of the 4-wheeler.

Helicopters were getting closer as the battlefield was full of bullets so each group may not have heard their blades spinning in the night hour. John Malone was running scared as he followed his cousin, who was like a jack rabbit bouncing around from tree to tree. He was firing his weapon and hitting bikers with precise aim as their bodies collapsed in the forest which surrounded the Venomous Vipers compound. In back of John's guys from the Militia, they were being erased from Earth as bullets ripped them apart from sub machine guns as shells were hitting the ground at a high rate. John Malone forced his finger to pull the trigger a few times. Each bullet missed its target as each time he ran and pulled the trigger. It was an argument between his brain and his finger.

Inside the clubhouse, Blade Runner was not liking what he was seeing on the monitors. From both sides, his guys were piling up dead. Blade Runner yelled orders through the mouthpiece, but it seemed like all their communication went dead as his fist slammed down on the bar. Blade Runner rose to his feet, checked his clip on his gun, and spoke to his sidekick who went by the Enforcer. He was a big burly guy with a long red beard who was carrying an AK-47 as his weapon of choice. Same weapon he recovered on a mission in the Middle East when he served in the Army infantry. "Let's get the fuck out of here," Blade Runner snarled as he bit down on his lip. They both went out the back service door of the club house.

Agent Miller, back behind the tree, popped out and fired a bullet taking out another snake in a jean jacket. Bullet went right in-between his eyes. Agent Miller was at the top of his class at the firing range, and he always loved Mel Gibson in *Lethal Weapon*, making the smiley face on the human target in the movie. "We have taken out their communications, over," said Agent Hawken in his earpiece.

"Roger that," which was good news as Agent Miller was closing in on the compound with his tag team of a FBI well-trained SWAT team.

Meanwhile Cassidy was pretty much crawling through the grass outside the shed on the compound. Her leg was being dragged as she crawled like a little tike with a semi pistol in her hands. She could hear World War III breaking out, as guns were being fired from all over.

Outside the compound, State Police invaded the staging area of the militia. At least ten squad cars with deputies with their guns drawn, rounded up 4 guys and their ATVs. High above them in the tree line, the Black Ninja of the Venomous Vipers could see what was going on. His sword still had a few drops of blood from the guy he beheaded. The communications were out. He could hear some of his brothers starting up their hogs in the distance. He could hear the helicopters now hovering like vultures looking for their prey. "It's time to walk away, Jacob," he said out loud to himself.

All those martial arts degrees. Serving all those missions while in the Special Forces. Training with the best Ninjas in the world. All the tournaments he fought in. All the underground fight clubs he spilled blood in. His mother would not want him in no biker gang. The thought of it was kind of a cool idea at the time. He took out the sword, jabbed it in the soil, and hit the road. "Maybe I'll open up that surf shop down in Key West." He looked like Spiderman zigzagging through trees with ease. The sword, which had the Venomous Viper logo on the blade, would be found years later by some hikers.

Johnny followed his cousin right into the Venomous Viper compound as the bullets seemed to stop whizzing by their faces. It was Johnny, Liam, and one other guy still left from the Militia. They heard motorcycles starting up. Over their heads, they heard helicopters.

The Blackhawks helicopters circling were unloading reinforcements. More FBI tag team soldiers were sliding down ropes entering the compound. The blades whirling above made the tree branches whip around, but that did not stop these guys who were well-trained and could climb out of a helicopter in their sleep.

Blade Runner and The Enforcer turned the corner but did not see what was on the ground. A single shot was fired as Cassidy, from the ground, put a bullet in the neck of The Enforcer as he fell down like a ton of bricks. The Enforcer dropped his gun, and his hands went to his neck as a volcano of blood went through his fingers. Both Blade Runner and Cassidy could hear the thud. Cassidy saw the perfect opportunity to put down the man that caused this entire situation in her life. She did not hesitate as she squeezed the trigger, but the gun jammed.

"YOU FUCKIN' BITCH, YOU HAVE BEEN A THORN IN MY SIDE!" Blade Runner's head looked like a stop sign. His veins were pulsating like he was injected with that special Barry Bonds seasoning. Cassidy threw the gun after nothing came out after the six squeezed. She could see him lumbering towards her.

Motorcycles were roaring down the pathways. The FBI tag teams were all unloaded from the helicopters. The tag team went after the Venomous Vipers on the run. It was like shooting ducks in a barrel as they picked these bikers off their bikes riding away. As the body went limp, the bike continued down the path, eventually crashing into a tree. One guy got shot and then a branch whiplashed him off the Harley as the bike fell over with one wheel still spinning and the engine still idling. Outside, the FBI were surrounding all exits they could think of as possible escape routes from this compound. They had the assistance of the state police, and it seemed like they brought every law man or soldier from the Tristate area and beyond, with their guns blazing. Some more bullets flew. More Venomous Vipers were erased from this planet. One Statey joked, "It's like the snake hunters in Florida getting rid of those invasive Pythons in the Everglades."

"Let's just hope none of those restaurants want these Venomous Vipers on their food menu like those Florida people wanting Python steaks on the grill".

The FBI and the State Police did take a few of the Venomous Vipers alive.

"FREEZE," was yelled out loud as Liam, Johnny and the other Militia stopped in their tracks. They did not see Agent Miller, and one other tag team FBI soldier, emerge from one of the buildings.

"PUT DOWN THE WEAPONS NOW," Agent Miller yelled.

"JAKE, IS THAT YOU?" Johnny was looking at his childhood best friend, from childhood to the days in high school.

"JOHNNY, YOU'RE ALIVE!!"

At this brief moment, the wheels were spinning in Liam's mind. The letdown of the guard by Agent Miller seeing his old friend. Johnny could sense it. Johnny could see his cousin's hand move. It happened so fast it was like a Western at high noon. Johnny got the words out barely, "No Cuz".

It was too late. In seconds, Johnny was the only one standing. Liam's bullet took out Agent Miller. Agent Miller squeezed one last shot while falling over, that took out the militia guy. The FBI tag team guy took out Liam. However, Liam squeezed the trigger twice and took out the tag team guy. "Cuz... Jake," Johnny was in shock as he dropped his gun. Panic ran through his body like some deadly disease. That's when he heard a scream. It was a woman. It was a familiar voice that he remembered from a long time ago. "No Way." Johnny picked up his gun.

Another scream. Johnny had no time to think about his cousin, Liam, or his best friend who were both dead.

Blade Runner was going ballistic on Cassidy. The Venomous Viper leader grabbed her by the hair and threw her against the side of the building. Cassidy hit her head hard as her vision got blurry and her broken shattered leg was absolutely throbbing. She thought she heard multiple gunshots a short distance away. She screamed, "Fuck you," over and over as he was about to pick her up again. She was able to land a good kick in his nut sack.

"Bitch," he muttered as sharp pain went through his midsection. He thought he had no time for this. He needed to get the hell out of here or he would be seeing a prison again. Before he went, since that psychopath Shark could not do the job, he was going to end this girl's life even if it were the last thing he did. Blade Runner put his beefy mitt right around Cassidy's throat and started squeezing the life out of her. Her eyes were popping out as he was choking the life out of her. Her eyes were blurry, but out of the corner of her eye she thought she was dreaming. How could it be? One word slid out of her mouth in between quick breaths, "Johnny."

Blade Runner could not understand what the hell she was saying. His back was turned as he had Cassidy pinned up against the wall. "Easy, you little bitch, it will be over soon. He squeezed her neck even tighter when he heard a popping sound.

Johnny stood there as smoke came from his barrel. "Cassidy..." His jaw dropped.

It was a direct hit from Johnny's gun, right in the side of the big man's biker jacket, as his hand released the tension around her neck. Blade Runner growled as he went for his gun in his holster, but it was too late. Johnny shot him again, this time right in the gut, and just like in the boxing match when Muhammad Ali knocked down Joe Frazier. The words, "Down go, Frazier," would have suited the situation as Blade Runner's big rump hit the ground. His hands tried to stop the blood from his midsection while his gun stayed in its holster. He now was gasping for air.

Cassidy slid down the side of the building she was pinned up against. "Johnny," she got out, as she was now in a sitting position and her eyes started tearing and her heart was beating rapidly.

Johnny looked at what this big oaf had done to his girl. Johnny just snapped. "I've been waiting for this for a long time, motherfucker." Johnny squeezed the trigger as Blade Runner was trying to butt walk away.

The bullet went right into Blade Runner's knee. "That was for my mom." Another bullet fired out of his gun, this time in the other knee.

Blade Runner squealed like a pig in heat. "That was for my dad."

Johnny emptied his clip and Blade Runner was a bloody mess as he lay lifeless. Johnny dropped the gun and went over to the love of his life as he got on the ground, tears flowing from his eyes, and hugged her.

"I've been looking for you," she managed to say sobbing.

"I never thought I'd ever see you again." As he was sobbing, they held each other.

It was like when they played the old Nintendo game. The original "Super Mario." How he got Mario to save the princess, which he has done in the video game and now in real life.

"You're my Mario," she said.

"You're my Luigi." They laughed, held each other tightly, and never let each other go.

THE END

The Southern Illinois charter of the Venomous Vipers was officially shut down. The authorities were able to turn the Venomous Vipers who were still alive after that small war that broke out at their compound. With the information they got from that charter, the FBI and other government authorities across the nation led successful raids on all of the Venomous Vipers compounds. Local police were able to put a halt to all the drug trafficking in each city where the Venomous Vipers did business. It was one big swoop with precise timing on that day where they took down the whole biker network, leaving no stones unturned.

TWO YEARS LATER

"NOW BATTING FOR THE SANTA FE BUZZARDS, #7 JOHN MALONE." The small crowd on hand gave him a round of applause.

Finally his first at-bat in some type of professional baseball, as he slowly walked up to the plate soaking it all in. It was a perfect Spring day. Not a cloud in the very sunny skies in the state of New Mexico. Malone had on a red helmet with the S &F in cursive. The Buzzard uniforms were white with red pinstripes. They looked like the old 1977 Chicago White Sox uniforms. That year they were known as the hit-men. He had black under his eyes and butterflies in his stomach, as he stepped into the batter box versus the El-Paso Scorpion pitcher. He was blinded by the tint off a gold star just for a second. Malone looked over by the dug out while he did some landscaping in the box and smiled at his wife, finally, Cassidy was in her Sheriff uniform. She was in her browns. Dark Brown pants with a tan brown shirt that had the gold Sheriff star pinned on her chest of her button-down shirt. Her belt had her gun and cuffs, and her hair was pulled back in a ponytail. She smiled looking through her state trooper sunglasses. Her leg had fully recovered. She walked with a limp though. With her bravery and how she was a great detective, she took the job in New Mexico. It was an offer they could not refuse. "GIVE IT A RIDE JOHNNY," she yelled.

They both needed a new start. The job paid well while he got himself back into baseball shape. Worked at his game. Then he tried out for the local team, and he made it. They were both living the high life as they put their past to rest. They knew it was a long road, but they had finally made it. Both their hearts from the long separation never gave up, even though they lived a very far distance from each other. The first pitch from the Scorpion pitcher was a laser beam, but outside as John took the first pitch. The Santa Fe Buzzards was just an Independent minor league team. It may be the start of something of a late career to the minors for John Malone, but that was too far into the future to think about that. It was great being in the game as he looked over, gave Cassidy a smile, and most importantly had his soul mate. The Scorpion pitcher, this time blew one by Malone right down the middle of the plate. "STRIKE," the umpire behind the catcher screamed.

John Malone stepped out of the box, did a quick practice swing, and glanced over at the third base line as something in his mind thought he was seeing things. It was his parents and two sisters, watching and rooting him on. He could not believe it as he went back into the box, concentrated, and looked at the wind-up of the Scorpion pitcher. As the right-hander delivered, he saw the ball come out of his hands. He leaned back, and waited on it very nicely, and with a leg kick got the big barrel of the bat on the ball. With a nice upper cut swing, the ball took off. He glanced over and saw his family on their feet in amazement. He dropped the bat and took off down the first base line. He saw the right field hustling back to the wall. He saw the ball travel over the Sid Sauce Hot Sauce sign in the right field corner on the left side of the foul pole. Everyone stood up and started screaming as John Malone's welcome to professional baseball first at-bat, was a home run. He slowed down after rounding first base. Went into his home run trot. Slapped five with the third base coach and looked at the seats where his family would have been. They were gone. He stepped on home plate and slapped hands with a teammate. He then looked into the sky and raised his hands up to the heavens where he knew they were watching. He knew his family were watching from the box seats in heaven. He knew his best friend, Jake, and his cousin, were also watching.

Those two who sacrificed their lives, will always have a spot in both their hearts. He headed to the dugout, but first made a pit stop and kissed Cassidy. They both were crying at this point with tears of excitement. Finally, what he wanted to do his whole entire life came true, with the game he lost his family doing. He was separated from his childhood sweetheart and best friend. Now the wait was over. He had both of those and he knew his family was also supporting him. It felt like a weight had been lifted off his shoulders. One which he had carried around for a very long time.

THE END